1765

# MOLLY LAKE
*in*
## Barely Afloat

*Also by*
SAMUEL ENDICOTT

*The Quebec Affair, 1759*
*The Treasure of Le Nain Rouge, 1773*

1765

# MOLLY LAKE
*in*
## Barely Afloat

## Samuel Endicott

GRIFFIN PRESS

Griffin Press
Cover and interior design, by David Moratto
www.davidmoratto.com


ISBN 978-0-9834343-9-9

*For Elaine*

N

*Manhattan Island*

H

F

*Quarry on Blackwell's Island*

G

*Newton Creek*

C

D

E

A

B

## LEGEND

A - Governor's Island
B - Buttermilk Channel
C - Colden's Mansion
D - St. Alembert's Home
E - Diamond Reef
F - Farm House
G - East River
H - Hudson River

# CONTENTS

# PART I

# First Shot

# CHAPTER ONE

MOLLY LAKE EMERGED from her family's cabin holding two muskets and their gear in her arms. She paused under the big oak to admire the sunrise and the beauty of the Mohawk River flowing in the distance. Molly liked mornings, and she had been anticipating this particular wake-up all summer. Today her beau, eighteen year-old Jean-Luc St. Alembert, was arriving. Molly wished the seventeen miles separating the family's cabin in Schenectady from the pier in Albany could somehow disappear.

Before heading to the barn, she glanced at the azure sky and noted its promise of agreeable weather. When she entered the barn, she greeted General Wolfe (the family's new horse) and began the process of harnessing the beast of burden to the wagon. General Wolfe turned to watch Molly and whinnied. Molly nodded to him, patted his flank, cinched and checked all the straps, and climbed aboard. Before she flicked the reins, she said, "You seem as eager as I am to get to Albany.

Peter Lake, Molly's father, was the next to come out of the cabin. Six feet one inch tall and muscular, thirty-two year old Peter frowned as he observed his sixteen year-old daughter steer the wagon toward the cabin. He had hoped Molly would forget about this fellow because he just didn't approve of her falling in love with a Frenchman from Canada. As Peter waited for Molly to bring the wagon around, he considered how his daughter had fallen head over heels for an enemy soldier. Shaking his head slowly, he watched Molly drive the rig to the cabin, but his thoughts drifted to the changes he had noticed in her since the family's return from the Quebec battlefield last October. Of course, none of this would be happening if the Huron hadn't kidnapped Marie and taken her to Quebec. Peter had taken Molly with him in his quest to get his wife back, and his daughter proved her mettle in one scrape after another. Molly still had freckles sprinkled across her cheeks and pert nose, and she liked to wear her auburn hair pulled back, but her face and figure had thinned ever so slightly as she physically matured.

"Hey, Lake, we want to talk at ya," boomed a rough voice from behind.

Peter whirled about. Two rent collectors from Mr. Van Rensselaer's estate, brothers named Vernon and Jacob Jones, were on horseback and riding toward him. Peter was a tenant farmer on the patroon's sprawling lands and one day in arrears.

Peter had the rent money in his cabin, but hadn't taken his payment to the Rensselaerwyck estate. His contract gave him until the fifth of the month. He intended to deliver it the next day—following the trip to Albany with Molly.

Vernon and Jacob dismounted. Jacob got into Peter's face and asked, "Mr. Van Rensselaer wants his money. You have it?"

"I'll deliver it tomorrow," said Peter matter-of-factly.

"Fork it over now, Lake, and we'll be on our way to the next deadbeat's spread."

Peter knew better than to pay the Joneses. The Mohawk Valley neighbors said these two thugs didn't always turn the money over to Van Rensselaer. Peter said, "I'll get the money to the Dutchman by tomorrow. That's a promise."

"Not good enough," said Vernon. He moved behind Peter and grabbed him. Peter struggled, but Vernon held him tightly. Jacob drew back his fist to convince Peter of the wisdom of paying right then.

Having observed the Joneses ganging up on her father, Molly sneaked up behind Jacob and slammed her musket's stock in the small of his back. The blow knocked him to his knees; he looked at Molly in shock.

"Let go of my papa, Vernon Jones, or I'll bash your good-for-nothing brother again," said Molly. Jacob cowered at her feet.

Vernon said, "That's big talk for a girl."

Molly pulled the musket back and said, "Here is how I see it. A few seconds from now, your brother, here, will have a heck of a headache, and you will have nowhere to hide. My papa will commence beating you to within an inch of your life. Is that how you want to start your day, Vernon Jones?"

Jones knitted his eyebrows as he contemplated the imminent thrashing. Molly figured she had made her point.

Jacob said, "For God's sake, brother, let the man go."

Vernon released Peter, and he and Jacob started backing away. "We're going, but if you don't pay the boss, we'll be back."

With his fists balled, Peter said, "Get off my property you silk-stocking wharf rats. And you tell the Dutchman, he'll get his money tomorrow." He watched the Jones boys mount up and ride down the dirt road. He turned to Molly and asked, "Were you really going to butt stroke Jacob?"

Molly stared at the Jones brothers until they rounded the bend. She placed the musket in the wagon, and said, "I never did like those two. Are we ready to hit the road?"

Peter asked sternly, "Well?"

"Yes, Papa, I would have."

Marie rushed out of the cabin and asked, "What happened out here? I heard angry voices."

Peter said, "The Jones brothers reminded me the rent is due. I will take it over to the Dutchman tomorrow. That's all." He turned to Molly and said, "Mount up; I'll join you in a minute. I want to speak with your mother."

"Alright, Papa."

Marie asked Peer in a frightened whisper, "The Jones brothers were here?"

Peter frowned and said, "Yeah." He picked up his hat from the ground and brushed off some debris. "It's a fine day when a man has to be rescued by his daughter." Intentionally changing the subject, Peter said, "I heard some interesting news at the trading post."

"Oh?"

Peter regarded his wife's stunning beauty and gave her full credit for Molly's good looks. Her long dark brown hair cascaded onto her shoulders, and (for an instant) considered allowing Molly to go to Albany by herself. "It seems King George has tightened his hold on Quebec. I heard tell the French returned with seven thousand troops, battled Murray's garrison at Sainte Foye, and then laid siege for weeks after the battle."

"More fighting," Marie said sadly shaking her head. "I wonder if Molly's friend took part."

Peter said, "Don't know, but this feller said each side lost about two hundred and another thousand were wounded. It seems the French came out on top this time."

"But, darling, you said, 'King George has tightened his hold on Quebec.' It isn't sounding like it."

"Well, I'm not finished, dear."

"Pray continue." She smiled at her husband.

"The battle didn't decide anything, though the enemy forced Murray to retreat behind the city walls. It really came down to which side was reinforced first."

"Well?"

"I'm happy to report that we won."

"Have you told Molly?"

"Naw, it will only make her fret. Her friend probably wasn't hurt, or his Indian pal, Opechwan, would have mentioned it when he stopped here in June to tell Molly of Jean-Luc's visit. I'll mention to her when we're on the road to Albany." Peter walked to the wagon and climbed aboard.

"You seem mighty eager to get to Albany," called Marie to Molly sitting in the wagon.

"Is it obvious, Mama?"

"Well, since you're prepared to depart without your food baskets, I'd have to say yes." Turning to her husband, Marie said, "Peter, wipe off that scowl from your face; I don't want you to making Jean-Luc feel unwelcome."

Peter rolled his eyes. They waited for Marie to fetch the food baskets. After Marie returned and handed them over, Peter nodded to Molly to begin the journey.

The time passed quickly for Molly, who had mental checkpoints along the route. Having made the run to Albany numerous times with her father, Molly mostly listened as her father discussed the details of the French army's withdrawal from Quebec.

When the Lakes arrived at the waterfront in Albany, Molly regarded the majestic Hudson River flowing before her. She strained her neck looking downriver and did see a distant vessel. As the boat approached, Molly brushed debris from her light brown flannel dress, pinched each cheek for additional color, and retied her hair behind her head. She turned to her father and asked, "How do I look, Papa?"

"You look fine, Molly." Peter knew this morning would be difficult, but as the suitor's transport neared, his stomach churned.

Molly said, Now Papa, act nice around Jean-Luc. He is real special." Molly placed her hands on her hips and said firmly, "I mean it."

Peter looked away, shook his head, and muttered, "Getting sassy she is."

When the ship carrying Jean-Luc arrived at the pier, chills of anticipation crawled over Molly's neck and arms, and she pondered whether it best to greet him in French, her second language, or English.

When Jean-Luc appeared on the gangplank, Molly waved enthusiastically. Jean-Luc waved and ran ashore. He and Molly hugged warmly. They separated only when Jean-Luc noticed Molly's father inching closer; he placed his hand out to greet her parent.

"It is good to see you again, Mr. Lake," said Jean-Luc in a heavy French accent. Peter coolly shook hands with the young man.

Molly's beau was taller than average and strikingly handsome. A shock of his dark hair had fallen near his eyes, and Peter noticed his athletic physique during their handshake. Even this dubious father picked up on the aura of confidence that surrounded the young man; and when the occasion required, Jean-Luc's Gallic spirit revealed a flair that inspired confidence in him. Shaking his head, Peter detected this fellow possessed an élan rare in a person of eighteen. Though for the moment those qualities deserted him in the presence of Molly's father.

Molly beamed and said, "That was well said, Jean-Luc." She turned to her father and said, "Jean-Luc is leaning English, Papa. Isn't that wonderful?"

Peter snorted. A deckhand followed with Jean-Luc's belongings and placed his bag down behind him. "Let me load your bag," said Peter.

"No, Sir, I will do it." Jean-Luc placed the bag into the back of the wagon, and Peter walked around to mount the front seat. Molly and her true love embraced. After hugging they kissed and kissed again.

Peter glanced over his shoulder at the kissing and said under his breath, "I told her not to get mushy in public." He shook his head.

"You look wonderful!" Jean-Luc said.

Molly beamed. She said, "Mama is dying to see you." Turning to her father, she said, "Papa, would you mind sitting by yourself? Jean-Luc and I have lots to catch up on."

Peter nodded sullenly. Molly lowered the wagon's rear panel, and she and Jean-Luc hopped on and sat with their legs hanging over the edge.

For an hour, the young couple talked in whispers, but the gist of the conversation was repeated statements of how much one missed the other. About halfway to the Lake homestead, Jean-Luc said, "I have come to ask your father a question."

"Oh, what kind of question?" asked Molly coyly. Jean-Luc smiled sheepishly. Molly hugged his arm and said, "I have only thought about you every day and night. Kiss me again." This time they kissed deeply only parting lips when General Wolfe shook his harness to alert Molly to her father's disapproving look.

Peter felt ambivalent about this visit. On one hand, he grown concerned about Molly not being married and her disinterest in the local boys. And this Canadian beau did seem to be from a prosperous family. From the corner of his eye, he saw another kiss. He decided to interrupt and blurted, "There was another battle."

Molly's eyes looked into Jean-Luc's face as he answered her father in English in his Montreal accent, "Yes, sir, I was at Sainte Foye... with Chevalier de Levis, and in Montreal afterward when we surrendered. The war is over and Canada is at peace finally. He lightly touched Molly's cheek and said, "I have come to see Molly, because — " Jean-Luc stopped in mid-sentence.

Peter remembered his own experienced with Marie's judgmental parents. He and his wife had been forced to elope, because his in-laws hadn't approved of him. He wasn't from Acadia, which disqualified him in their view. Noticing the young man's nervousness, Peter changed the subject and asked, "What brings you to the Mohawk Valley?"

Molly looked at her French Canadian beau and said, "He came to see me, Papa, What a silly question." Peter smiled sheepishly. Molly blurted, "Jean-Luc wants to ask you something."

Peter looked at Jean-Luc with quizzical arched brows. Another awkward silence ensued.

Jean-Luc sputtered, "That is correct, sir." He cleared his throat and asked, "Um, perhaps when we are able to speak in private?"

Peter drove the wagon onto his farm and up to their log cabin. He was pretty sure he knew why a nervous suitor would trek two hundred miles through the forest to ask a young lady's father a question. Peter turned to Molly and said, "Unhitch the horse and wipe him down."

To make this ordeal a little less trying on the young man, he put his arm around Jean-Luc's shoulder and said, "In that case, let's walk to the cabin. We'll talk there."

When she heard men's voices in conversational tones approaching,

Marie walked outside and saw her husband with another coming up the path.

Peter called, "Honey, it is Jean-Luc."

Surprised and delighted, Marie rushed out and warmly hugged Molly's beau. "You're looking well, Jean-Luc. Your journey wasn't difficult, I hope?"

"It went well."

"And your parents?"

"They are fine, thank you."

Peter said, "He has come all the way from Montreal to ask me something." When Jean-Luc wasn't looking, he rolled his eyes

Marie gave her husband a subtle frown, smiled sweetly at Jean-Luc, and said, "Well, dinner will be ready in a bit. You two sit and talk." She then knitted her brows in a subtle signal to her husband for him to behave himself.

Peter did feel sympathetic to the young man, but the fellow was French! Nevertheless, he was determined to be hospitable and said, "Let's have a smoke under the elm."

Settling on two wooden stools in the shade of an elm tree, Jean-Luc and Peter took out their pipes in almost synchronized fashion. As Jean-Luc removed his tobacco pouch from his pocket, he spotted a stone grave marker ten feet away. It was Molly's baby brother, Little Pete. He had been killed by a Huron when her mother was abducted in '59. Peter tapped his pipe against his boot more from habit and not because any residue remained. Jean-Luc imitated him and then offered Peter his tobacco pouch. Graciously accepting (although he had his own), Peter silently filled his clay pipe. After puffing with a match's flame flaring inches above the bowl with each inhalation, Peter settled back and waited for Jean-Luc to finish firing up his pipe. When his visitor had his tobacco glowing, Peter asked, "What ever became of your uncle?"

Jean-Luc's demeanor turned momentarily melancholy. He said softly, "Actually, I brought accusations against him when I reached Montreal. Governor Vaudreuil, refusing to act, dismissed them. The governor even retained my uncle's services until after the Sainte Foye battle... if you can believe that? They allowed Uncle Francois to resign, and he sailed to France. However, the latest ship from overseas brought news of his arrest. He was to be tried for embezzling from the king. My family is, of course, humiliated."

"I didn't mean to embarrass you, I'm sorry I brought it up, and yet, I cannot honestly say I feel bad for him. We will not speak of him again. I believe you traveled from Montreal to ask me something."

The moment of truth had arrived. "*Oui*... Molly and I... um, what I'm trying to say..." Maybe he should just blurt out his question, but he summoned inner strength to remain calm (having rehearsed his lines several hundred times), Jean-Luc said, "Molly and I would like your permission to marry. I love her very much." Fearing a negative response, Jean-Luc forced himself to look into Peter's eyes and asked, "May we have your blessing?"

Though anticipated, Peter, nevertheless, felt a bit thunderstruck when the actual moment arrived. Struggling to conceal his misgivings, he took a long puff on his pipe. After exhaling Peter said, "I have no doubts, Jean-Luc, concerning your affection for Molly... or hers for you. But I must ask you..." Peter felt that, seeing as how this fellow was not from around Schenectady, he needed to know more, "How do you plan to support Molly?"

Jean-Luc's tension ebbed. He had rehearsed his answer as he had traveled. "I have some money set aside..."

Good... good, thought Peter, at least he is a saver and responsible. He seems to have his eye on the future.

"... to enter business." Jean-Luc continued, "I thought Molly and I would settle in one of the cities on the coast, perhaps New York. Of course, Molly and I need to discuss that further, but I would like to start a shipping enterprise. I feel the future is unlimited in that area. Don't you agree, sir?"

Peter drew on his pipe and nodded. "Yes, I do, particularly if the crown continues neglecting this corner of its empire." Peter looked around for Marie. He knew his petite Acadian wanted to know everything. "Well, Jean-Luc, I think it is time we see how Molly's mother feels."

Jean-Luc nodded. "Marie, dear, could you come outside a moment?" Marie exited the cabin wiping her hands on a towel. As she approached the two men, Jean-Luc respectfully stood (Peter followed a moment later). "Darling," Peter began, "Jean-Luc wishes to wed our Molly. He has asked our blessing."

Marie knew her husband liked this young man. She liked him too. "That's wonderful," she said, "We are happy for you both." Jean-Luc felt exultant and thought he would burst. Then Marie voiced a maternal concern. "I think your mother and father would appreciate an opportunity to become acquainted with Molly before you announce your engagement."

"Oh, yes, my parents would like that."

"When could your parents meet your fiancée?"

Their discussion continued, and a half hour later, Molly returned from the barn. She had (understandably) rushed through her chores. Jean-Luc beamed when he saw her. He stood abruptly and said, "If I may be excused, I would like to speak with Molly." Peter and Marie nodded and Jean-Luc excitedly ran to meet his girl.

As he approached, Molly asked with coquettish delight, "Did you have a nice talk with Papa?" Jean-Luc's wide smile divulged the answer. With the sun setting, she and Jean-Luc touched their foreheads together. In blissful silence, they stood united and determined to never allow kings to separate them.

# CHAPTER TWO

NEW YORK CITY FIVE YEARS LATER
OCTOBER 10, 1765, 10 A.M.

MOLLY WALKED OUT her front door and locked it behind her. She had endured a rough night tossing and turning in her bed. Molly felt the letter in her pocket and pursed her lips. She had carried it ever since it arrived. The sender had asked for a secret meeting. But there was another issue causing Molly to have such fitful sleep. Weeks before his latest voyage, Molly noticed her husband spending long hours on his ledger. He made his entries in the late evening, and his new routine was worrying Molly. Something was troubling her partner, and she walked pensively up the street in the direction of their shipping business. With two blocks remaining she heard a familiar voice call out, "Molly Lake!"

It had been over five years, and it took her a few moments, but she recognized the person calling to her. Molly adopted a mock scolding stance with hands on hips. "My name isn't Lake anymore, good sir; it is St. Alembert now." She couldn't help feeling a little nervous seeing her old deck officer. She liked John Andrews, and noting the navy selected him for promotion, was happy to run into him.

He hurried across the street smiling broadly and holding his arms wide. After bear hugging Molly, he held her to arms length and said pleasantly, "Married life agrees with you. You look amazing. I take it from your last name that you married the French chap from Canada."

Molly beamed and said, "Yes, I did. We married the summer after the fighting ended." Noticing his new rank, she said, "I see you have been promoted. Congratulations *Commander* Andrews. My, your new epaulets certainly set off that uniform."

"Thank you, Molly. I would imagine you also have made a few adjustments since leaving the frontier. How does city life agree with you?"

"I like it. For one thing, I'm wearing more dresses. Upriver, I didn't have much use for frills." Molly looked down at her light brown, linen dress. "But our business keeps me too busy to become overly sentimental about the back country," she said in a white lie.

"Are your parents doing well?"

"Mama is wonderful, but you know Papa; he is a restless breed. He doesn't like being a tenant farmer—never will. Now, enough about him, please tell me why you wrote in such a mysterious manner?" Molly asked lightheartedly. "I have taken your letter everywhere since it arrived sounding all secretive and such." She pulled the envelope from her dress pocket and playfully poked Andrews with it. "You have my complete attention, Commander."

Andrews looked about the street, saw a handful of pedestrians and a beggar on the corner, but nothing seemed suspicious. Exercising prudence nevertheless he said in a whisper, "We shouldn't discuss it here."

Noting the seriousness in his voice, Molly resisted the urge to tease further and said, "In that case, there's a grog house on the next corner that serves scones with tea. I may die of curiosity first."

Commander Andrews smiled and thought that's the Molly I remember. He was prudent to move from the street; the beggar had been observing his encounter with Mrs. St. Alembert.

Watching the wife of the man he wanted to encounter meeting with an enemy naval officer did not surprise him though it aroused his interest. The vagrant continued scrutinizing them until they entered the grog house.

When Molly and Commander Andrews walked through the door, Andrews motioned for the proprietor to seat them at a table away from the windows.

The beggar stood and walked to the grog house door, but attired as he was chose not to enter. He peeked through the window and saw them take a table away against the far wall. Thinking it better to move to the alley, he shuffled to the rear door. When the grog house owner came out with some garbage, he eyed the vagrant with an unpleasant expression and said, "Get out of here," and waved him away. "You're not welcome." The beggar said nothing and submissively slunk away. After the owner went back inside, the beggar returned to the street and peered into the window. He observed Molly and Andrews chatting. He then took a seat on the sidewalk near the door. There he feigned taking a nap. Frustrated that he could not eavesdrop on their conversation, he waited patiently for them to finish.

Inside, Molly inquired about their old shipmates and Commander Andrews did his best to bring her current. Then Molly said, "I cannot wait another second. Why did you write? You have been mysterious?"

"Molly, I am here as a representative of the Navy Board. They need the assistance of well placed colonials and I believe you are a person that can help us."

"Me? How can I help the Navy Board?"

"Trouble is brewing—financially, I mean. The empire is heavily in debt, and I'm afraid taxes are heading higher throughout the realm."

"Oh, not again; I knew it," said Molly shaking her head. "And they are already high." Molly started to wring her hands, but stopped herself.

Commander Andrews said, "See here, England supplied both the men and money to defend the colonies. The Mother Country is burdened with war debt and needs New York's help."

"So they're shifting it onto *us*? I recall hearing about wars in Europe, the Caribbean, and even India, during the same period." Struggling to avoid sounding argumentative, Molly said, "Well, you still haven't told me how I can help this Navy Board."

"In this political climate, Molly, we are anticipating problems. As you know, custom enforcement has been lax, but Parliament intends to tighten up collections. As they do, we feel certain there will be those who abuse the situation—on both sides." Molly looked puzzled. To elaborate Commander Andrews said, "We anticipate tax evasion attempts from the colonists... organized tax evasion. We have heard a rumor of a secret organization formed to harass customs agents."

"I haven't heard that," said Molly pursing her lips.

"That is why I'm here. They are quite secretive."

"What do you want of me?" asked Molly.

"We need to stop this movement. Will you help me?"

"Of course, but I'm confused."

"I want you to learn who these people are and tell me."

"I don't know," said Molly rubbing her chin. "Snitching isn't in my make up."

"It isn't snitching, Molly. You can do New York a favor by helping us avoid bloodshed between the crown and colony."

"I don't like it."

"Look at it this way, Parliament recently authorized seizure of vessels involved in smuggling. If you help the crown, you will win powerful friends in the government and might just bank a favor or two. That would come in handy someday. We simply want you to keep your eyes and ears open. Parliament is well intended, and our purpose is to prevent bloodshed... from either side, or at least stop it quickly. We just want to keep peace in the empire."

"You want me to report the names of members of some secret organization whose name I don't even know. How can I do that if they are so secret?" asked Molly.

"Let's take baby steps. When one of our customs agents is attacked, try to learn who assaulted him."

Molly looked at the window thoughtfully. She said quietly, "I did hear about the burning of the customs agent's house in Plymouth, Massachusetts. I didn't know what to think... he was only doing his job."

"That's right, Molly, he was only doing his job. Please recognize this discussion involves us, and only us. You must tell no one of our meeting."

Molly frowned and remained silent. After a tense moment she said, "Commander Andrews, I have a husband. He is a shipper and could help me learn of this secret group. Besides, Jean-Luc and I," she looked at the floor a second and then added, "we don't keep secrets."

"I appreciate that, I really do, but you are the only colonial I trust. And your husband *is* a Frenchman." Molly's eyes flashed anger. Commander Andrews quickly added, "So you can understand my reticence. But that doesn't reflect on your loyalty." Molly folded her arms and looked away.

"Is that all the Navy Board wants?"

"Knowing you as I do, I'm certain your business *is* above reproach." Commander Andrews paused a second and asked, "Your business is above reproach, isn't it?"

"Of course," said Molly.

"So I think you're positioned perfectly within the coastal community and with your trading contacts, well, I know you understand the importance of keeping commerce harmonious."

Molly fidgeted in her seat and felt ill at ease. The thought of informing on fellow New Yorkers felt improper.

Commander Andrews noticed her discomfort and said, "I hope I haven't misplaced my trust."

Molly's eyes lowered slightly as she remembered the last war and the many scrapes she had experienced fighting beside this man. Molly said softly, "No, your trust isn't misplaced."

He asked, "So... will you help?"

She looked Commander Andrews in the eye and said, "I just don't understand why I must keep this from my husband. Why, he could do a much better job of this than I."

"Molly, the war involving England and France may be over, but we all recognize the peace is temporary. The Bourbons are nursing a grudge—they always are. They will cause mischief in the Americas where possible. If they see a chance to separate the colonies from England, they will inject themselves. You can see that, can't you?"

"France may be England's enemy... but my husband is not. He enjoys living here."

The grog house proprietor came to their table and placed two servings of tea and a plate of scones on the table. Commander Andrews waited for him to walk away before continuing. "I know you, Molly. I know your mettle. We served in wartime together." Commander Andrews's frustration bubbled to the surface. "Look, don't be naïve — your husband..."

Piqued Molly said, "His name is Jean-Luc."

"Your husband, Jean-Luc," Commander Andrews was trying hard not to offend, "is an English citizen by marriage... but, frankly, only by marriage. It's reasonable to assume his loyalty remains with France. If he knew of an arrangement between us... if he told a friend of the Bourbons... it would place my life, and this mission, in jeopardy." Molly pursed her lips, but didn't challenge Commander Andrews' reasoning. He quickly added, "Besides, you'll be helping your king, your husband, and your family's business at the same time."

"Good enough. But couldn't you get the same information from the News Board?" Molly glanced away in the direction of the window and noticed a man peering in. "Isn't that the beggar who was sitting on the corner?" she asked.

When Commander Andrews looked up, the beggar pulled away from the window. Andrews' conversation with Admiral Boscawen before he left for New York flashed in his mind —

*The admiral's aide escorted him to the door of Admiral Honorable Edward Boscawen's office. The admiral was a visionary leader — one who could foresee effects of poorly thought through policies. In truth, Admiral Boscawen often said that anyone who understands human nature could duplicate his management style. Andrews stood before the admiral's desk at attention. When Boscawen looked up,*

Andrews saluted. Admiral Boscawen returned the salute and
looked over the man in front of his desk. Andrews had come
recommended by his former commander, John Wheelock, an
officer respected in the sea service. Pointing to the chair to his
side, Boscawen said, "Take a seat." After Andrews seated
himself, Boscawen continued, "We're sending you to the
Americas, Commander." Andrews' expression did not
change, but being married, an overseas assignment would
upset his wife. "Parliament is raising taxes on the American
colonies and giving the customs agents carte blanche on
collections. The Minister of the Exchequer has even offered to
share money with naval captains derived from the sales of
confiscated vessels used by colonial smugglers."

"Yes, sir, I've been following this in the newspaper."

"Good. Upon arrival, there are several things I want you
to do."

"Excuse me, sir, but where in the Americas?"

"Yes, of course... the Port of New York on Manhattan
Island... first, reconnoiter the shippers and determine a
reliable individual to assist you. It will need to be someone
established, but don't pick one of the Dutch patroons. I think
that would be a dangerous choice. Develop a working
relationship with that person and have them report to you the
names of any of our captains they know to be abusing this
policy." Commander Andrews hadn't heard anything to make
this mission too difficult. Admiral Boscawen continued, "The
other aspect of this mission is for you to identify treasonous
individuals who harass our customs agents. Resistance in the
colonies to these tax incentives is growing and becoming
more organized. That concerns me."

Commander Andrews said, "There has been talk for
decades now about the Americas splitting from us. So the
admiral thinks higher taxes and a policy of confiscating
smugglers' vessels will push them towards that end?"

"Yes, I do." A knock on the door interrupted Admiral Boscawen. "Come in."

Captain Lord Harry Powlett (the admiral's executive assistant) stuck his head in the door. "I have an urgent dispatch from our agent in Cherbourg. I thought the admiral should see it right away." Captain Powlett walked in, handed Admiral Boscawen the message, and left.

After scanning the document, Admiral Boscawen said, "John, this reports two French agents departed in late December for New York. This will complicate your mission I think. The agent thinks they are headed to Manhattan Island also."

"Do we have descriptions?"

"I am afraid not."

"And if I find them... what does the admiral want me to do?"

"Oh, well obviously, I want you to interrogate them to discover why they're there, their contacts, et cetera... then eliminate them."

Andrews' mind returned to the present and he stood up abruptly. Molly said, "Oh, let him be."

Alarmed by the sudden move in his direction, Count de Charnay fled into an adjacent alley.

When Commander Andrews reached the street the beggar was nowhere in sight; Andrews placed his hand inside his coat and gripped his pistol. He edged toward the alley entrance and peered around the corner. The alley looked empty. Deciding the beggar wasn't worth pursuing he returned to the table.

Molly said, "You scared me half to death. It was only a beggar looking for food, wasn't it?"

Commander Andrews said, "I can't be sure, but I was afraid they would know I was here." He forced a smile.

Molly asked, "Is this request of yours placing me... and my husband... in danger?"

"No, not at all," said Commander Andrews. He didn't like being deceitful. After sipping his tea, he said, "You'll help us then?"

"Sure, I'll keep my eyes and ears open. I'm more than happy to report anything I hear. Just don't ask me to snitch on the shippers."

Commander Andrews smiled for the first time since they got to the grog house. "Agreed, now look here, I'm about to be late for an appointment. I'll be in touch." He stood and walked out into the street.

Count de Charnay had shed his beggar's garb in the alley. He walked back to the street corner with a completely new appearance. De Charnay watched the Englishman exit the grog house from a block off and began following him. He was careful to maintain a guarded distance. When Andrews neared the wharf, the paladin halted. He watched the Englishman approach the frigate H.M.S. Durham. After walking the gangplank, Andrews saluted the Union Jack on the stern and said to the ship's officer of the deck, "Request permission to come aboard."

The officer of the deck nodded.

"Please tell Captain Mowbray that Commander Andrews is here to see him."

"He is expecting you, sir, the captain's quarters are below the poop deck."

"I can find them," said Commander Andrews smiling. He walked to Mowbray's door, knocked, and waited patiently. When he heard, 'Enter,' he stepped inside. Captain Mowbray sat behind his desk and said, "Commander Andrews, come in." Captain Mowbray pointed to a chair.

Andrews smiled and sat down. "Sir, I am here as a courtesy call and wanted to let you know I was in town."

"Yes, well..." Mowbray could see from Andrews's uniform that this officer was not assigned to a warship. "What's your business here, Commander Andrews?"

"Admiral Boscawen directed me to assess the effectiveness of the implementation of the Navigation and Stamp Acts." Captain Mowbray laughed. Unable to discern the connotation, Commander Andrews asked, "Did I say something humorous, sir?"

"Sounds bloody boring to me." Captain Mowbray's remark surprised Commander Andrews; he realized the captain had ditched the niceties found in the hallways of the Navy Board. "In plain language, Commander, does that mean you are here to assess the navy's role in implementing the customs acts?"

"Well, yes, of course, sir. I have no authority with the Customs Office."

"You 'staff hens' are all alike. Why don't you steer clear of the gobbledygook desk-bound sailors use to impress each other." Commander Andrews's face flushed crimson. "Look, Andrews, I am a simple man trying to follow orders. The Durham is here to assist the local customs lads in their collections efforts."

Commander Andrews said, "I'm sure they appreciate your support." Captain Mowbray leaned back in his seat with a pleased expression. "Is the smuggling situation as bad as I have heard?"

Mowbray sat up and said, "Worse—it is utterly pervasive. However, I will soon have these waters under control. You see, the Durham is intimidating to the criminals. When a smuggler sees me coming, he knows he's as good as caught."

"Sir, how many Yankee vessels have you 'caught?'"

"Well, none yet—we just arrived," said Captain Mowbray uncomfortably. "We're providing support to the customs office in other ways as well. When customs needs to search a building, my marines will assist them. However, tonight, I am sending them out on a different matter. My marines are going out on a recruiting trip." Captain Mowbray leaned forward and asked, "Care to go along? You can get your feet wet."

"Thank you, but, no," said Commander Andrews, "I've been on my share of press gangs."

Captain Mowbray laughed and decided he liked the young officer after all. Commander Andrews wrapped up the visit and departed the Durham.

From a building corner, Count de Charnay observed Andrews

leave the wharf. He determined to search the English officer and determine if he posed a threat to his mission. De Charnay raced through an alley until he gained a full block on Commander Andrews. When Andrews passed the corner Count de Charnay clubbed him with his pistol's butt. Andrews staggered forward and fell. Stunned, he struggled to kneel and felt the lump on his head. Realizing he had been attacked, he whirled to face his assailant. Though stunned from the blow, he grabbed his attacker by the lapels, but succeeded only in ripping away a button. He tried to wrestle his mugger to the ground, but the paladin punched him in the jaw, and Andrews fell unconscious. Then Count de Charnay dragged him behind the buildings and rifled his pockets. When he discovered Andrews was armed, he shook the pistol's powder from the frizzen, tapped its barrel against a nearby tree until the ball rolled out and tossed the weapon to the ground. He examined Andrews' money pouch but found a few notes but nothing to ascertain his purpose. He disdainfully flipped the money pouch onto his victim's chest and walked away.

The next thing Commander Andrews felt was the shock of cold water splashing onto his face. He blinked several times and sat up. Molly was standing over him and a man he didn't recognize. Molly said, "Commander, this is Schout Jack Freeman; he is the sheriff of New York."

Commander Andrews forced a weak smile.

"Someone tried to rob you, sir," said Schout Jack. The lady here said you chased a beggar you thought was watching the two of you."

"My assailant wasn't a beggar. This person was dressed in quality clothing."

Schout Jack furrowed his brow. "That doesn't sound like a thief." The sheriff helped Commander Andrews to his feet and then asked, "Is anything missing?"

Commander Andrews felt his pockets, spotted his money pouch and pistol on the ground, and picked his wallet up to examine it. "My money is all here."

"There is something on the ground though," said Schout Jack. Molly picked up the button and handed it to the sheriff. "This is gold button has a cock's image impressed onto it. Your attacker lost it in the struggle. This is a good clue. I don't think there are too many coats in the city with buttons like these." Freeman stroked his chin and said, "We have an attack, but no theft. That's interesting. I'll need you to give me a description — to be thorough."

"Yes, of course."

A shaken Molly said, "I should be getting into the office. My husband is scheduled to return this evening."

Schout Jack nodded and took Andrews by his elbow. He walked him the short distance to his office and sat him into a wooden chair, and said, "After you give me a description of your attacker, I'll accompany you to your ship, Commander."

Andrews said, "I'm not assigned to a boat at present."

"Oh?"

"Actually, I was on my way to your office to ask your cooperation." Schout Jack leaned forward. "We had a report that two French agents recently sailed from France and we think they are here in New York."

"Are you some kind of a spy chaser?" asked Schout Jack.

"The Navy Board prefers the term counter-intelligence, but no, not really."

"Seems like y'ar whether you wanna be or not."

Commander Andrews smiled and said, "Perfectly accurate assessment, Sheriff. May I have your cooperation in this matter?"

"Why, sure, son, but have you considered these spies may now be chasing you?" asked Schout Jack.

"You're suggesting a preemptive strike by my quarry, eh? Perhaps the hunter is now the hunted."

"Looks that way." Schout Jack leaned back and stroked his mustache thoughtfully.

# CHAPTER THREE

THROG'S NECK
TUESDAY, OCTOBER 9, 1765, 5 P.M.

EW YORK'S FALL winds gusted across the schooner's beam
propelling sea spray over her deck. Wet and chilled to the
bone, Jean-Luc St. Alembert steered his ship under the late
afternoon sun and reddish sky. For three hours, the anxiety aboard
had been building and he saw the stress in the faces of his crew. Over-
head, the gulls circled like vultures waiting to devour a desert carcass,
seemingly biding their time for his schooner to be overtaken. As his
cutwater plunged through the three-foot waves, Jean-Luc wondered if
Lady Luck had finally abandoned him.

Molly's husband was following a westerly heading across Connecticut's southern coast, known as the Long Island Sound, and the
voyage had been hellish. The choppy sea made the going difficult and
weak stomachs churn. Not knowing whether prison, poverty, or both
were in store when the pursuing frigate sailed within range of its cannon added to his worries. As Jean-Luc's schooner dashed for the New
York spit, Throg's Neck, he raised his spyglass and grimaced. Atop
their pursuer's mast fluttered the Union Jack. "Just as I suspected," he
said under his breath. Jean-Luc watched the trailing frigate's stem rise
and fall parting the frothy seas in synch with his own. The two ships

glided through the white-capped seas as though partners in a nightmare waltz.

Looking behind repeatedly, Jean-Luc could see the empire's warship closing the gap. He estimated his pursuer could fire a warning shot across his bow within a half hour. However, he had experience with eluding customs vessels. With the uncertainties of tides, currents, and winds, he would never strike his sails until all hope evaporated. Just as he was turning the corner on profitability, his brief career as a commercial shipper looked to be entering its denouement only because his pursuer was faster. Plus his usual tactic of ducking into a cove wasn't feasible, because the frigate on his tail was close enough to observe any deviation in his course and to bottle him up.

As he approached Throg's Neck Jean-Luc thought of his usual feelings of relief at having the most difficult leg of the voyage in his wake. But today it was becoming increasingly obvious that the frigate would soon force him to heave to. Shouting to Henry he said, "Let's take her around the spit."

Watching Jean-Luc spin the wheel and the deck crew adjusting the lines on the belay pins, Henry whispered to the angels, "We need a miracle." Either it was *Aeolus*, the god of wind, or Providence, but an invisible power granted his wish. At that sublime moment the air stream shifted and began gusting out of the south.

Jean-Luc immediately recognized the implication. His schooner had already entered its turn, and for the first time in an hour, he thought escape possible. With his sailors scrambling across the rigging to complete the schooner's course change, Jean-Luc remained outwardly serene and ordered, "Prepare to secure the lines... coming about... steady..." The deck hands stood by the belay pins and mainsail sheets and the topmen held tightly to their positions as they readied to adjust the boom's angle to capitalize on the wind shift. After all, being chased by an imperial warship focuses one's mind powerfully. Responding to the situation, the skipper and his crew functioned as a single entity to maintain top speed, which is how Jean-Luc captained his vessel. After completing his tack he had his bow pointed toward the setting orange star. The southerly wind filled his canvas and sent his schooner surging.

The other skipper also recognized what had just come to pass. When his bowsprit lurched downward like one who has stubbed a toe and his pennants fluttered backwards, he knew his chase couldn't continue. His frigate was 'in irons'—the nautical term for a sailing vessel pointed into the wind. Without propulsion the fuming captain faced the frustrating dilemma of either performing time consuming tacks to keep wind in his sails until the ship could creep around Throg's Neck or terminating the chase. If he performed the necessary maneuvers, he risked running aground which would end his naval career (in addition to being a courts-martial offense). Or avoiding that fate he certainly would fall hopelessly behind regardless.

Captain Melton Mowbray, the warship's commander, turned away to rub his temples attempting to relieve the stress. His head throbbed and it felt like another migraine coming on. As he watched the suspected smuggler escape, all he wanted was just to lie down.

Back on the schooner, Henry Charles's long blond locks swirled in the wind complementing his boyish grin. The senior topmen shouted, "The telltales are blowin' strong, Skipper. We have them dancin' a merry jig. If I warn't twenty feet in the sky, I would be doing the jig with them. Aye, t'is beautiful to be at sea."

Jean-Luc turned his attention to the small ropes attached to the sails that indicate whether its trim is optimum, and nodded confidently for the first time since the pursuit began. Telltales stream rearward when the sails are producing optimum speed, and St. Alembert's telltales were virtually straight back in these southerly gusts. Observing the afternoon sky, Jean-Luc noted the first reddish hues outlining the clouds over distant Manhattan Island and their weather implications. Since the imperial warship apparently no longer posed a threat, he relaxed for the first time in hours, and in visible relief, beamed at his topman. He had out sailed the empire's tax collector again. This late afternoon, he looked forward to a routine docking and a pleasant reunion with his wife.

When the wind shifted suddenly moments ago, Jean-Luc winked at Henry. It appeared to all that they had outrun the empire's tax ship. On the smuggling runs Henry noticed that his skipper loved to maintain the crew's spirits in the fashion — as the French might say, *"le bout en train"* — or 'the life of the party.' But when his business was on the line, the skipper employed extraordinary concentration. Henry admired his employer's mastery of sail trim and his concern for the crew's welfare was obvious to the most cynical tar.

Turning to his favorite employee aloft, Jean-Luc shouted, "We were lucky with that wind shift."

"Picked a supportive occasion," answered Henry through cupped hands. "What do you suppose that frigate's skipper is doing now? I'd venture it ain't no happy dance."

Jean-Luc turned and observed his more powerful pursuer performing a perfect box haul, which is akin to a nautical U turn. At first, Jean-Luc thought the empire's ship had not planned it, but after considering the expertise required to execute that move between the bays Eastchester and Little Neck, he whistled softly in admiration and realized his good fortune in escaping such a skillful mariner.

"Skipper, I had me misgivings for a few," said Henry descending from the lubber's hole. Holding onto the shrouds, the top man stole one final glance at the king's ship. "Be it me or have ye noticed his majesty's navy acting powerful keen on boarding us of late?" Henry dropped to the deck and he positively beamed.

Jean-Luc nodded with a distant look, because he was thinking of the risk in evading customs. "They want the empire's colonists to cough up tax money, and they are serious now. Yes, I've noticed," said Jean-Luc. "They want to pay down the war debt, and believe the purpose of a colony is to support the mother country. Neither will I succumb to tyranny, nor will I pay for their wars. And now, they have given customs agents and navy captains a wicked incentive."

"What would that be?" asked Henry.

Jean-Luc rubbed his chin uneasily and said, "Well, if he had caught me and been able to prove me a smuggler, he would have confiscated this old boat, sold it, and pocketed half the money."

"Sold the schooner? Oh, they can't do that. Can they?"

Jean-Luc patted the ship's wheel and said softly, "Sorry old girl, I did not mean to hurt your feelings."

Incredulous, the topman looked into Jean-Luc's eyes hoping to see a clue that he was joking. Appalled when Jean-Luc nodded grimly and didn't change expressions, Henry said, "That would ruin the company, Skipper."

"Yes, it would ruin any of the shippers." Jean-Luc verified his heading with the compass before returning his attention to Henry. "You and I were not even born when they passed the Molasses Act in '33. That tax made an outlaw of every New York trader." Jean-Luc's expression turned grim, "The difference between then and now is the customs agents were not motivated, were easily bribed, and their enforcements were lax. Plus no one got upset ten, even five years ago, because the revenue agents still would not go to the trouble to pursue commercial vessels. But now... with this incentive... everything has changed."

"I still don't see how they can keep your ship or the money."

"That is the reward parliament holds in front of them to motivate collection agencies. I am afraid that peace with France gives them time to think up these schemes. And they raised taxes each of the past four years." Henry shook his head. "And next month they will require us to purchase stamps for official documents." Jean-Luc turned his attention back to the ship's heading. He knew he was operating outside the law. He wanted his shipping business to operate in the black without smuggling, but knew his competitors were either doing just that or somehow grossly underpaying the tax. "Our taxes are higher than ever, Henry, and parliament must raise money to pay the soldiers that are here now. After all, it is costly stationing troops on the frontier."

Aboard the empire's frigate, a debate was heating up between the captain and the customs agent. John Robb, said, "Let's put a cannon ball into him. That way we can identify him in port by the damage."

Captain Mowbray shook his head and said, "That is a bad idea."

"He is getting away. Our prize is slipping through our fingers," said Robb.

"Simply because he is running from us doesn't justify—"

"I'm not allowing that smuggler to escape. I'll take responsibility."

Mowbray scratched his chin and shook his head. Resigning himself to Robb's rashness, he said, "Then use the 'smasher' on the foc'sle, but it probably can't reach. We'll be out of range for certain, if I turn for a broadside."

Robb ran to the foc'sle and took the stubby barreled cannon near the bow. He placed the quoin on its bed and sited the barrel above the other ship's silhouette. The quoin, a wooden wedge marked on its side with elevations, assisted with distance corrections. He then lit the touchhole.

Henry flinched when a distant cannon's report sounded astern. Jean-Luc shouted, "Everyone down!" The crew braced for a horrendous impact. One tension filled second lapsed and then a water geyser erupted fifty yards astern.

Shocked, Henry said, "They've never fired at us."

"What kind of government fires on its own commercial vessels?" asked Jean-Luc.

Henry looked at the customs ship and answered, "Obviously, if we keep smuggling, Skipper, they will do it again." He stood and brushed deck debris from his clothing.

Rubbing his neck thoughtfully Jean-Luc said, "They tried to damage us so they could identify this vessel at the pier."

Henry nodded. He continued watching the other ship and wistfully asked, "What are we going to do?"

"What can we do? I do not have a good answer. If we pay customs and our competitors do not—we will go stomach up."

Henry smiled and said, "You meant to say 'belly up.'"

Jean-Luc pursed his lips and said in his French accent, "Yes, 'belly up.' If we do not pay, and are caught, they will seize the ship and its cargo. Either way, I will lose all."

Jean-Luc's melancholy underscored the truth of his statement. He turned over the wheel to Henry walked to the stern rail. There, brooding on his conundrum, his mind drifted to his marriage of four years. Jean-Luc adored his wife and didn't regret marrying a New Yorker. Working together, they had made their shipping business profitable after just three years. They had a cozy home and six small market boats servicing the river trade from the Manhattan Island to the Long Island Sound and the Rhode Island coast. With these six boats and their old schooner, they had built their business by transporting pig iron, tar, lumber, barrel staves, flour, molasses, and miscellaneous goods within New York's coastal and inland communities. In addition to those vessels he and Molly had taken a loan to acquire four goelettes to increase their market share within the smaller communities along the inlets and tributaries. Jean-Luc wisely seized any niche abandoned by the larger shippers (and frankly every bit of income helped). His prize possession though was still the run down schooner, Marie.

And yet, as in any marriage, frictions surfaced from time to time. His wife had returned from Canada with a war hero standing as a spy for General Wolfe during the siege of Quebec. Jean-Luc, on the other hand, had fought the English under first General Marquis de Montcalm and then General Chevalier de Levis, but on the defeated side. As a result of his being French Canadian in colonial New York, he struggled socially and experienced a disadvantage in business. Once married and living in the New York colony, he felt early (and often) the colonial bias against anything French. For over two centuries, New York's colonists had considered France their natural enemy. That animosity hadn't abated with peace on the colony's northern border. For another, the couple had precious little discretionary income. Though far from destitute, they agreed to pour their earnings into debt reduction on the goelette loan and, of course, keeping up the maintenance on the vessels. Yet Jean-Luc couldn't argue with his wife's recommendation of paying employees and creditors first and neither truly chafed at their modest lifestyle.

On a larger perspective the French-Canadian husband felt bitter toward the English Parliament that appeared to covet the colonies' maritime success (of which he played a small part). Jean-Luc correctly sensed that legislative body's desire to bring their New York colony under control and the English upper class's resentment of the *nouveau riche* that had emerged in the American colonies. For domestic peace Jean-Luc attempted to curb his carping about King George and the actions of the government.

At first, colonial shippers ignored the English customs agents, but as the authorities stepped up enforcement, they tried (successfully) to bribe them. But when that stopped working, they resorted to evading payment by smuggling. Jean-Luc and other New England ship owners felt they could abide control, but not if it came with unreasonable taxation—especially since they had no representative in Parliament other than their ineffectual colonial agent. It became obvious to the St. Alemberts and the New York business community that Parliament struggled with managing a global empire.

But Jean-Luc also struggled on a personal scale. His neighbors, with their resentment of his French ethnicity, frustrated him daily with their aloofness. He tried to make friends at church and establish friendly contacts with the other shippers, but any broadmindedness on their part was superficial. Jean-Luc all too well understood his modest inroads socially were because of his wife's war hero position. Nor did his fare-thee-well status at such a young age assist his quest for inclusion in the community. Though untrue, his competitors assumed that his father had given him the funds to start his business. These gentlemen, many of them Dutch patroons, were self-made men and decades senior in age. But it was on the open sea that Jean-Luc felt the joy that comes from being in control of one's business and the ship's helm. His sailors appreciated his hands-on leadership, business acumen and keen eye for commercial opportunities; plus the fact that they worked for a prosperous enterprise gave them secure feelings about their futures. Yet, despite the esteem of his employees, as a Frenchman in New York, he remained socially isolated.

# CHAPTER FOUR

Throg's Neck, NY
October 9, 5:35 P.M.

Customs agent John Robb angrily slapped the foc'sle railing of the navy frigate and turned away from the unloaded cannon. Having spent the last two days aboard a warship pursuing one Yankee ship after another he suspected of carrying contraband, he wanted a prize—desperately. When he first sighted the American's sail, bolts of exhilaration had flashed through his body on the hope of confiscating a smuggler's vessel. Since the schooner appeared to flee as soon as it spied the warship, he had fixated on the potential future income. Seizing a vessel of that size would be his first step toward an anticipated fortune. Standing on the quarterdeck watching the quarry escape, he had thought what a feather in my cap that would have been.

A New York customs agent for two months, he was finding the job frustrating. Robb discovered it to be devoid of social status and satisfaction. Thirty-four years old and unmarried, he sailed for the Americas in the unfortunate circumstance of having been disinherited by his rich estranged father. Wanting to begin his new life with a positive start he had eagerly sought this colonial customs position in the hopes of quick riches, wooing a colonial beauty, and proving his father wrong about him. But two months in the America's found him futilely chasing, but never catching, New York shippers and finding himself in the royal governor's doghouse for his ineffectiveness.

When the Yankee accelerated around Throg's Neck, Robb knew it meant he would be summoned to the governor's office tomorrow morning to explain another week of unfilled revenue coffers. And because he had not improved the tax bottom line the governor was concluding rapidly that he lacked the will and/or the skill to perform his post. As he watched the fleeing smuggler, he knew that (if only he could hold on to his position) it was a matter of time before he caught a big prize, earned the governor's favor, and turned around his situation.

Robb remembered that at his London customs training, Prime Minister Grenville delivered the graduation address. He and forty-nine other agents, all qualified for duty in the far-flung empire, envisioned great wealth when informed that they could sell confiscated ships (American or not) found smuggling or in some cases under reporting cargo quantities... and pocket half the money. Of course, he must share with any royal navy captain whose warship materially assisted in a capture. Well, that wouldn't be a problem, Robb thought, I won't need to confiscate many. Before long I'll be back in the social circles of 'my kind.'

The adept mariner who completed the commendable box haul maneuver, Captain Melton Mowbray, walked across the poop deck and said to Robb, "He had too great a lead by the time we spotted his sail. Besides, smugglers cannot count on wind shifts saving them every time. We'll yet catch a Yankee smuggler." From Melton's tone, Robb discerned the navy captain didn't count the American colonials as actually English.

"'Next time' won't help me tomorrow. Governor Colden is going to summon me to that worn spot in front of his desk reserved for customs agents. He's certain to demand an explanation. Blast the luck!"

"Don't ye be worrying, Johnny Boy," said Captain Mowbray slapping the disheartened customs agent on the back. "You'll survive. An ass chewing never killed anyone. You stick with me. We'll catch that scoundrel and many more of his sort. I've been ordered here to enforce the laws, and, by God, I will do just that. Before you know it we'll be bringing in one Yankee vessel after another for resale... and sooner rather than later."

Robb looked away. "Well, I really wanted to catch this one."

"We would have, you can be sure, but I'm short handed. Perhaps you noticed our slowness trimming the mainsail." Robb nodded. "I'll rectify that when we berth in New York."

"You intend to send out press gangs, don't you? You know, dragging men off the street—dragging fathers away from their wives and families—won't endear you to the Yankees. They detest press gangs. In my few short months in this horrible backwater, I know that much to be true. I've observed their reactions."

"Perhaps tis true what you say, Johnny Boy, but that is the price they pay for our protection. I think it's a fair exchange, don't you?"

"But isn't there another way?"

Captain Mowbray seized his opportunity to lecture Robb about the uneven tax burdens concerning Americans and the English aristocracy. Emphasizing his point he wagged his finger and said, "There is something wicked with an economy in which one people at great expense protect another and it is the other that obtains the wealth. Don't you agree, Johnny Boy?"

"Of course, yes. England ought to have lower taxes. England does the fighting." Robb's cold eyes fixed on the stern of the escaping ship, and with Captain Mowbray, watched their lost prize disappear down the East River on a westerly bearing.

"Do you think you could recognize the ship at the wharf?"

The question hung in the wintry wind. Mowbray's shake of the head reflected his misgiving. Finally, he said, "Doubtful, he had his nameplate covered. We never got close enough for a good look and one schooner looks like any other." Mowbray walked beside Robb and watched their potential prize vanish behind Throg's Neck.

Later Jean-Luc sailed past Ryker's Island. He mentally checked off the river isles because they indicated the time remaining before the vessel berthed. Listening to the sails beating made him feel the ship wanted to reach home as badly as he did. As the schooner glided past Blackwell's Island in the early morning moonlight, he thought two down one to go, and daydreamed of being under the blankets with his wife.

When they passed northward of Governors Island and tacked to starboard, Jean-Luc said, "Helmsman, give Diamond Reef a wide berth. Remember, it extends over half a mile out." Diamond Reef, rocky shallows running northward from the island, had hampered mariners for a century on the Hudson River approach.

Their bowsprit turned into the Hudson River and toward their berth. Setting aside the recent memory of the pursuing warship, Jean-Luc reviewed his schedule for the day ahead. His thoughts were momentarily interrupted as Henry called for orders to reef the mainsails. The schooner slowed to a crawl using only the bowsprit skirts to make headway and maintain control. Home safe, the Marie glided into its berth.

# CHAPTER FOUR

Manhattan Island
October 10, 8 a.m.

As the newest member of the French king's inner circle, Count Geoffrey de Charnay was getting a feel for life as a provincial peasant—only he was on official business on Manhattan Island. He sat on a street corner near the city's wharf and begged for alms. His real purpose—to make contact with the French Canadian shipper—would be the first step of his mission. A lad sprinting in his direction from the docks caught his attention. "Boy," said Count de Charnay in English, "what is the name on that ship that came in last night and is now unloading?"

"It's the Marie, sir," said the youngster.

"Thank you, boy; here is something for your information." Momentarily forgetting his assumed station in life, Count de Charnay reached into his hat's collection and offered a shilling coin to the lad.

The youngster looked at the coin, pondered the generosity of the beggar's offering and ratty appearance, and said, "I cannot accept this, Mister. You appear in want—more in need than I of this money." The lad returned the coin to the beggar's palm, smiled, and ran around the corner.

Count de Charnay chastised himself for his slip and dropped the coin into his hat. He thought over his plan to identify this shipper. He remembered afterward his need to meet with his associate from Ireland. As he observed the Marie's unloading, his mind wandered to a poignant memory of his Irish partner. Thirty-eight years old now, he had been but eighteen years of age at the time he first led men into battle. It was the year 1745, and the French were battling the English in yet another of a long series of conflicts—this one, the War of the Austrian Succession. Though a satisfying recollection, he never smiled whenever the memory surfaced. Those mental images now flooded into his consciousness—

*He had been peering over a stonewall, attempting to detect English sappers and grenadiers probing his position. His battalion commander had assigned him a critical point in the defensive line. Protecting the army's left flank, he had occupied the fortified Redoubt D'Eu that stood on the edge of the dense forest known as the Bois de Bary. His provincial unit had been called into service during a critical phase of the war. The French army, led by Marshal Maurice de Saxe, outmaneuvered the enemy's army and tempted them to attack his formidable defensive position. The inexperienced twenty-four year old second son of English King George II, the Duke of Cumberland, appeared to be taking the bait. The French (with an Irish regiment in reserve) occupied the rear of a slope that ran between the villages of Fontenoy and Antoin in Belgium. Captain de Charnay worried that his soldiers (actually neighbors living in the vicinity of his family's estate), having performed adequately in yesterday's skirmish, would face the brunt of the assault. He believed it would be nigh impossible to hold his ground.*

*First Sergeant Pouliarez ran in a crouch and knelt beside him. Pouliarez, thirty years older, sported a handlebar moustache. The two went way back, indeed, Pouliarez was a village elder in the province. He asked, "Captain Geoff, perhaps we should increase the size of our listening posts."*

*Captain de Charnay considered the proposal and said, "That is a good idea; it will boost morale and help the sentinels remain alert." He opened his spyglass and peered through it slowly moving the lens from left to right. After shutting his telescope, he said, "Cumberland is certain to attack here; I have no doubt of this. Double check the ammunition and redistribute as necessary."*

*Pouliarez nodded and disappeared into the night's veil. Captain de Charnay thought it a good idea to nap as there would be no time for rest once the battle was joined. He awoke an hour later when men from his listening posts scrambled over the wall. One whispered, "The enemy is formed and are now on the march, Captain."*

*Moments later the first sergeant rejoined de Charnay. Pouliarez glanced at the sky and said, "We will have the sun in our eyes."*

*With gallows humor, the young captain answered, "Well, they'll have the afternoon sun." A messenger approached and informed the captain to feed his troops. Captain de Charnay said, "I like this. The marshal positioned us back from the crest. It protects us from their cannon."*

*Ninety minutes after his men had their breakfast, the Scots Greys and the Highland Regiment approached the foot of the slope. Marching shoulder to shoulder with their muskets pointed forward, Captain de Charnay observed their massed formation, glanced at Pouliarez, and frowned. Both men believed the ensuing battle would be sanguine. As the English surged forward with drums beating and bagpipes blaring, De Charnay bellowed, "Ready!" He and his villagers, reflecting their steely resolve, brought their weapons to their shoulders. When the enemy advanced inside musket range, he screamed, "Fire!"*

*For the next three hours, Captain de Charnay's infantrymen* exchanged murderous gunfire and alternated bayonet charges. They fired volleys into Cumberland's ranks one time after another. Twice the enemy had to be repulsed by hand to hand fighting. Captain de Charnay's exhausted soldiers had suffered heavily, and yet, his villagers had not broken. Growing concerned that they could not repulse another assault, he looked behind him for an indication the reserve might relieve them. Seeing none, he turned to his village elder and said, "We cannot wait here. We are going to attack."

"That is suicide, Captain," said First Sergeant Pouliarez objecting.

"On the contrary, we will be slaughtered if we remain here without ammunition. Attacking is our only chance."

Marshal de Saxe, keeping a close eye on this critical sector from his vantage point, chose that moment to unleash his hidden reserve—The Irish Brigade—soldiers forever known as The Wild Geese.

Shouting their battle cry, "Remember Limerick and Saxon Perfidy," the blue uniformed expatriates were eager to cross bayonets with their historic tormentors. Charging through de Charnay's dog-tired men (who cheered as only those experiencing a life saving rescue) the fresh reserves, a regiment commanded by Colonel Jeremy Dillon, smashed into the depleted Scots Greys and Highlanders and drove them down the hill.

Marshal de Saxe observed his success. Knowing his main body was exhausted he chose not to pursue Cumberland. Though beaten badly on this day, eleven months later Cumberland would later save his reputation on the Scottish field of Culloden, and it would be the Scottish clans who paid dearly for Saxe's decision not to destroy Cumberland's army.

The commander of the Wild Geese gave the command to break off the pursuit at the foot of the hill, though his warriors continued hurling insults at their retreating, bloodied adversaries. Watching the English withdraw, Col. Dillon heeded Mars' warning, "At the moment of victory, fasten your chinstrap." He quickly reformed his regiment.

With the Wild Geese occupying the bottom of the slope, de Charnay's men took a well-earned breather. Seeing no indication the enemy planned to counterattack, Col. Dillon decided to confer with the exhausted French leader whose resolute defense prevented Cumberland from penetrating the line. He found Captain de Charnay holding his dying first sergeant in his arms, Col. Dillon put his hand on de Charnay's shoulder and said, "I have never witnessed such a display of valor, Captain. I congratulate you and your men."

Captain de Charnay didn't look up, but wiped blood from his wounded comrade's face. He said, "We were out of ammunition. These men," he motioned with his arm, "these soldiers around you are farmers from my province." Shaking his head sadly, he said, "We lost so many. This is the worst day of my life."

The compassionate Irishman knelt beside his French ally, placed his hand upon his shoulder and said, "Laddie, we Irish say, 'No matter how long the day, the evening will come."

"But one must first survive the day." Captain de Charnay motioned toward Dillon's soldiers, "Your men also fought superbly. The timing could not have been better. Cumberland's men would have slaughtered us."

Col. Dillon motioned to a tree stand five hundred yards away and said, "I watched the battle from there. I was close by the marshal."

"And what did you see?" asked Captain de Charnay.

"Your soldiers were incredible. But we could also tell they had exhausted all ammunition—and themselves."

"The marshal made a timely decision then."

"We Irish have another expression for an occasion such as this one."

"And what would that be?"

'Two people shorten the road.'"

Captain de Charnay said, "If you are trying to cheer me up, sir, it is working. Are there any more Irish expressions you wish to apply to the moment?"

Col. Dillon laughed and stood. "Bury your friend. I should get back to my men. Perhaps, we will meet again."

"I would like that," said Captain de Charnay sincerely. As he watched the Irishman walk away Captain de Charnay never expected their paths to cross again—

When another passerby dropped a coin into his hat, Count de Charnay's thoughts returned to the present. He glanced up at the donor, and said, "Thank you, good sir. God Bless." Then his eyes moved to the governor's mansion where he spotted his colleague observing him from a window. When he saw his old friend, his mind's eye summoned their meeting eleven months earlier. This pleasant meeting had occurred at the king's palace:

—It had been morning, December 22, 1764, when he was hurrying across the snow-covered grounds of Palace of Versailles. He had been late for a meeting with the king, Louis XV, and the Minister of the Marine, Nicholas de Berryer. Five years earlier, King Louis elevated him to that august circle of twelve royal surrogates, known as Paladins, because a vacancy had opened with the death of Captain Rene d'Alquier—the last paladin killed on assignment. French kings choose paladins according to personal criteria—for example, Count de Charnay had been chosen for his legendary courage, flawless command of the enemy's language. As de Charnay entered the king's anteroom, the secretary motioned he should hurry in. Shutting the door behind him, de Charnay observed the king, Minister de

Berryer, and an older gentlemen chatting amicably. "Please accept my apologies, Your Highness." Glancing at the visitors, de Charnay nodded. The king waved his hand toward a chair. As Count de Charnay sat, he thought, the man sitting beside the minister looks familiar.

"We were discussing an important development," began King Louis. "The American colonies are exhibiting unrest. Taxes appear to be the cause." Count de Charnay nodded respectfully. "It is our policy to limit our enemy's influence when and where we can. One way we accomplish that is by reducing England's revenue streams. That is why we wanted to see you today."

"How may I be of service to your majesty?"

"We are sending you and this man—" The king had forgotten the visitor's name.

Minister de Berryer quickly added, "Jeremy Dillon, Your Highness." De Charnay glanced at Dillon who, upon seeing the paladin's startled look, smiled subtly.

"—Dillon, yes, of course—to the Americas. Through our network in London we have managed to place Monsieur Dillon in the mansion of the New York governor." Turning to his paladin, the king said, "Count de Charnay, I want you to work with Monsieur Dillon. In addition, when you arrive in New York contact the son of a prominent family of New France by the name of—" King Louis' eyes searched the ceiling for the young man's name.

Minister de Berryer injected, "Sieur St. Alembert's son is named Jean-Luc, Your Highness." Turning to Count de Charnay Minister de Berryer said, "St. Alembert fought in the colonial militia with Marquis de Montcalm and Chevalier de Levis in the last war. We believe he will be receptive to your proposal."

"And what is my proposal to the young St. Alembert?"

"Encourage him to become involved with the American movement that wants independence from England," said Minister de Berryer. "He now resides on Manhattan Island.

"I see," said Count de Charnay.

"However, there is one snag," said de Berryer.

"Oh?"

"This fellow married an English colonial and the wife is no shrinking violet. She served in the English Navy at the siege of Quebec. She made quite a name for herself, and we understand she is fiercely loyal to England. " A wife who fought with Wolfe and a husband who fought with Montcalm — an interesting union, she must be a tempting morsel to get our man to the altar," said Count de Charnay.

"It is possible she could complicate your mission," said de Berryer.

King Louis interrupted by asking, "Did you just say the contact married a female that fought with Wolfe?" The king snapped his fingers and said, "Nicholas, didn't a war dispatch mention an English woman shooting Captain d'Alquier in New France?" Turning to Count de Charnay, he said, "Geoffrey, investigate that, and if it is the same person — take care of her. After all, how many English women were there with Wolfe?"

"As you wish," said Count de Charnay, but his expression showed doubt.

"What is wrong?" asked King Louis.

"Only, Sire, eliminating the wife of the man we hope to get to help our cause seems — "

Minister de Berryer's showed discomfort with this question. King Louis said, "Count de Charnay, I thought of that, of course. Avenging a paladin of ours is a higher priority. Do it so the young man doesn't know. Is that a problem?"

"No, Sire."

*After the meeting ended and the three stood in the
anteroom, Minister de Berryer asked Count de Charnay,
"Have you met, Col. Dillon?"*

*Smiling, Count de Charnay said, "Yes, he once saved my
life." Reunited, the two buddies hugged warmly as a
surprised Minister de Berryer looked on.*

Count de Charnay's psyche returned to the present. He nodded at
his colleague in the window.

Dillon also nodded and then turned to his new supervisor, the
colonial governor, Cadwallader Colden. "Is there anything else the
governor wants before I take my noon break?"

Governor Colden waved him off and continued to read his dispatches. As Dillon walked across the room, Governor Colden said
absentmindedly, "Oh, Jeremy, before you go, throw another log onto
the fire, won't you?"

# CHAPTER FIVE

## October 10, late morning

Jean-Luc debarked and walked briskly toward his office. One hundred feet behind him strolled three men disguised in sailors' garb tailing the young entrepreneur. The tall, handsome man was James DeLancey; the scion of the DeLancey fortune. The other men were temporarily unemployed ship captains Isaac Sears and Alexander McDougall. They wanted to observe Jean-Luc for possible anti-tax sympathies, and if they found him sympathetic to their politics, they intended to recruit his help.

Jean-Luc wanted terribly to fit in, had observed his fellow owners striding in a hurried manner walking to work and emulated them. His Gallic outlook seemed at odds with these English. He passed by 'The Fields' where the crown's troops drilled, but keeping to form didn't glance at the soldiers marching. Continuing up the street, he passed two shopkeepers chatting outside their businesses.

After Jean-Luc passed, the first commented on his gait, "Appears our French gentleman has a hot meal waiting."

"Or the bailiff on his heels," said the other and both laughed heartily at Jean-Luc's expense.

Oblivious to being the butt of their joke, Jean-Luc crossed the street and walked another block. There he encountered a ragged drifter sitting cross-legged by the door of Montayne Tavern. Jean-Luc had passed this tavern a hundred times, but had never seen this destitute person.

The poor wretch wore dark clothing, had a cowl over his head, and salt and pepper beard stubble. In front of the wretch laid an over turned wide brimmed hat. The hat was so dusty that it appeared to have been trampled by cattle. He beseeched pedestrians for alms; Jean-Luc pitied him and dropped two coins into his hat.

The beggar said in a gravelly whisper, "Merci, Monsieur St. Alembert."

Stunned, Jean-Luc cocked his head and looked closely at the beggar, but wasn't able to see his features. In French, Jean-Luc asked incredulously, "Who are you?"

The beggar glanced left and right and noted the three men down the street. Satisfied they could not overhear, he said in a whisper, "I am an Emissary of the Master."

Jean-Luc had heard that phrase only once before in his life, but would never forget it. Unsettled, his voice quivered as he said, "If you please, present your left arm." The beggar held up his hand and the loose cloak's sleeve fell revealing a tattoo on the right forearm that read '*MISSI DOMINICI.*' "There are only twelve men in France with that tattoo—the paladins." Jean-Luc squinted to examine the beggar, but didn't recognize him. "How do I address his Excellency?"

"I am Count Geoffrey de Charnay."

In a whispered rasp, Jean-Luc asked, "Count de Charnay, pardon me for asking, but why are you here—sitting like this?"

Count de Charnay motioned with his head to the tavern behind where he sat and said, "Let us go inside. I will tell you."

During the siege of Quebec, Jean-Luc encountered a paladin and learned that these twelve representatives of the king of France speak for the king in distant governmental matters and affairs of state. He also knew the king authorized some of them to assassinate as necessary. The French aristocracy considered paladins human treasure; enemies of the king feared them.

And Jean-Luc had learned not to cross swords with one. Puzzled, Jean-Luc entered the tavern. Seated in the middle of the room were two men talking quietly who only glanced at him as he took a table next to the wall. Moments later, the paladin entered, but walked with a despondent gait of someone homeless and not with a confident step of a French aristocrat. He stood humbly by the chair and waited for Jean-Luc to gesture for him to sit. The paladin pulled back the chair beside Jean-Luc. The tavern keeper looked up from his task of towel drying tankards and scowled at the vagrant's appearance. After all, his tavern was not a seedy dockside dive, but a meeting place of businessmen who talked the language of commerce. Jean-Luc observed the waitress looking to her boss for an indication whether she should serve the odd pair. Displaying obvious antipathy, the tavern keeper grunted his assent, but only because he recognized Jean-Luc.

Lowering his voice, Jean-Luc said, "Excellency, why are you dressed like—this?"

Count de Charnay replied in a whisper, "When we are abroad, a paladin often travels incognito. It is not safe for my king if his enemies know we are out of the country. And even though our realm is at peace with the English, I, too, would be in peril if they knew of my presence. They would be curious as to my purpose. They would probably insist on knowing."

Jean-Luc asked, "How may I be of service?"

Count de Charnay smiled for the first time. He said, "I have heard good things about you," and placed his hand on Jean-Luc's arm. Count de Charnay pulled his hand back quickly as the waitress approached.

Placing her hand on her hip in an impatient stance, the waitress said without enthusiasm, "What can I get you?"

Count de Charnay looked down humbly. Jean-Luc took the paladin's cue and said, "Two sherries, if you please." The waitress nodded sullenly and sauntered away. Neither spoke until she returned with two glasses filled with the brown, Spanish wine.

She said, "Folks don't order this much." Jean-Luc smiled politely and she shuffled back to the bar.

Count de Charnay said, "Jean-Luc, you appear to be a prosperous businessman."

"Thank you, Excellency, but in truth, our business is struggling. Parliament is sucking us dry with their levies. We make payroll and meet our loan payments, but that does not leave much for my wife and I to live on. But, of course, you did not come here to hear my problems."

Still whispering, Count de Charnay said, "While we are in the tavern, Jean-Luc, I must ask you to refrain from addressing me as 'Excellency.'" Blushing, Jean-Luc nodded. Count de Charnay continued, "I am sorry to hear of your issues. It will be better for you when this colony is no longer subjugated by the English."

"Certainly, but I do not think that will ever happen."

"Why assume that?"

"I do not understand.

"You see, King Louis retains 'observers' among the English colonies. We have heard reports of unrest. I am here to substantiate those reports and to act of them if they are true."

Jean-Luc blew softly through his lips and said, "Well, I am not surprised. It is obvious the colonies resent a parliament that wants them to pay for England's wars."

"Precisely, my friend, it is not just. And that brings me to the purpose of my visit. King Louis wishes you to be my assistant."

"Me? How?"

At that moment, DeLancey, McDougall, and Sears entered Montayne Tavern and quietly took a table in the corner. To ensure they weren't eavesdropping Count de Charnay subtly looked them over as they seated themselves. Satisfied they could not hear, he returned his attention to Jean-Luc and tapped the table in emphasis. He said in a harsh whisper, "By joining with a group that advocates separation. There are groups in other colonies, and it would be a boon to France's foreign policy if we can detach New York and the other colonies from England."

"Excellency, my marriage to an English colonial makes me an English citizen. I am now a New Yorker."

Count de Charnay condemned Jean-Luc's assertion. "No, you are not. You are French. Your marriage to a foreigner does not change that."

"I beg to differ."

"I see." An awkward silence followed and an offended Count de Charnay's eyes flashed anger. The young shipper looked nervously down at his glass on the table. Unaccustomed to having to debate, an annoyed Count de Charnay pushed back his chair and stood. DeLancey looked over at the beggar, but after a glance, returned to his conversation with his two companions.

Jean-Luc quickly said, "Please, sit." Count de Charnay slowly sat down. "I am willing to seek membership in one of the anti-tax groups. I will do this to help New York."

At that moment, John Robb, and his associate, Douglas Lising, entered the tavern and took a table across the room.

Robb said, "Finally. Some progress yesterday."

Lising asked, "What happened?"

"That wily Dutchman, Van Cortlandt—I caught him under re-porting his rum puncheons and ells of woven cotton. I've got the old Dutchman now."

"So you've caught one of the big fish in a lie, have you? He's wealthy, John. Old Pierre will try to draw out the litigation."

"Time is on my side. I'll bring him to either his senses or eco-nomic ruin. It'll be his choice."

"My but you are ambitious—going after Pierre Van Cortlandt." Lising then poked Robb and said, "I recognize that fellow, John." Lising nodded toward Jean-Luc. "He's a newcomer on the wharf." Lising snapped his fingers and said proudly, "His name is St. Alembert. I heard he's bankrolled by his father."

"St. Alembert? Sounds French." said Robb.

"He moved from Montreal after taking a Yankee bride."

Robb scowled and with a voice dripping with disdain said, "What kind of woman marries a Frenchman? Look who he drinks with—that vagrant doesn't belong in this tavern." Robb looked around and whis-pered, "A shipper, you say, do you think he smuggles?"

"Probably," said Lising.

"Can you hear what he's saying to that street wretch?"

The bar maid, having just served DeLancey's table, came to Robb's table and (hating the tax man as much as the next lass) asked dryly, "What you two want to drink?"

Robb ignored her and continued inspecting the young merchant. Lising spoke up, "Bring us two ales." Answering Robb's earlier query, Lising said, "Nah, can't hear a thing, John."

Robb and Lising had no idea that the people at the adjacent table —DeLancey. McDougall, and Sears, were tax activists. The people at DeLancey's table now observed both groups with interest. "What luck, Isaac, we've front row seats," said DeLancey. He was a thirty-three year old scion of the DeLancey fortune, and you couldn't find a New Yorker more involved in politics or anti-tax than him. One wouldn't label him a patroon, (his ancestry was French Huguenot after all—not Dutch), but you could sort him with the prominent members of New York colonial society. DeLancey's companions were middling sorts who did not merit inclusion in his exclusive social circles. Sears and McDougall's occupations were rabble-rousers and enforcers for their betters. When DeLancey (or another patroon) wanted something done, Sears or McDougall did it. DeLancey had it on his mind to learn more about the young shipper, St. Alembert, and intended to approach him in the near future.

Oblivious to those watching him, Jean-Luc tried to placate the paladin. He asked, "Do you have news of François Bigot? What became of my uncle?"

"Ah yes, the family 'black sheep.' We arrested him when his ship docked at Cherbourg. We charged him with embezzling from the king. He faced charges in a Parisian court. But he bribed his jailer and fled before the court could convict him. He was sentenced *in absentia* in December of '63. However, we know where he is. He is in Neuchâtel, Switzerland, no doubt in comfort and spending his stolen millions."

Jean-Luc frowned. Then he shrugged his shoulders and asked, "Will France enter Switzerland and bring him to justice?"

Count de Charnay scratched his chin and said, "International relations are delicate. One of my peers is negotiating his return. Interestingly, when a friend of mine broke the news of the loss of New France, the famous Voltaire was in the room with the king. Do you know what the esteemed state philosopher said to our distraught monarch?" Jean-Luc shook his head. Count de Charnay said, "'After all, sire, what have we lost—a few acres of snow.'"

Jean-Luc looked down at the table and shaking his head sadly said, "He really said that? A few acres of snow? Monsieur Voltaire also has a talent for understatement." He took a sip of wine and asked, "Have you been an Emissary of the Master long?"

Count de Charnay said, "Actually, I was elevated following the death of Captain d'Alquier. Since you were at Quebec, did you ever meet him?"

Jean-Luc coughed. His sherry had gone down the wrong windpipe. "Oh, yes, I met him. We got along well, I believe. I was with him when he died."

Count de Charnay nodded and asked innocently, "You were? Interesting." That confirmed in his mind that Madame St. Alembert was the woman his king wanted eliminated.

Lising leaned over to Robb and said, "John, that fellow is the one with the fleet of small boats."

"So?"

"So, he services the small routes the big boys are quitting."

"Good for him," said Robb with sarcasm. Though he couldn't overhear what the young ship owner and the beggar said to one another, he did detect Jean-Luc's French accent. He said, "Oh my word, Douglas, that man is French! Did you just say he was a newcomer to the wharf?" Lising nodded. "Then I shall take particular pleasure in collecting his taxes." Robb continued scrutinizing Jean-Luc. With his face contorted in disgust, he said, "French accents are like fingernails on a chalkboard." The tavern waitress approached and carelessly banged the tankards upon the table sloshing some of their contents over the rim.

Lising said in disgust, "Could you try being careful?" Jean-Luc glanced over at the commotion, but took no particular notice of the men. Lising leaned over and whispered, "Look, John, they're even drinking sherry!" Count de Charnay detected the men at the next table had said something about him and Jean-Luc and he looked over at Lising.

"What you staring at?" asked Lising with a sneer believing it would be easy to bully a beggar.

Count de Charnay peered from under the brim of his hat at Lising, but he only answered the offensive question with a malevolent smile. Although unaware he had provoked an experienced assassin; Lising noted the beggar's expression and realized he may have disturbed a sleeping rattlesnake. DeLancey, McDougall, and Sears tensed at this unexpected clash and exchanged nervous glances; they feared having to intervene should violence erupt involving the men at the adjacent tables. Correctly sensing this person wasn't to be pushed, Lising chose to turn away and not badger the vagabond further.

Returning his attention to Jean-Luc, Count de Charnay said, "Let us depart. I am pleased to note the king's trust is well placed."

Jean-Luc did not protest the paladin's statement, but to clarify he said in a whisper, "What I promised was to seek an opportunity to unite with other shippers in resisting these unfair economic policies." The paladin nodded understandably and he and the young shipper pushed their chairs back and stood.

"Excuse me," Robb said with his voice dripping with antagonism, "but aren't you *Monsieur* St. Alembert... the shipping proprietor?" Clearly Robb thought it would be good sport to harass the neophyte.

Jean-Luc replied in his heavily accented English, "You have me at a disadvantage, sir. Who, may I ask, is inquiring?"

"John Robb. I am employed by the crown to collect customs. I'll be dropping by your office next week to officially present myself."

Jean-Luc said, "In that case I will look forward to your visit." He turned to leave, but stopped, and turned back and asked, "Need I prepare in any way?"

"Oh, I wouldn't go to any bother. I'll review a few of your manifests to justify my visit. It will be routine, I assure you, old boy, rather a social call, if you will."

"Until next week," said Jean-Luc with a half-smile. He stepped forward and led Count de Charnay out the door.

As Jean-Luc exited, Robb glared at the young businessman and said, "I'll bet he has paperwork covering his arse. They all do."

"Of course he does," said Lising. "Reviewing his books is a waste of time. I think you'd have more luck if you surprised him."

"What do you mean?"

"Use that search authority you learned about in the customs course."

"What search authority?"

"The Writ of Assistance—it has been around since '51. That is what our people are using in the Massachusetts Bay Colony. You search his business or his house, and St. Alembert will get the message that you are serious."

Robb asked, "What grounds will I use to obtain the warrant?"

"That's the beauty of the Writ. You don't need grounds— just suspicion. Besides, we suspect this fellow is a smuggler—both of us. He and the others, they all do it. When Colden sees you taking positive action, maybe then, he'll get off your back."

"Good idea." John Robb pursed his lips and nodded. He liked the idea of reviewing the books of this French Canadian.

# CHAPTER SIX

ROBB KNOCKED AND then tentatively entered the spacious office of the New York royal governor. Governor Cadwallader Colden's male secretary, the elderly Jeremy Dillon, gently closed the large oak door behind Robb; it creaked and groaned imparting an ominous impression of a pharaoh's crypt. Seated behind an ornately carved cherry desk (complete with the exquisite carvings of the English crest on the frontispiece and with claw and ball legs) sat the seventy-seven year old acting royal governor. Sitting before the bewigged Governor Colden was the commander of the *HMS Durham*, Captain Melton Mowbray. Governor Colden gestured for the customs agent to take the chair beside the captain. As he sat, Robb noted the many honors hanging on the governor's wall and the embellishments of power that included the English flag and a staff holding the royal escutcheon of the Hanoverians. The office was luxurious, and the anxious Robb considered the irony of its lavish appointments being transported across the Atlantic via Yankee shipping that probably had avoided customs.

Governor Colden came straight to the point. "Captain Mowbray has been telling me how yet another Yankee shipper escaped paying customs."

Suspecting the captain may have laid yesterday's failure on him, Robb said in a noncommittal tone, "I see."

"Yes, he has been outlining that unusual change of wind direction."

"That is correct, Governor, the Yankee schooner took flight when he spotted our sail. We were about to capture him at Throg's Neck when the wind shifted and left us 'in irons.'"

"Nevertheless, Agent Robb, the government has nothing to show from your futile chase. Though your official conduct is above censure, that fact remain."

Oh, oh, here it comes thought Robb. He and Captain Mowbray exchanged concerned looks just as the old governor began wheezing.

Governor Colden poured a glass of water from his silver pitcher and sipped its contents. Fighting to control a nagging cough he swallowed with great difficulty before continuing. "Your collection record is abysmal, and Parliament, not to mention the king, wants results." With his unsteady hands the governor slowly picked up a sheet of paper on the corner of his desk and said, "Just this morning I was comparing your figures against your predecessor. There has been a decline." Governor Colden feebly flipped the paper back onto his desk in a disgusted manner.

He failed to mention that my predecessor also mysteriously abandoned his post and hasn't been heard from thought Robb.

"Whereas I am not holding yesterday's failed effort against you," the governor continued, "the fact remains this office cannot function properly without an improvement in your collection figures." Robb squirmed in his seat and saw with his peripheral vision the navy captain also fidgeting. However, Captain Mowbray wasn't accountable to Governor Colden for his performance (though he had tried to soften the governor's disappointment). But if the old boy wasn't blaming his customs agent for yesterday then who else could be culpable but the navy, thought Robb. "And yet, sir, my tenure shows improvement in retail revenue collections. "Governor Colden steepled his fingers and said, "Piffle. True enough, Agent Robb, but retail sale revenues are a fraction of what the customs duties would be and they won't finance this colony past midmorning. Our office—"

"But, sir, I have inherited these issues. My predecessor wasn't able to collect import revenues with any degree of success, and I might add, the challenges of my office are colossal."

"I've heard all of your predecessor's excuses, Agent Robb. Exactly what challenges are you referring? Have you new difficulties to append?"

"Well, first, the shippers' schedules are rubbish, what with winds and tides being huge variables. I have tried to anticipate their returns and intercept their ships for inspection, but it is inexact. Then the Yankee coast is immense. A smuggler can put in anywhere." Seeing the old man scowl, he quickly added, "Practically."

The old governor knitted his brow and grimaced. He said, "Tell me something I don't know. This is my second time as governor. I am aware of the smugglers' advantages."

Robb laid out his defense. "And only recently have we gotten naval ships to supplement our own. I know that with the navy's assistance I will be able to improve customs collections. But it will take time for the navy's presence to be felt."

"And yet, Robb, you either improve your figures or—you'll force me to return you to London."

"But, but, sir." To Robb a return to England as a failure was the worst fate imaginable.

"No 'buts.' I want the prime minister's cabinet off my back," said Governor Colden.

Captain Mowbray said, "If I may interject, sir, Robb won't fail. We'll catch Yankee smugglers and improve your revenue. We would have been successful yesterday, but the wind shifted. I also believe I could have caught him a bit earlier, but I'm short of crew."

"If you are trying to instill confidence, Captain, that argument did not succeed."

"Governor, I will send out press gangs. They'll return the *Durham* to full strength within days."

Governor Colden slowly pushed back his chair and walked to his window. With his hands behind his back he pensively looked out over the busy city street. "Couldn't you sail up the coast and kidnap *their* citizens? If you impress men from New York, I'll be listening to their complaining drivel for days." Colden turned back to Robb and Mowbray and said, "That's a start, Captain Mowbray, and press gangs may bring your ship up to full strength, but, given the revenue status, I would rather face angry citizens than an angry prime minister."

Sensing Captain Mowbray was winning the governor's favor and he desperately needed to do likewise, Robb's mind raced. Stalling for time until a moment of inspiration hit him, he said, "Governor, if I may, I have a plan of action."

"Really?" asked Governor Colden suspiciously.

"I will begin a series of searches of the local shippers' warehouse and residences. I will root out their contraband. The shippers must hide their inventories somewhere, and I will find them."

"What legal basis will you employ?"

"I will use the Writ of Assistance."

"So you're going to dust off that old regulation, are you? Well, good luck. A Massachusetts barrister, a chap by the name of James Otis, developed a huge following by opposing that law. Do you not expect the same will happen here?"

"Sir, we all understand the pressure to produce. But the writs are legal. I studied Otis's argument. He drew a great deal of attention in London legal circles, and we reviewed his arguments in my customs courses. But more importantly, sir, his arguments didn't win his case."

Governor Colden stood. Musing over the dilemma connecting the inevitable colonial complaints against press gangs and his prime minister's insistence that the colonials pay their share, he turned and said, pointing a bony finger at Robb, "Find your contraband and bring me a Yankee smuggler. I want to make an example of him."

# CHAPTER SEVEN

MOLLY WALKED UP behind Jean-Luc as he sat at his desk working the ledger. She gently massaged his neck for a minute as he continued to work. After totaling a column, he placed his quill pen on the desk and allowed himself to enjoy his wife's soothing touch.

"That feels wonderful," he said.

"Jean-Luc, said Molly kneading his shoulders, "how can you tell if a shipper is smuggling?"

"Hmmm, that is the spot," he said. After a minute he looked up at Molly and said, "Dear, practically everyone smuggles. Go to the wharf and select a ship—there you'll find a smuggler."

"Everyone?" asked Molly. Unsure of what her husband's response would be, she asked, "Does *Monsieur* St. Alembert smuggle?"

Jean-Luc opened one eye (cocking an eyebrow) to determine whether Molly's question held unpleasant implications for him. Viewing Molly's concerned expression with wariness, he said, "That is an unusual question. What prompts your inquiry?"

"Oh, I began thinking about that customs agent from Plymouth, Mass, they chased from their region. And then there was our own customs agent that mysteriously disappeared six months ago; I was wondering whether you might be in danger on our wharf.

"Do not worry about me, darling."

"Well, how do you know there is smuggling? How does one tell?"

"Wife, the signs are everywhere—if one knows where to look."

"Give me a 'for instance.'"

"Let me see—oh, all right, a ship that refuses to show his flag." Molly pursed her lips and looked out the window. Jean-Luc continued, "Flying the wrong flag is a pretty good indicator, too. And there is the ship plying waters that are known smuggling routes or sails unusual routes."

Molly said, "I was thinking of indicators on the wharf. Only a customs ship could detect smuggling on blue water."

Jean-Luc smiled and asked, "So you want to know the clues when a ship is in port?"

"Yes, that is what I'm after."

"Then look for unexplained cash. Cash stored in odd locations is a strong gauge. I have even heard stories of cash stored with the cargo." Once more Jean-Luc stole a glance at his wife to read her expression, but her pursed lips told him she hadn't heard what she wanted. "Another way to spot a smuggler is accounting irregularities."

Molly massaged his temples as Jean-Luc closed his eyes. She suddenly stopped and Jean-Luc's eyes popped open warily. "I won't be finding St. Alembert cash laying about the cargo will I?" Molly laughed at her joke.

"Molly, really! Our cash is in the bank!"

"Before I forget, darling, have you deposited the funds from the shipment to Mr. Hanson in Connecticut?"

"Yes, I did that already."

"Old Mr. Hanson paid you? Finally! Then you are going to continue carrying pig iron and lumber to him?"

"Yes, but, beginning last week, only lumber," said Jean-Luc without looking up.

Molly thought I would have sworn I saw them loading pig iron for the Connecticut run last week. She watched her husband close the ledger and place it in his desk drawer. He stood and said, "I need to get something from the ship before I forget." After Jean-Luc departed through the front door, Molly tiptoed over to his desk and sat in his chair. As she pulled open the drawer where her husband kept his ledger, she felt a loose floor board beneath her feet. "What's this?" She got onto her knees to examine the board and discovered it lifted up. To her shock, she found an identical ledger to the one in the desk drawer. After examining it, she concluded that Jean-Luc's hand had made the entries.

She rarely walked to the wharf at night, but she was concerned and intended to confront Jean-Luc about the hidden ledger. Before placing a flintlock pistol into her handbag, Molly put on her heavy shawl and cap. As she approached the pier where the Marie floated snugly bound, she saw a good for nothing hanging around the corner.

One ogled her and to Molly's great annoyance, asked, "Looking for someone to while away some time, Miss?"

Molly recognized the idler and answered, "A kind offer to be sure, Mr. Brown, but no, thank you."

Startled at being recognized, the married neighbor slunk away. Molly neared the family schooner and detected no sign of activity. She looked about and could see sailors preparing to depart on the morning tide, but they were working on ships some distance down the wharf. The adjacent ships appeared quiet and minimally lit. Molly decided to board the *Marie*.

She took a whale oil lantern from the main mast hook, and after lighting it, descended the companionway. She walked the short distance to the corner of the fore section of the orlop, Molly found what she expected—residue from the pig iron shipment to Mr. Hanson in New London. "What is he up to?" she asked aloud. Then Molly walked to the captain's quarters and went inside. There she placed her lantern on Jean-Luc's desk and opened the middle drawer. She pulled a pile of maps out and examined them in the lantern's dim light. They were unmistakably drawn in Jean-Luc's hand. Molly held the charts closer to the light and scrutinized them through squinted eyes. "These are 'hidey holes,'" she said quietly. "Jean-Luc is using these gunk holes for smuggling. I'm going to wring his neck."

Meanwhile, Jean-Luc was meeting with Count de Charnay for a drink at the tavern. Two glasses of sherry sat on the table. They were discussing the young shipper's progress in joining an anti-tax group, but their conversation had met an awkward pause. Count de Charnay finally said, "Come, let us finish our drinks and take a walk along the wharf. I need some brisk air." Jean-Luc didn't relish the thought of leaving behind the toasty tavern fire, but picked up his glass, and swallowed the wine.

As they closed the door behind them, a cool, autumnal breeze blew across their path, and the flapping of the ship pennants could be heard a block away. To be polite, Jean-Luc asked about RhÔne-Alpes, the province where de Charnay's ancestral home was situated. Count de Charnay grew sentimental as he answered Jean-Luc's queries.

Rounding the corner, the wharf stretched for several miles with blue and brown water commercial vessels of various capacities. Jean-Luc proudly pointed out his firm's schooner.

Count de Charnay noticed a dim glow emanating from below deck and asked, "Is that your night watch's light I see?"

"It can not be. I have no scheduled watch tonight. If you will excuse me, I should investigate. You do not need to wait for me, Excellency, I will shoo away this intruder—whoever it is." Jean-Luc stepped onto the gangplank.

Count de Charnay said, "I could remain here in the event you need assistance."

Jean-Luc shook his head and said, "That will not be necessary. It is probably a teenager. I can scare off whoever it is. *Au revoir.*"

"Then I will bid you, *"Bon chance et adieu."*

Jean-Luc watched the paladin walk up the street, and when he had disappeared in the night, he boarded the gangplank and walked warily toward a confrontation with the trespasser. As he reached the gunnel, Jean-Luc had second thoughts about going this alone, but the paladin had already departed the wharf.

Hearing footsteps on the gangplank, Molly blew out the candle. She angrily muttered, "If that is a thief, he just made a huge mistake." With her adrenaline surging, Molly was determined to defend her property. She took out the pistol and cocked the flint. She sidled to the companionway and climbed the steps to view the intruder. Molly watched the shadowy figure jump onto the deck and furtively approach the companionway. She tiptoed backwards and hid behind the door of the captain's quarters. The intruder descended the steps silently and crept toward the door. He went inside and walked to the desk. Molly pointed the pistol at him and had her finger on the trigger where she applied the slightest amount of pressure. The intruder lit a match and in the lantern's glow, Molly recognized her husband. She quickly let the flintlock down onto the pistol's frizzen. Molly stepped out. "I almost shot you."

Relief washed over Jean-Luc. "I thought someone was burglarizing the *Marie*. I was in the area, saw the lantern's light, and boarded to investigate." Jean-Luc started toward Molly, but her stern expression stopped him in his tracks. Molly took a step toward the lantern. Puzzled Jean-Luc asked, "Why are you here, darling?"

"Jean-Luc, I could brain you with the butt of this pistol right now."

"What have *I* done?"

"For starters, I discovered, quite by accident, the ledger you keep under the floor." Jean-Luc bit his lip, because he knew his deception was over. "It is obvious you are breaking the law, and on a routine basis," said Molly.

Jean-Luc tried to smile. He said, "I can explain. Let us go home where we can talk?"

"Fine!" Molly grabbed her wrap and stormed out. She stomped up the companionway and walked to the gunnel in a huff where she stopped to wait for her husband.

Jean-Luc nervously blew out the lantern. He locked the door, and walked slowly up the companionway like a man on his way to the gallows. He knew full well there would be the devil to pay when he got home.

Meanwhile, Count de Charnay had not walked away, but had held back to observe Jean-Luc through the cabin windows. When he saw him speaking with a young woman, he rightly assumed it was the American wife; the woman King Louis wanted killed. Tonight is a perfect opportunity to check this off the list. He gripped his pistol and quickly checked its powder.

While Molly waited at the gunnel for her husband, she was thinking she could talk sense into him when they got home. And she knew something else, she couldn't remain angry with the man she loved. Molly's thoughts of their rift and their soon to take place family discussion caused her to become careless about safety. Silhouetted with the full moon behind her, she presented a perfect target.

Count de Charnay stood in the shadow of the schooner adjacent to the *Marie*. He quickly glanced about the wharf surroundings and was satisfied that he could escape down the alley. The shadows hid him from the woman's observation. He went to one knee and rested his barrel on his left forearm. De Charnay sited down the barrel and aimed for Molly's torso. He uneasily squeezed the trigger. The paladin's gun belched its deadly musket ball.

Startled by the blast from below, Molly fell backward onto the deck. She lay still for a second trying to determine what had just happened.

Hearing the gunshot Jean-Luc raced across the deck. He knelt beside Molly and asked, "Are you hurt?"

She looked into her husband's eyes. Visibly shaken Molly said, "Someone just tried to kill me."

Jean-Luc's confusion turned to anger. He said, "Hand me that pistol."

Molly sat up and examined her clothing. She found the entry and exit holes. "The ball went between my legs." Jean-Luc tried to take the pistol. "No! I want to use it on whoever shot at me." Molly stood, checked its pan for powder, and bolted for the gunnel. Jean-Luc leapt to his feet and was immediately behind her. They dashed down the gangplank, and upon reaching the pier stopped to listen for footsteps of the fleeing shooter. The streets stretched out with no pedestrians in sight. The would-be killer was long gone.

A sailor from the adjacent schooner called down, "I heard a gunshot. Is anybody hurt?"

Molly said, "No one is hurt." She examined the hole in her dress, and said softly, "He missed."

Jean-Luc ran several steps in each direction looking for the person who had tried to kill his wife. He searched his mind for whom could have done it or why.

Frightened, Molly knelt on the deck and pondered whether this attempt on her life was tied to her accord with Commander Andrews. She resolved then and there she needed to get out of town for a spell and would accompany Jean-Luc on his voyage upriver.

Upon arriving at their home, Jean-Luc built a small fire in the stove and began to boil some water for tea. Molly undressed and got into her flannel nightgown and sleeping cap. His gut churned, and tonight's attempt left them both visibly shaken.

# PART II

## Patroons

# CHAPTER EIGHT

OCTOBER 18, 11 A.M.

JEAN-LUC ENTERED his office and found Molly at her desk with her head in her hands. He rushed to her side and asked, "What is it, darling?"

"I feel dreadful."

"Then you should return to bed."

"No, no, I'll be fine. I had this nauseous feeling yesterday, too, but, after a while, it left. I think I could use some fresh air, though." She stood, crossed the room and opened the door. The chilly breeze that blew in felt refreshing especially with the warm sun beaming into the room.

Jean-Luc said, "Then, I will just sit at my desk and do some work. That way, I can keep my eye on you." After settling in and opening his ledger, he began entering figures, totaling columns, and balancing the books. As Molly stood in the doorway, shouting could be heard coming from the up the street. Jean-Luc asked, "What is going on?"

Molly shook her head and walked outside. From the porch she observed a noisy crowd of about fifty moving in her direction. "Something has those people riled up, Jean-Luc." The disturbance was still a block away when the neighbor's five-year-old boy, Billy Sherman, ran up.

Billy tugged on Molly's dress and said, "Mrs. St. Alembert, they have one of yours."

"What do you mean, Billy?"

"The lobsterbacks! Mama said to run tell you they have your sailor."

Molly looked again at the crowd coming up the street toward her home and recognized their employee. Incredulous, she stammered, "Henry?" Baffled, Molly studied the raucous swarm moving toward her and now understood what Billy was trying to say. Henry walked in leg-irons escorted by a squad of royal marines. Molly shouted over her shoulder, "Jean-Luc, come quick! A press gang has Henry."

Hearing the gravity in his wife's voice, Jean-Luc burst through the door. "What did you say, darling?"

"It is a press gang coming this way, and they have Henry Charles."

Jean-Luc looked at the crowd. When he spotted Henry, he rushed into the street holding up his hands gesturing for the marines to stop. The sergeant in charge looked upon Jean-Luc as an insect needing to be squashed. The mob had made the sergeant fearful and he didn't want to stop—or to talk.

As soon as Henry recognized Jean-Luc, he called out, "Skipper, don't let them take me!"

"Clear a path. We're on the king's business," the sergeant demanded. The crowd had encircled them and now posed a serious threat to the marines. The men in the crowd had their fists balled and the women who carried brooms shook them angrily at the marines.

Jean-Luc stood his ground defiantly. In his French accent, he said, "I am Captain St. Alembert, this man's employer. Why do you have him in leg irons?"

The sergeant in charge, a man named Johnston, was newly arrived in the Americas and a veteran of the Seven Years War in Westphalia. Sergeant Johnston narrowed his eyes at the sound of Jean-Luc's Gallic accent. Over his shoulder, he mockingly said to his subordinates, "This here gent is a Frenchman." His subordinates, already apprehensive, grew even edgier as the crowd inched closer to them. The lobsterbacks glared irritably at Jean-Luc. "We haven't time to chat, Frenchman.

Stand aside. King's business." When Jean-Luc didn't budge, the Johnston narrowed his eyes and growled, "Didn't you hear me? Stand aside."

Jean-Luc said, "Since when does the king kidnap his subjects?"

The sarcasm in Jean-Luc's voice enraged Sergeant Johnston. "Watch your smart mouth."

"I demand you release my employee," said Jean-Luc.

"Demand, you say? Here is your response, Frenchman." Johnston smashed his musket's butt into Jean-Luc's jaw.

Jean-Luc crumpled onto his back at Johnston's feet. The people in the crowd gasped and backed off. They knew of the young shipper, but few had social contact with him. But observing his defiance of the press gang, they became enraged when he was knocked to the ground. Furious, one woman began beating a marine with her broom and screaming, "Go home, lobsterbacks!" The crowd inched closer taunting and insulting the press gang.

Johnston felt that if his detail could get to the wharf their shipmates would reinforce them and they'd be safe. He jerked Henry by his arms and pushed him forward. Henry looked back at his skipper lying in the dirt, but when a royal marine jabbed him in the small of his back with his musket, he turned around quickly.

Molly had watched her husband confront the royal marines. Seeing the violence, she bolted from her porch. When she reached Jean-Luc, the press gang had advanced to the corner with the angry crowd hot on their heels. Molly knelt and placed her husband's head in her lap. Fighting back tears, she tried to revive him. She looked around for help and saw Mrs. Sherman who she recognized and had seen dozens of times around the neighborhood. The Shermans lived two doors down.

Looking at Molly with sympathy, she rushed over and said, "The king's navy ought to leave our men folk be. Is your man all right?" Molly didn't answer, but examined his bleeding jaw and wiped away a tear.

Will Sherman came out to see what the commotion was about. He, too, came over and knelt beside Jean-Luc and looked compassionately at Molly as she held her husband in the dusty street. Mrs. Sherman said, "I will be right back with a pan of water and a clean cloth."

When Mrs. Sherman returned, she handed Molly the wet cloth. Taking it, Molly said, "I'm obliged for your help. You're both good Samaritans." The strangers smiled. Molly wiped Jean-Luc's brow and dabbed his bleeding mouth with the moist cloth. Jean-Luc's leg jerked and he moaned softly. He blinked several times. Molly said, "Be still, darling."

Mr. Sherman said, "Take it easy, fella."

Jean-Luc looked around slowly and blinked several times; he then dabbed at his jaw. He held up his hand to examine the bleeding.

The neighbor woman said, "Sir, you should go straight to bed."

Jean-Luc struggled to get to his feet and the man reached down and assisted him. Molly said, "As soon as I get you under the covers, darling, I'm going down to Governor Colden's office to complain. I'll ask him to intervene for Henry."

"Henry! Where is he?" asked Jean-Luc softly. He blinked several more times trying to clear his blurred vision and his throbbing head.

"The press gang took him to the wharf," said the man. "They'll be putting him on their ship."

"I am going to get him back," said Jean-Luc. "Do you know which ship?"

"Oh, it be the *Durham* for sure, but you're wasting your time. Folks here have tried to get the king's warships to release men before. But they know how to handle angry wives, brothers, and fathers. You won't get anywhere at the wharf but another busted lip."

Regaining his equilibrium, Jean-Luc stood and brushed the dust off his clothes. "Then I shall go to Governor Colden's office," said Jean-Luc as he took several unsteady steps.

Molly called after him, "Wait! You're not going alone," and ran to his side. The Shermans looked at each other and shook their heads.

When Jean-Luc and Molly reached the governor's office, Jean-Luc flung open the large oak doors and angrily demanded of the governor's secretary, "I want to speak with Governor Colden."

Alarmed by the young man's demeanor the old indentured servant employed as the governor's secretary, Dillon, stalled and said, "Governor Colden is with someone. May I ask the nature of your business?"

Jean-Luc said, "I want to speak with him about an employee the navy impressed today. The press gang came from the *Durham*."

"I see, um, well, please take a seat. I'll arrange an audience with the governor when he is finished," said Dillon.

Jean-Luc said, "There is not time. You either tell him Jean-Luc St. Alembert is here or I am going in unannounced. The ship could sail at any time." Dillon faithfully stood his ground. Jean-Luc brushed past him and said, "I must see the governor immediately," and jerked the door open.

The door banged loudly against the wall, and Governor Colden looked up from perusing the latest London dispatches. Determined, Jean-Luc and Molly strode to the desk. Jean-Luc slammed his palms on the desk's top and said, "Governor, a press gang grabbed one of my employees. They have taken him to the *Durham*—just now! I insist you intervene."

Without responding to Jean-Luc the governor turned to his secretary in the hall and said with icy coolness, "What's the meaning of this, Jeremy?"

"He barged past me, Governor; I tried to stop him," said Dillon.

Jean-Luc leaned over the governor's desk and repeated his demand, "You must stop this impressment. The man has a family. He is an important employee."

Noting this intruder's countenance, Governor Colden decided the wiser course of action was to mollify the man. Hoping a soft voice would turn away wrath, he smiled and said softly, "And to whom am I speaking?"

Molly said, "We are the St. Alemberts. We are the proprietors of St. Alembert Shipping."

Noting Governor Colden's unchanged expression, Jean-Luc said, "Sir, the citizens of this city well remember the impressments of '57."

Governor Colden smirked and said, "And how old were you in

'57? A teenager from your looks, I'd wager. Do you really remember that?"

"I'm old enough to hear my competitors say the English navy surrounded the city and impressed eight hundred men in an illegal round up. The navy must not be allowed to impress New York's merchant sailors."

"I perfectly understand your feelings, young man," said the governor buying time.

At that moment, Robb and Lising entered the building with papers needing the governor's signature. The two customs officers stopped outside the governor's office, peered inside and saw St. Alembert and his wife before the governor's desk and Dillon five feet behind them.

Robb asked, "Governor, may we enter?" Governor Colden wouldn't take his eyes off Jean-Luc long enough to respond. Dillon stood ready to physically intervene should the young shipper threaten the royal governor.

Jean-Luc would not be placated easily and said, "You understand, do you? Then stop the impressment!"

When Robb heard Jean-Luc's tone, he sensed an opportunity to act as the governor's personal defender. Rushing inside, Robb said to Dillon, "Go to the wharf and inform Captain Mowbray of the situation. You'll find him on the *Durham*. I'll remain with the governor." Dillon hesitated.

Governor Colden said, "That is a good idea. Go, Jeremy, please."

Molly said, "I wouldn't interfere, if I were you." The two custom agents ignored her. Molly warned her preoccupied husband, "Jean-Luc, behind you." She stepped in front of Robb and Lising.

Jean-Luc spun around to face Robb and Lising and said threateningly, "Do not interfere."

Robb said, "Shall we throw him out, Governor?" Governor Colden didn't respond, and Robb interpreted his silence as consent. "See here, you ruffian. You're coming with us." Robb grabbed Jean-Luc's arm, but Jean-Luc angrily jerked it away. Now Robb sensed throwing out the young intruder wasn't to be as easy as he had imagined. When Robb tried to grab Jean-Luc's arm a second time, the angry shipper slapped his hand away and took Robb by his lapels. Jean-Luc's eyes flashed.

Governor Colden said, "See here, St. Alembert, this is a royal customs officer. You two need to get along. Unhand him this instant."

Jean-Luc reluctantly released the shaken agent. Robb said with a quivering voice, "Now you'll be leaving."

Standing to the side, Molly said, "We aren't leaving until the governor assures us he will intercede on Henry's behalf. We want our employee released."

Robb turned and angrily said, "Be quiet, woman. Nobody asked you anything!"

Governor Colden shook his head sadly. He felt the situation might have defused, but now Robb had been sarcastic with the man's wife.

Jean-Luc drew his fist back and punched Robb in the jaw. The blow sent the agent over a chair and into the wall. The force of the blow knocked the governor's memento, old Pieter Stuyvesant's peg leg, from the wall. As Robb hit the floor, Jean-Luc whirled to face Lising, but the assistant did not want to clash with the athletic younger man. The standoff continued for several tense moments.

Summoned by Dillon, Captain Mowbray and ten armed royal marines rushed into the room. With his sword drawn, he pointed it at Jean-Luc and said, "Take him into custody, Sergeant." Jean-Luc, with Molly at his side, stood with balled fists. The sergeant was the same man that had smashed Jean-Luc in the face.

Molly stepped forward and confronted the captain. "None of this would have happened, if you hadn't sent out a press gang. We want our employee released."

Governor Colden said, "There's no need for brutality, Captain. This gentleman and his wife were just leaving." Captain Mowbray frowned, reluctantly sheathed his sword, and stepped aside.

Jean-Luc asked, "Will you order our employee returned, Governor?"

Captain Mowbray said with a sinister smile, "If you're referring to the sailor we just recruited, he's one of my crew now."

The annoyed governor glared at the naval officer. He didn't

appreciate his prerogatives being stripped by an indiscreet subordinate. He could be more diplomatic instead of the typical bull in a china shop thought Governor Colden.

Jean-Luc looked angrily at Governor Colden who averted his fierce gaze. He said, "Let us leave, darling."

As soon as the St. Alemberts exited, Lising rushed to Robb's side and helped revive his unconscious associate. Robb sat up and rubbed his sore jaw; he then shook his head trying to clear the fog. Resentment and humiliation seethed in his breast. On an elbow Robb stared at the young shipper leaving with his fetching wife. Jean-Luc had everything Robb coveted—: a business, a fine looking wife, and, he presumed, a respectable place in society. And now this French-Canadian immigrant had disgraced him in front of the governor. Robb was furious and wanted vengeance. He snapped at Lising, "Place that peg leg back upon the wall." Lising carelessly returned it to the nail in the wall; it hung crookedly.

When Governor Colden heard the building's front door shut, he said, "I'd like a word in private with Captain Mowbray and Robb." The ten marines and Lising quietly left the room. Dillon closed the door behind the others and remained in the back. He had been wisely instructed never to leave the governor alone lest someone make an inaccurate and difficult-to-refute claim about what had transpired.

Governor Colden asked, "This shipper, St. Alembert, is he clean?"

The chastened Robb said meekly, "I haven't checked him out yet."

"Do you have reason to suspect him of anything?"

Robb said, "Well, no. But he is no different, Governor. These colonial shippers smuggle, sir."

Ignoring Robb's unsubstantiated remark, Governor Colden said, "When do you plan to inspect his ledger?"

"I'll do it this week."

Governor Colden nodded. He began to straighten items on his desk. He said, "As you suggest, St. Alembert probably *is* smuggling. Use a writ of assistance. That will get you into his home and send a powerful message to others."

Robb said, "I'll search his alright. I will begin with his domicile. It will all be perfectly legal."

Disturbed, Dillon could not remain silent and said, "Governor, a man's home is inviolable."

Captain Mowbray turned toward the aged secretary and said derisively, "Only in England." Mowbray turned back toward the governor. No one noticed the secretary's visage turn crimson.

Governor Colden said, "The royal marines could be at his disposal, couldn't they, Captain?"

"Yes, of course, Governor."

"Robb, afterward, I want a full report. You both are excused"

"Yes, Governor."

Robb and Captain Mowbray exited the governor's office. In the foyer, Captain Mowbray said, "Plan the raid. You need only inform me of when."

Robb motioned to Lising to come closer. "Lising, we will be calling on the St. Alemberts soon."

Lising stiffened and asked, "When?"

"Soon! Very soon." Robb stared into space and thought I need a plan in the event we don't uncover anything. He continued to think about what vengeance to exact from this young *émigré*. He thought for St. Alembert's sake I better find contraband. If I don't, destroying his business will be only the beginning.

Dillon approached the governor's desk and asked, "Will the governor need me further?"

Governor Colden said, "Straighten Stuyvesant's peg leg."

Dillon regarded it a moment, and adjusted it slightly. "May I ask why the governor wants this old thing in his office?"

Governor Colden looked up and thought a moment. After a pregnant pause, he said, "It reminds the Dutch that we English are now in charge." He returned to straightening his papers. Dillon turned to leave. As an afterthought, Governor Colden said, "Jeremy, there is one thing."

"Yes, Governor?"

"Fetch that good for nothing sheriff for me first thing in the morning."

Governor Colden watched Dillon leave the mansion. He muttered, "It's strange that I know so little about him—he's a good worker."

Jeremy Dillon, a spry fifty-five, was known in Ireland as Viscount Connaught of County Westmeath. Wealthy from the rents collected on his considerable lands, Dillon's ancestors had fought the Roundheads under Cromwell, and his family despised the English wherever they met. And yet since arriving in New York, Viscount Connaught had grown to hold Yankees in high regard. He had fought England repeatedly on the battlefields of Scotland, Ireland, Belgium, and France, and he was angry over the treatment toward his family and neighbors by the English conquerors. He had formed Dillon's Regiment of the Irish Brigade and had crossed the channel to continue Ireland's struggle against England in the War of the Austrian Succession. Young Irish mercenaries, the Wild Geese, had followed Dillon into the service of the Bourbons. Dillon and the Wild Geese fought beside his childhood friend, Viscount Mountcashel, who also commanded a regiment in France's Irish Brigade. Together, Connaught and Mountcashel routed the English army in a ferocious counterattack during the Battle of Fontenoy in '45.

When King Louis XV wanted to send an espionage agent into New York with his paladin, Dillon made the short list. He had been in Paris when his Scotch-Irish connection caught the attention of the French king. His wonderfully falsified highland brogue endeared him to Cadwallader Colden during the employment interview in London while the governor was visiting on business. The governor immediately purchased his passage and entered into the indentured servitude contract with his new employee. Convinced he was bringing a fellow Scot on board, Governor Colden couldn't be happier with his selection.

# CHAPTER NINE

OCTOBER 19, 2:00 P.M.

O N THE WAY home Jean-Luc reflected on his clash with the customs agents. As his indignation grew, he decided to become involved in the anti-tax movement. His strides reflected his frustration, making it difficult for Molly to remain by his side. He desperately wanted Count de Charnay's counsel. When Jean-Luc and Molly arrived at their front door, he turned to her and said, "I must run an errand."

Molly said, "Jean-Luc, you suffered a solid thump today. Your gash could bleed anew; come in and lie down."

"I promise to rest when I return. I really must do this." He took Molly by the hand and looked toward the horizon; he said wistfully, "It has been a long time since we have seen Montreal. I miss Canada."

Molly watched her dejected husband turn and walk up the street. His slumping posture made her feel sad. Jean-Luc hadn't told her his destination and his state of mind troubled her. Molly watched him until he turned the corner. She opened her door, but stopped when the aroma of Mrs. McTavish's baked bread wafted over her. Normally, she loved the smell, but today, it made her feel like vomiting. *What is wrong with me? I think I'll lie down until it is time to meet Commander Andrews,* she thought.

In the meantime Jean-Luc approached Montayne's Tavern, but didn't encounter Count de Charnay. He decided he would wait ten minutes. As he paced near the entrance, to his surprise, the governor's secretary rounded the corner, smiled, nodded, and entered the tavern. Both astonished and curious, Jean-Luc tarried for a moment before his curiosity drew him inside. He waited for his eyes to adjust to the room and then noticed Count de Charnay in his disguise sitting quietly. Jean-Luc saw Dillon walk to the bar and order a mug of ale. The secretary paid for his beverage, looked around the room nonchalantly, and then departed after one sip. How interesting, thought Jean-Luc, as he turned toward Count de Charnay whom he noticed had also been watching the secretary.

De Charnay motioned for Jean-Luc to sit and asked, "What happened to your jaw?"

"Courtesy of an English press gang," said Jean-Luc touching his wound gently. "Excellency, my shipping colleagues and I live under impossible tyranny. This outrageous taxation— this cruel practice they have the nerve to call impressment, it is too great a burden. I have nowhere to turn. This government has made it impossible. Conditions get worse by the day. If doing as you ask will help me and my fellow citizens, then I will do it."

De Charnay asked, "Are you not splitting hairs?"

"Draw what conclusions you will, Excellency, but I wish to keep faith my new homeland and with myself. My reasons are important."

Count de Charnay cocked his head and held both hands apart as if to say he would not argue. Changing the subject, he asked, "Why did they hit you?"

"A press gang from the *Durham* snatched one of my employees, and— "

"And you tried to stop them? My foolish young friend, have you not learned there are times when one needs allies. A wise man once said to me, 'the road traveled is shorter with a friend.'"

Jean-Luc grinned. "It hurts to laugh, Excellency. Then he shook his head and asked, "What do I do now? I am willing to help this resistance movement you describe. Do I wait for someone to contact me?"

"No, I doubt they are prepared to do that. They undoubtedly are monitoring events, but that remains conjecture. Evidence a resistance movement exists abounds in Massachusetts, but I have not found concrete proof here. I have this feeling that it is only natural the movement's organizers will expand their struggle. A month ago they burned the house of the customs agent in Plymouth, Massachusetts. They are doing something about the tyranny. But I have not learned any of their identities. You can be sure the English authorities are trying, also."

"I wish there were men like that in New York," lamented Jean-Luc.

"There is one," Count de Charnay said firmly.

"Good, I will start by contacting him. Where can I find him?" asked Jean-Luc.

"He sits in front of me."

"Oh, be serious, Excellency. Please, I am still a start-up shipper, not a firebrand. I do not know how to begin."

"Begin by demanding your sailor's return."

"Do you want me to get slugged again?"

Count de Charnay frowned and said in a chiding tone, "Stop acting impotent. You have a family to provide for and a business to protect."

Acutely embarrassed, Jean-Luc said, "How can I accomplish what you suggest?"

"Be creative." The paladin leaned closer and said, "If you get your man back I guarantee the Yankee resistance will notice."

Several blocks away, Molly closed her front door and hastened to the café where she had agreed to meet Commander Andrews. With each step she thought of her husband's quandary and grew angrier about a situation seemingly spinning out of control. By the time she arrived at the café, she was upset. Commander Andrews had already taken the table by the wall. Molly entered the restaurant and saw that she and Commander Andrews had the entire establishment to themselves. Mid-afternoon hour seemed an ideal time to converse if one wanted privacy. Molly took a seat, but noticed Commander Andrews standing for Molly's approach (an interesting statement concerning her status as a young, businesswoman with a promising future).

Commander Andrews detected Molly's mood from her expression. "Is something wrong?" he asked.

"I'm having a bad day."

"Oh?"

"Yes, it began with a physical attack on my husband and has gone downhill."

"Is there anything I can do?" asked Commander Andrews sympathetically.

"Well, now, we're here to discuss abuses by naval authorities, if I recall correctly. Let's begin with the abuse my husband suffered."

"And the navy is responsible for the attack on your husband?"

"A press gang took one of our employees—a topman on our schooner."

"And your husband tried to stop them?"

"Yes, and for his efforts he received a musket stock to his jaw. These thugs came from the *Durham*. Are you familiar with that frigate?"

"Yes," said Commander Andrews.

"Do you know its captain?"

"I've met him."

Molly's anger simmered. "The impressment of a valued employee followed by a physical attack on my husband, well, I'm mad enough to bite a nail in half."

"Molly, no one hates impressing sailors more than the ones who do it."

"Really?" Molly's voice contained sarcasm, "I would have guessed the one being impressed hated it more."

"It is an odious practice, but you are well acquainted with the hardships of navy life. We struggle everyday with manpower shortages in the sea service and men simply don't volunteer to be sailors in the numbers necessary to crew the ships."

"Can you arrange the return of our employee?" Molly asked with no sympathy for Andrews's rationale.

Commander Andrews looked down and said, "Probably not. My mission to establish a monitoring network on political unrest in the colonies. I could jeopardize that by going off-course."

"That was a convoluted way of telling me that England doesn't want to lose her lucrative revenue stream that flows from this side of the Atlantic."

Commander Andrews knew full well that Molly could be cheeky, and this certainly was one of those times.

"Well, then, tell me what you know of the *Durham*'s commander," Molly said.

"His name is Captain Melton Mowbray. I know that the Navy Board's promotion committee passed him over for commodore. I'm sure he was terribly disappointed."

"Anyone would be," said Molly sarcastically.

"Captain Mowbray has had a solid career and I understand he is a skillful mariner. He wasn't with us at Quebec. He was stationed in home waters and assigned coastal defense."

As Molly processed this information, her anger began abating. She said, "That is a necessary duty, I suppose, but I would hardly imagine it would make an impression on the promotion committee. Anything else?"

"Others say he lacks tact and imagination."

"What do you mean?"

Commander Andrews scratched his cheek and leaned back in his chair. "Rumor has it that he wasn't promoted because he follows orders literally."

Molly nodded and leaned back in her chair mirroring Commander Andrews. She was thinking over what he had said about Mowbray. "Papa always said that there were two types of men not worth a hoot. One doesn't do as he is told and the other only does what he is told."

Commander Andrews smiled and said, "I always thought highly of your father."

Molly sat quietly thinking for a period staring at the door. Commander Andrews was thankful her anger was ebbing. He waited patiently. Molly slowly raised her head and looked Commander Andrews in the eye and said, "I will do as you ask, but— I haven't been feeling well lately."

"Oh?"

"And I don't know if my health will permit me to be as vigilant as you would require."

"I'm sorry. It isn't anything serious, I hope. Perhaps we should forget about this."

"No, no, it comes and goes. Right now I feel fine. I've thought it through and I'll do it. I think you and the Navy Board are sincerely trying to keep a lid on things." Both Molly and Commander Andrews smiled. She stood and said, "By the way, Jean-Luc and I are sailing upriver on the morning tide. It will be good for us to get away."

"When will you return?"

"We'll be away about a week. We're visiting Papa and Mama."

"Be sure to say hello for me."

"That will make them happy." Molly shook his hand, and walked out. Commander Andrews felt pleased with himself. His mission was on track.

# CHAPTER TEN

OCTOBER 19, 9:00 A.M.

MOLLY BREATHED A sigh of relief as she stepped aboard and took the schooner's wheel. She and Jean-Luc were sailing upriver and, for the next week anyway, were leaving their troubles behind.

Jean-Luc barked out, "Away aloft," and his topmen began to climb the ratlines and shrouds to the bound sails on their booms. Not that anyone held back, but Jean-Luc shouted, "Come on. Get the lead out."

Something is bothering him thought Molly. She turned to their employees on the wharf and ordered, "Cast off."

Under Jean-Luc's vigilant eye, the deck hands coiled the lines in a neat spiral. He believed one could tell a great deal about a seaman from the condition of the ship's ropes.

Molly watched their sailors scrambling aloft and recalled the first time she observed a ship departing and how remarkable it all seemed to her. She expected their schooner to sail the pleasant one hundred forty miles to Albany in three days. Molly enjoyed sailing the Hudson because navigation was simple and the shoals and shallow areas were well marked. Her husband had scheduled stops at Philipse Manor at the Upper Mills, Van Cortlandt Manor, and Albany. In Albany, they planned to rest the crew and take a side trip to Molly's parents' leased farm on the banks of the Mohawk River.

In New York City, Sheriff Schout Jack Freeman approached the secretary's desk with unease. The town's folk called him 'Schout Jack,' (*schout* is Dutch for sheriff, and they intentionally mispronounced it as 'shoot.' The forty-year-old senior lawman for Manhattan Island wasn't clear why the governor wanted to see him, but he didn't view it as positive. Born from the union of an English sailor and Dutch farmer's daughter, Jack spoke fluent Dutch, but his English tongue was haunted by that accent. Popular with the citizenry, he was forever suspect in the irascible governor's view as too soft for the job. In truth, the families made sure he and his deputies never had to buy a meal. All of this contributed to Colden's disapproval felt of the even-tempered cop. Schout Jack had a hawk-like face, a bushy mustache, and ruddy complexion befitting an active man doing an outdoor job.

Dillon greeted him with a smile and motioned to a nearby chair for Schout Jack to wait for his audience with the governor. Dillon knocked on the governor's door, stepped inside, and asked, "Is the governor ready to see Schout Jack—I mean Sheriff Freeman?" Governor Colden nodded glumly, and Dillon turned back to Schout Jack and said, "You may go in now."

Schout Jack walked quickly into the governor's large office with his hat in his hand. He nodded respectfully toward Hardheaded Pete old Governor Pieter Stuyvesant's artificial leg hanging on the office wall and sat down.

The respectful act annoyed the governor, but Schout Jack didn't care. Governor Colden glanced up and said, "Freeman, I don't think you approve that I keep Stuyvesant's peg leg on the wall."

Schout Jack answered in his natural soft-spoken manner, "It isn't really an issue with me, Governor, but there are Dutch families that find it offensive."

Governor Colden scratched his cheek as he contemplated Schout Jack's assessment. He then asked, "What can you tell me about these troublemakers?"

"Why, Governor, the incident ledger was a one pager last night. We ran in some drunken sailors, but it was peaceful most all evening, sir," said Schout Jack. In the governor's presence Schout Jack always ratcheted up his accent.

"Dammit, Freeman, I mean the rabble-rousers. Have you heard talk of strangers in town? If I abide sedition in my colony, the king will think me weak."

Schout Jack scratched his neck and said, "Governor, this town don't need outsiders to rail against his majesty. We have plenty of angry folk right here on this island. There's no need to import any."

"All the same, Mr. Philipse has complained to me on several occasions squatters from Connecticut and Massachusetts trespass and establish homesteads. I'm concerned that some of them may be political types infiltrating our colony. When was the last time you went up to his manor to run off squatters?"

"I don't never go, Governor. Mr. Philipse uses his own hired hands to run off those unfortunates. My force is small, and besides, he is out of my jurisdiction. This island gives me and my boys all the bad behavior we can handle."

"I suppose you heard about the unfortunate customs agent in Plymouth whose house was burned by the rabble-rousers?"

"Yes, sir, I read it on the news board."

Colden slammed his palm down on his desk and said pointedly, "I don't want any government property burned here. Between the African arsonists in our midst and ordinary carelessness, the fire department is fully committed."

"Shouldn't you be having this talk with the fire chief, sir?"

"Dammit, Freeman," Governor Colden's voice showed the stress these meetings always produced. "What I want from you is to keep your eyes and ears open for Massachusetts agitators. If any are coming here to start trouble I want to know. Could you please just do that?" asked Colden sarcastically.

Schout Jack's easy drawl just about sent the dour Scot over the edge. "Yes, sir, I think I could manage." Schout Jack stood, turned to leave, stopped, and said, "I believe you're correct; I've heard talk of anti-tax agitators, but they ain't coming from Massachusetts—or Connecticut even."

"Well, man, where are they coming from?"

"What I've heard is they's from across the big puddle." Schout Jack walked to the door.

Clearly agitated, Governor Colden raised his voice, "What are you doing about it?"

"I'm looking for them, Governor, and when I find them, I'll arrest them. Then they'll be your problem." Schout Jack politely nodded at Dillon in the back of the room and left.

Dillon's expression didn't change, but he felt anxious. He slowly stood and said, "Governor Colden, I am not feeling well, may I take my leave for the remainder of the afternoon? I am in no shape to be of service."

Galled by the meeting with Schout Jack, Governor Colden waved Dillon off with his gaunt hand. Dillon bowed, tidied his desk, gathered his coat and hat, and departed. He walked quickly to Montayne's Tavern, and seeing Count de Charnay in vagrant's garb seated on the ground near the door, nodded once and then walked inside. From the sidewalk, de Charnay could observe Dillon inside the tavern. When Dillon ordered an ale, drank a sip, and left, de Charnay knew his colleague needed to speak to him. As Dillon exited Montayne's, he knelt and dropped a coin into de Charnay's hat and continued. After five minutes, the beggar stood, poured his hat's contents into his palm and ambled into the alley behind the tavern. He untied his donkey (the animal lending credibility to his disguise) and began the journey to the Rock.

Dillon rode his horse and arrived at the Rock, the site where a roving band of Indians 'sold' Manhattan Island to the Dutch for a reputed twenty-four dollars in wampum. Most don't know the legend omits the Indians laughing as they rode off, since in the aboriginal culture, land was possessed only by the Great Spirit—not man.

Seated on a boulder, Dillon waited and watched an hour for his friend to come bouncing up the hill on the donkey. When Count de

Charnay was spotted approaching the Rock, Dillon started snickering at the spectacle. When de Charnay stopped his donkey, he looked sheepish at first, but then fell into the spirit of his friend's amusement. "What? I'm in disguise," he said.

"It's just the sight of a paladin of France's royal court on a jack-ass," said Dillon now holding his sides and roaring with laughter. He slowly regained his composure, but still had to wipe a tear from his eye. Finally, he said, "The old man met with Schout Jack Freeman," said Dillon.

"Who is he?" asked Count de Charnay, rubbing his backside gingerly.

"Someone we don't want to run into. He is the sheriff, and folks say not to let his folksy demeanor fool you. Schout Jack and the governor discussed the resistance movements in Massachusetts—and here. They somehow know foreign provocateurs are on the island, but they do not know their identities—I mean our identities. The governor pressured Schout Jack to find us. When the anti-tax gang in Massachusetts burned the customs agent's house, well, that got everyone's attention."

"The Massachusetts group burned the house—not foreign agitators. Tell me more about the governor."

"Oh, he is in his mid-seventies, I believe, and was born in Ireland to Scottish parents. His father was a minister who couldn't afford to fund his son's medical practice. So Colden came to the Americas in 1710 as a committed Whig to the principles of social justice. He has a keen interest in nature, enjoys a widespread reputation as a natural scientist. He still corresponds with the leading scientists in Europe. But his commitment to social justice didn't endure. He has alienated the powerful landowners. They hate him because he wants to reduce their political and judicial influence."

"It sounds like he is still, as you say, a 'committed Whig.'"

"I see how you could conclude that, but his motive is to increase his power and wealth. He just cannot stand the idea that Dutch patroons control court appointments on their properties."

"These patroons dispense justice on their own property? That is interesting, because in France, if a legal case interests the king, then we paladins do that."

"The Patroons even decide cases involving the death penalty."

"New York, it seems, has a power struggle, and quite a bit of dissension. That is encouraging."

"And all the more reason we must shield the anti-tax groups until they can mature. One of the resistance leaders is a man called Captain Isaac Sears. If this sheriff arrests him, it could cripple the movement."

"I do not think France is yet prepared to militarily intervene for these anti-tax groups. We are still recovering financially from the last war. For the foreseeable future, my country will not be able to help these Yankees.

Dillon asked, "What do we do?"

"I met with the young shipper, and encouraged him to join them. But we also need to keep Captain Sears and his men out of trouble." De Charnay rubbed his chin and asked, "What else do you know about this sheriff?"

"I have only learned he cares little for the governor and enjoys irritating him. He is popular with the people and seems honest enough. His position is elective and carries a certain independence from the governor, which chafes the old goat. The governor does not care for him either. He cannot bully him. I'd say Schout Jack is in his mid-forties, slender, wears a bushy mustache, and has a modest police force of four deputies. So I rather admire the man."

"Anything else?"

"Yes, since Schout Jack knew of foreign agents in New York, is it possible someone at Versailles betrayed us?"

"Betrayed?" Count de Charnay was wide eyed; he had been operating as if he was invisible to the authorities. Mentally reviewing suspicious courtiers, he in turn eliminated each name. "No! I doubt it. More probable an English agent reported our departure. I have observed a naval officer here who is not assigned to a ship. I think he is some type of government envoy. More likely he contacted the sheriff and reported the intelligence."

"Why do you think he is an agent?" asked Dillon.

De Charnay said, "I observed Madame St. Alembert meeting with this man. My attempts to eavesdrop were unsuccessful, so I decided to interrogate him. Someone interrupted us before I could begin." De Charnay stood and began pacing with his hands behind his back. He stopped and asked, "Where are you staying?"

"I am in a small flat near the governor's mansion—a block from the wharf and the army barracks."

"I want us to move to a room in the same building where Sears is staying to better monitor him."

"I can do that."

Count de Charnay saw something that made him smile. He tapped Dillon on his shoulder, pointed to a ship on the brown ribbon of water leading north, and asked, "Do you recognize that vessel, my friend?'

Dillon gazed on the ship for a few seconds and said, "No, Geoff, sorry."

"That is the St. Alemberts' schooner. I am working him into our strategy. Remember the king and the minister mentioned him during the meeting. For one, he struggles financially with the taxes, and has begun smuggling as a means of opposing this evil empire."

"Perhaps he smuggles just to keep his business profitable," suggested Dillon.

The paladin smiled sheepishly. "Well, either way. He is going to be prominent in this colony someday, and we want him working with us."

Dillon walked over and patted his friend on the back. "Killing his wife could foil our plans.

Disgusted with the directive to kill a woman, especially one whose death would be counterproductive, de Charnay said, "My sovereign wants it done. I cannot argue."

"And if the king wants it done, what can you do?" asked Dillon.

"I have learned she is the same female who shot my predecessor—that much is certain."

"She is as good as dead, then" said Dillon.

"Perhaps—perhaps not. She seems to lead a charmed life. Last night I had her in my sights, but a noise startled me and I missed," said de Charnay.

"There will be other chances," said Dillon. He patted his friend on the shoulder and said, "I'm glad I don't have that hanging over me." For a few moments, the two men watched the schooner below in silence. Then Dillon continued: "I have been thinking about something also, Geoff. When I watched that lad and his wife standing up to the governor, something inside me stirred. We were sent to separate these colonies from England. When they separate, I want to be a part of what they build."

"What about your estate in Ireland? Do you not want to go home? Do you not want to drive the English out of Ireland?"

"I thought that was what I wanted, but these New Yorkers seem so—"

Count de Charnay looked puzzled and asked, "What?"

"They seem so optimistic, Geoff, these Yankees are destined to tame this wild land. I want to be part of it."

Having lied to his associate about the assassination attempt, de Charnay looked at him with a quizzical expression.

Dillon said, "Aren't we a pair, Geoff? I am an Irish Viscount who wants a new start in this strange new land, and you, a paladin, have orders to kill the wife of the one man who can help us accomplish the mission."

De Charnay said in jest, "There is no hope for us."

"On the contrary, my friend, maybe there is hope for us yet."

# CHAPTER ELEVEN

OCTOBER 20

ELOW THE RISE where Dillon and de Charnay observed the schooner, *Marie,* sailing past the Yonkers' confluence with the Nepperhan River, Molly stood on deck as her wind-blown auburn hair danced about. She pointed to a huge redbrick manor house and its adjacent saw mill and asked, "Darling, doesn't that house belong to Frederick Philipse?"

Jean-Luc smiled and nodded. He said, "He owns the entire east bank from over there to beyond our first stop. You see, he and the other patroons positioned their mills near the confluences to use the power of the river to turn their mill wheels and the location affords them easy access to the Atlantic."

Molly said, "That was smart. Maybe we will expand into timber harvesting someday."

"Darling, they get their lumber from their tenants as partial rent payment; they write it into their leases. The tenant farmers are required to bring their trees to his sawmill. You and I don't have the land or the enslaved Africans to compete with his monopoly." Jean-Luc added as an afterthought, "Perhaps someday."

Molly's head jerked around as she asserted, "Oh, no, we'll not own human beings. We shouldn't judge others, but you and I won't make our living from wickedness."

Jean-Luc said, "Fine, darling," and winked at her. A strong puff sent the schooner on a surge and he nodded to Henry to haul in the sheets to take advantage of the stronger breeze. With the sails taut, the Marie's deck tilted a degree in response.

Molly felt blissful as she watched the mainsail canvas straining against the spar and sheets, and leaving the memory of the murder attempt in her wake helped. She observed Jean-Luc giving the crew orders and her confidence in him eliminated past misgivings about sailing the reaches of the river. The *Marie* cruised past forested high-rising banks and nimbly 'gave a coat of paint' to a marked shallow area meaning Jean-Luc had steered the schooner close on purpose. Two hours later they began the approach to the mouth of the Pocantico River. As their topmen reefed the mainsails, Molly observed the Philipse family's other gristmill and white washed, two story administrative buildings. A dozen mallards flew in low in front of their bowsprit and landed with a splash near the mill flume. These manors, formerly patroon-ships of the Dutch colony, New Amsterdam, belonged to three of the wealthiest original Dutch families in the Hudson Valley. The patroons had adapted readily when the English wrested control of their satellite in 1664. In addition, these and the other wealthy Dutch clans main-tained residential and commercial presences among New York City's thirteen thousand citizens. Their upriver manors were surrounded by their commercial enterprises and vast tracts of real estate that domin-ated the east bank between the Hudson River and the borders with Connecticut and Massachusetts. To manage their far-flung commercial enterprises (not to mention their tenants), patroons invariably built several homes besides their main domiciles in Manhattan. More im-portantly these powerful families had been clashing repeatedly with Governor Colden over their century-long domination and near-totali-tarian power.

Jean-Luc tied off at the pier of Philipse Manor's Upper Mill. The weather had cooperated wonderfully and the sun sparkled on the tranquil waters between the river and Philipse's dam. Molly spotted Mr. Philipse on the pier with his overseer, an aging gent named Elbert Aertse. Accompanying them was his enslaved miller, Caesar. The trio waited for the schooner to tie up. At age forty-three, Frederick Philipse III owned the mill and farm, and appeared in robust health, but he rarely visited his Pocantico Mill. He preferred living in the city. Jean-Luc hustled down the gangplank to confer with the patroon and overseer. This being one of his infrequent visits, Freddy Philipse took the opportunity to probe the new shipper on issues of import, and deemed it better to do so upriver. Philipse controlled the politics and commerce of the Westchester region, and the St. Alemberts felt compelled to court him for a portion of his business.

Mr. Philipse said, "St. Alembert, are you transporting my order?"

"Yes, sir." answered Jean-Luc, "And good morning. I have your dry goods and nails in the quantity requested." Molly walked up and stood quietly beside Jean-Luc.

Philipse said, "Fine, but I have a problem. Aertse forgot to order nine-penny nails, so we'll need a crate of those. Three shillings is fair, isn't it?"

Jean-Luc glanced at Molly, and the husband-wife team smiled in such a manner as to be undetectable by others, because Molly knew her husband would counter the lowball offer. Jean-Luc said, "I'm sorry, Mr. Philipse, but all nine penny nails on board belong to the Van Cortlandt order." Without saying 'No,' Jean-Luc signaled the three-shilling offer would have to be raised, because to a skillful negotiator, offers never get worse after the first refusal.

Mr. Philipse said, "Look here, St. Alembert, I'm a generous man, but not excessively so. I've given land to my church for its glebe and rectory, but I'll not allow you to take advantage of me. I won't be robbed on my own property."

Before Jean-Luc could respond, Diamond, one of Philipse's enslaved Africans, pointed toward the manor house in the distance and said, "Look, Miss Elizabeth is coming."

Elizabeth Philipse, at thirty-three years of age, was notorious in the Westchester region for driving her surrey at breakneck speeds. She had two passengers in the rig with her, and the sight obviously distressed Philipse who had his hands on his head. Polly, his beautiful younger sister, sat with her new husband in the rear seat and held her bonnet in place. "Those four black stallions are going to be the death of someone someday," he moaned. Worried about his sister, and her husband, Colonel Roger Morris, he said, "Oh, my word, she's going to kill them."

Philipse and Jean-Luc suspended their haggling to watch the surrey dashing along the dirt road. Returning from visiting friends in the village of Sleepy Hollow, Elizabeth pulled the reins back as the surrey careened onto the path before the planked dock and halted it in a billowing dirt cloud. The passengers, Col. and Mrs. Roger Morris, stepped down laughing nervously.

Col. Morris said, "What a chauffeur you've married, Freddy. Yes, quite exhilarating, don't you agree Polly?"

Mrs. Morris straightened her bonnet, smoothed out her dress, and nodded with a smile.

Two young Africans, George and Diamond, ran to the surrey and held the horses by their bridles as Mrs. Philipse tied off the reins. Philipse and Col. Morris assisted their wives to the ground. Elizabeth asked guardedly, "Who have we here, Freddy?"

"Dear, the St. Alemberts are from the city. They are new shippers." Elizabeth gave a disinterested nod in the St. Alemberts' direction, but actually she looked them up and down from the corner of her eye. Without revealing her emotion, Elizabeth thought, anyone can look good at twenty-one, dearie, but I have wealth. Mrs. Morris stepped forward with a warm smile and shook Molly and Jean-Luc's hands. Mr. Philipse continued, "Roger, you'd be interested to learn that Mrs. St. Alembert served with Wolfe during the war."

Col. Morris asked, "Really?" Molly nodded shyly. "I fought with Wolfe. Were you with the Royal Americans, my dear?"

Elizabeth stepped forward and said, "Our Roger is quite the war hero. He fought on the Plains of Abraham." Turning to Molly, she asked condescendingly, "What was it you did, dear?"

Molly matter-of-factly said, "I was a powder monkey on the *Pembroke*."

Col. Morris thought a moment and then said, "The *Pembroke*? Ah yes, Wheelock and Cook's ship—a splendid frigate. It led the fleet to Quebec."

Molly smiled at one of her fondest memories and said, "Yes, we did."

Philipse interjected, "Don't let her humility fool you, my dear, this young lady spied behind enemy lines, as I hear it." Caesar, the enslaved African that operated the Philipse's grinding wheel, approached Mr. Philipse while wiping his hands on a dirty cloth. He stood patiently waiting for an opportunity to get a word in.

Col. Morris ignored him and said, "Really, I didn't know the general had a spy inside Quebec. You must tell me all about it."

With the conversation on Quebec Jean-Luc's countenance darkened and he shifted uneasily on his feet. He wanted to finish the negotiations over the nails.

Mrs. Philipse didn't want to give Molly a chance to say anything. "I'm sure it's quite a saga, dear. You'll have to tell it to us some other time, won't she Freddy?"

Polly Morris said innocently, "I want to hear it now. Molly would you like to come to the house for some tea?"

Jean-Luc hastily spoke up, "Today isn't a good time. We really must set sail soon if we are to reach the Croton River by nightfall."

Molly took her cue and added, "We're due upriver in only a few hours, Mrs. Morris." Turning to Jean-Luc, she asked, "Is the cargo unloaded, dear?"

Morris said, "We promise not to keep you long. We'll retire to the parlor. We would so enjoy hearing your story, Mrs. St. Alembert."

Elizabeth frowned imperceptibly, but didn't protest further. She said to the young African standing to her side, "Diamond, tell Massy and Dina to drop what they're doing and bring some bread, butter, and cool spring water to the parlor."

Diamond nodded and ran toward the dairy barn. He found them milking the dairy cows.

Jean-Luc watched his wife enter the two-story, white washed house where the Philipse's stayed when they came to the upper mills. He turned to Mr. Philipse and said, "I may not be able to sell you the nails in the quantity requested for the price suggested, but I could be persuaded to part with some in trade for a barrel of your flour."

Philipse wrinkled his nose as though the counteroffer disagreed with him. But Caesar spoke up and said, "We need'n those nails, Mr. Philipse. I can't finish the mending of the mill wheel if I don't get them nails. Yes, sir, we need them something bad."

Caesar's revelation made Freddy pinch the bridge of his nose in exasperation and shake his head. He grumbled, "Thank you, Caesar, for reminding me." Under his breath he said, "In front of St. Alembert." George grinned broadly the entire time.

Jean-Luc glanced at Caesar and was certain he had said that in front of him on purpose. I'll bet he does minor sabotage practically every day, thought Jean-Luc. He smiled at Caesar though both masked their enjoyment of Philipse's humiliation. "Is it a deal, Mr. Philipse?" asked Jean-Luc, extending his hand.

"Deal," said Philipse. He shook Jean-Luc's hand unenthusiastically. He turned to George and Caesar and said, "Help the crew off load my purchase. The St. Alemberts are on a schedule and I need a moment for a private word."

Philipse and Jean-Luc walked slowly to the wharf beside the St. Alemberts' schooner. Molly glanced at her husband and Mr. Philipse walking side by side from the parlor window while relating a much-abbreviated version of her Quebec saga for her hosts.

Philipse asked, "Tell me something, St. Alembert. How is business?" Not waiting for Jean-Luc's reply, he continued, "The Crown is levying ghastly tax increases. I'm certainly struggling to meet my commitments. How are you managing?"

Jean-Luc's first thought was to tell this wealthy busybody to mind his own business, but he controlled his tongue and said, "My wife and I are meeting our obligations, Mr. Philipse. Thank you for your concern."

Philipse said deceitfully, "Well, of course, they're denting our profits. Well, I don't mean to intrude, but I have been growing concerned about the colony's future. And I know that many of my friends find it a strain to pay these new customs." His vast wealth made any new customs superfluous. He then said slowly, "I'm sure many are manipulating their manifests." He stopped to study Jean-Luc's reaction, but seeing the young shipper remain poker faced, he said, "How are you remaining profitable? Are you paying these exorbitant customs?"

Jean-Luc hesitated. He looked into Mr. Philipse's eyes to discern his level of candidness. Maybe this man could become an ally. When Mr. Philipse smirked, Jean-Luc decided to sidestep the query. "Mr. Philipse, of course, I am paying the duties on my shipments." Jean-Luc felt a twinge of unease because he detested lying. But he managed to throw out, "We should pay our taxes, should we not?"

"Oh come, come, my boy. Everyone knows the new customs are pinching shippers. Being new to the business, it must damage your profits utterly."

"I am managing, but thank you for your concern."

Realizing he couldn't trick the young man into divulging anything, Mr. Philipse tried a new approach. He needed a juicy tidbit to offer Governor Colden in exchange for greater autonomy in his manor's legal affairs. Trying to inquire into his political leaning, Freddy said, "Perhaps you've heard of men forming an anti-tax organization? It would seem to me a natural course to take for men uncomfortable with their added tax burdens."

Jean-Luc nodded thoughtfully and said, "Yes, it seems natural." Turning the tables on Philipse, Jean-Luc asked, "Have you heard of any such groups?"

"Actually, I have," said Philipse thoughtlessly. "I suspect James DeLancey. I think he would do just such a thing. He has made numerous comments concerning unreasonable tax increases to pay for *their* war. Their war, indeed, the crown supplied the army to protect us. Isn't that so?" Freddy didn't wait for Jean-Luc to reply. "DeLancey even makes it sound like England and the colonies are not one and the same."

Unable to build a rapport with the young shipper, Philipse said, "Let's join the others while we wait for our people to complete the off-loading."

Jean-Luc felt like shouting for joy. He had outmaneuvered Philipse and now he had a name to contact. He had never met James DeLancey, but he would make discreet inquiries, and try to engineer a meeting. As he and Philipse walked up the stairs to the parlor, they could hear George yell from the gangplank, "We finished, Mr. Philipse."

Molly said, "Well, I suppose that's my cue. We really are on a tight schedule and must take our leave. Thank you, you've been wonderful listeners. Mrs. Philipse, I am most appreciative of your hospitality."

Elizabeth said, "Nonsense, darling. You only got started, and I know Roger wants to hear all about the spying part."

Col. Morris said, "Promise us you'll finish the story on your next visit."

Molly said modestly, "I promise."

After Molly and the others walked back to the pier, Elizabeth said to her husband, "I almost forgot, Freddy. We agreed to loan two hands to Joanna." Without checking with Jean-Luc, she turned to George and said, "Fetch Massy and Dina. I promised Mrs. Van Cortlandt she could borrow them for the week. She's having some sort of get together." Molly looked beseechingly at Jean-Luc sending the message not to agree to transport enslaved Africans.

Jean-Luc recognized his wife's look of displeasure. He took her aside and whispered, "If we don't transport them they will just have to walk the Albany Post Road. And after all it is only two to three hours upriver."

Molly and Jean-Luc rejoined the group. Molly said, "Oh, darling, I'm sure we can afford a favor for our gracious hosts."

Philipse said, "By the way, St. Alembert, when will you return to the city? I may have additional cargo for you to transport."

Jean-Luc said, "We will probably return in seven days. I will be in the office the following morning."

As the St. Alemberts and the two girls walked the path from the gristmill to the pier, Elizabeth asked discreetly, "Freddy, did you get any information?"

Frustrated by his inability to entrap Jean-Luc, Philipse said, "He wouldn't admit to anything."

Elizabeth asked, "But you do think he underpays, don't you?"

Watching the St. Alemberts board their schooner, Philipse smiled and waved to the young shippers. Then he said, "Without a doubt. This new requirement to place stamps on all official documents has to be pinching the middling sort, especially a small businessman like St. Alembert."

"Then I think you should report him. But be sure to get something for your information. We want that dreadful Scotsman to stop attacking us."

"Elizabeth, I will visit the governor soon. Colden should agree to back off on his rhetoric towards this manor. But he is determined to break our political hold on our lands."

After boarding the schooner Molly said to the two young girls, "Stand by the foc'sle. You will not be in anyone's way there and will be safe." Massy and Dina looked frightened and Molly's heart went out to them. She understood their heartache from being separated from their loved ones. Molly smiled, but Massy and Dina quietly held hands and would look only at one another.

Philipse turned to his foreman, Aertse, and said, "I shall be using the office in the house for the next hour. I have an important letter to draft, and wish not to be disturbed." Aertse nodded.

Jean-Luc stood on the quarterdeck as the schooner headed out into the river. Molly came to his side and they watched the brown weathered grist mill and white manor house until the Hudson River's vegetation blocked the view. Little did the St. Alemberts know that at the next stop their young marriage would face its greatest challenge.

# CHAPTER TWELVE

Two hours later, the schooner nestled against the Van Cortlandt's pier, and Jean-Luc's deck hands quickly secured the lines. As soon as the gangplank hit, Molly debarked; Massy and Dina followed dutifully. A short distance up the Croton River Molly could see the Van Cortlandt's ferry crossing with passengers, horses, and wagons. Molly shook her head in admiration at the numerous revenue streams Van Cortlandt Manor generated. The Van Cortlandts had amassed a huge fortune also. Molly figured in the tenant farms, the ferry, and a boarding house; on top of that there was a farm for their personal needs.

Joanna Van Cortlandt, age thirty-five, bustled down the footpath to where they stood. She put her arms around Molly and gave her a welcoming hug. Massy and Dina stood quietly nearby. Mrs. Van Cortlandt said to Molly, "It's so good to see you again. We've been looking forward to you and your husband visiting with us."

Molly had met Mrs. Van Cortlandt on an earlier visit and was on friendly terms—though still only an acquaintance. She responded to her warm greeting and smiled warmly. Molly said, "We were full and by the entire leg, Mrs. Van Cortlandt."

Noticing Massy and Dina, Mrs. Van Cortlandt stepped back and said, "Youngsters, I am happy to see you, too. You may go to the kitchen now. Bridget will tell you what your chores are." The African girls nodded and walked toward the brick house. Turning back to Molly, Mrs. Van Cortlandt said, "Come, Mrs. St. Alembert, we are host to some folks who would like to meet you."

Molly said, "Please call me, Molly."

Mrs. Van Cortlandt put her arm around Molly's shoulder and said, "I will do so and I want you to call me, Joanna."

"But Mrs. Van Cortlandt, I mean, Joanna, my husband and I are in work clothes. We should change if there are to be formal introductions." Jean-Luc hustled down the gangplank and stood beside his wife.

"Welcome, Mr. St. Alembert." Mrs. Van Cortlandt turned back to Molly and said, "Your attire is of no import, Molly. It is you and your husband the others are anxious to meet. These are sensible folk; they watched you arrive, and perfectly understand your dress." They turned to walk to the house when Mrs. Van Cortlandt said out of the blue, "Molly, your complexion is wonderful. It simply radiates."

Molly smiled and said, "Thank you, but I have my moments when I feel simply awful."

With a smile, Mrs. Van Cortlandt said, "I shouldn't wonder."

Eight years senior to his wife, Pierre came down the front stairs to greet the St. Alemberts. Though the Van Cortlandts were rich, the Philipses' financial empire dwarfed their assets. Yet Van Cortlandt, too, held enslaved Africans laboring around the manor and assisting with his enterprises. In addition to owning the ferry spanning the Croton River and connecting the Albany Post Road, he owned the nearby gristmill, sawmill, tavern, and hundreds of profit-generating tenant farms. He shrewdly sited his house where the Hudson and Croton rivers met and (as had Philipse) added to his largess by charging vessels to dock at his pier. In addition, he had an operation that reaped the marine bounty of the river only a stone's throw from his home.

Van Cortlandt Manor was a two-story red brick dwelling with a sloping roof, eight freshly painted white columns, and a long portico.

The stairs started from opposite directions and met at a landing before becoming one leading to the portico. The entrance to the home was a large, dark brown Dutch door that Mrs. Van Cortlandt had insisted upon to allow in fresh air and yet kept the small children's whereabouts known.

Molly observed six people standing by the front door and said, "I hope we are not intruding. We and your foreman can handle the off-loading of your order."

Van Cortlandt said, "Not at all, these are old friends and while you're here I want them to meet you two. But I actually don't employ a foreman, unless you will allow me to count my sixteen year-old, Philip?"

Jean-Luc said, "Of course, sir. But I should report that your order is short a barrel of nails. Mr. Philipse insisted on a barrel that he needed. I do have the other barrels on your order to keep you going until I can get back with that absent barrel."

Pierre shrugged and said, "Well, no matter, those of us upriver must stick together. More to the point, Freddy is an old friend of the family."

When the foursome ascended the steps Van Cortlandt said, "Jean-Luc, Molly, I'd like you to meet our friends. This," he motioned towards a couple several years senior to Mrs. Van Cortlandt and him, "is Philip Livingston and his lovely wife, Christina."

Jean-Luc awkwardly stepped forward, shook hands, and smiled.

Molly, self-conscious of her deck clothes, demurely curtsied and said, "It is a pleasure to meet you."

Together, the Livingstons smiled and politely stepped aside so Pierre could steer Jean-Luc and Molly forward to Philip and Catherina Schuyler, Stephen and Catherine Van Rensselaer (both twenty-three), and then thirty-three year old, James DeLancey. He then said, "Christina is Stephen's sister."

Molly asked innocently, "Are you all related?"

Mrs. Van Cortlandt said, "Honestly, Molly, marriage between our valley families is so common you would think our offspring should have two heads and three feet." Molly politely laughed, but Mrs. Van Cortlandt's jest contained a kernel of truth.

Pierre ushered the group inside the house for refreshments. Molly and Jean-Luc felt honored and a bit overwhelmed by this unexpected attention from the colony's well to do. Molly remembered her father saying such awful things about the landowners, especially the Van Frogs, but they're very nice actually. Pierre poured the stemware personally handing out the glasses. As he approached Molly with a glass in his outstretched hand, he stumbled. Molly gave a little cry as she anticipated the contents dribbling down the front of her blouse. To her astonishment, the glass didn't spill a drop. Pierre had pulled his favorite hoax —the goblet with the false top. As everyone laughed Mrs. Van Cortlandt playfully slapped her husband on his chest and said to Molly, "Papa only plays his trick on those he likes, Molly."

Jean-Luc leaned over and said, "He really fooled you, sweetheart."

Being a good sport Molly hugged Pierre and joined the laughter. She understood it was a jest emanating from affection and not malice. She complimented his joke. Van Cortlandt quickly poured her another glass of wine (this one real) and said, "Now that the St. Alemberts have been initiated into our circle, I would like to propose a toast—To New York, may she always respect the natural rights of her citizens." The group murmured their agreement and sipped their wine.

Philip Schuyler said, "Pierre, I must add my sentiments. May I?"

"Yes, of course."

Schuyler raised his goblet and said, "To the return of representative government."

Molly looked at Jean-Luc to read his reaction. Clearly, these manor families thought ill of the empire's recent and closer supervision.

After sipping from his goblet James DeLancey said, "Here, here, well said, Philip." Molly looked the thirty-three year-old in the face and saw his enthusiasm for defying authority.

Jean-Luc thought, this is the man I want to speak with.

James DeLancey asked his host, "Pierre, may I throw in my humble toast?"

Van Cortlandt glanced questioningly at Mrs. Van Cortlandt. She nodded, and he said "Of course, James."

"Then I shall cry, 'To the end of tyranny.'" His voice dripped with hostility.

Molly winced and hesitated before sipping her wine. DeLancey's sentiments could only be described as seditious.

Jean-Luc grew exhilarated that these new acquaintances expressed feelings he'd had since settling in New York. He echoed DeLancey to punctuate the notion, "To ending tax tyranny."

Mrs. Van Cortlandt noticed Molly's uneasy expression and said, "Why don't we send the gentlemen off. They can go to the tavern and we ladies will get to know one another better? Is that agreeable, Pierre?"

Van Cortlandt took his wife's cue, and with a wave of his arm, gestured for the men to mosey down the brick walk to the tavern three hundred feet away; Mrs. Van Cortlandt motioned for the women to seat themselves. Molly looked out the window and saw six children walking up from the river. They ranged in ages from sixteen to three. The sixteen-year-old boy held a fishing pole and a string of fish. The oldest girl carried the three-year-old boy. Molly asked, "Are those your children, Joanna?"

"Yes, Pierre allows our sixteen year old, Philip, Sundays off—to respect the Sabbath." Mrs. Van Cortlandt sighed and added, "Well, St. Peter was a fisherman, so I hope the lord understands my son's love of fishing." Molly smiled, and Mrs. Van Cortlandt refilled her guests' glasses as she asked, "Do you want a family, Molly?

"Oh, yes, very much. We'll start one as soon as we get our business on its feet."

Mrs. Van Cortlandt smiled said, "Pierre and I felt the same when we were your age."

Mrs. Livingston said, "It is interesting that you have mentioned the future, Molly, because our husbands will be talking to your husband about New York's future."

Mrs. Schuyler added, "Well, someone must attend to it. Especially since our king and his parliament only want to tax and tax. Why, I believe they're green with envy."

Molly asked, "What do you mean, Mrs. Schuyler?"

"The lords and ladies in England have taken note of the wealth building in the colonies, but they are convinced our sole purpose is to produce wealth for them. I don't think that is why our families crossed the treacherous ocean. Do you?"

Molly was quiet for a moment. She thought the English Army risked all to secure New York from Indian war parties. Now these Van Frogs wished the redcoats would leave their shores. Molly considered the seditious talk inappropriate. She shook her head and agreed with Mrs. Van Schuyler, "No, I don't," but her friendly expression masked her misgivings over Catherina's statement. It seemed to her these Van Frogs and elites had prospered greatly from England's protection the last hundred years, but now seemed resentful when asked to pay for the military forces stationed in the Americas.

"Molly, just coming from Manhattan as you have, do you have any news about this new tax requiring us to place stamps on everything?" asked Mrs. Van Cortlandt.

"They will arrive any day."

"My husband and his business associates are furious. Honestly, I don't know where this tax will lead," said Mrs. Van Cortlandt.

Mrs. Van Schuyler said, "Philip says it will lead to violence. I'm sure my husband will be interested in your husband's stand on these assaults on our prosperity—and liberties. But I'm guessing your husband is also a man who cherishes liberty, Molly. You must be very proud."

Molly felt conflicted. She was flattered the manor families were including her and Jean-Luc in their gathering, but she had a terrible sense of apprehension about the future and the anger they felt. Yes, the taxes from overseas frustrated her at times, but weren't they all loyal English subjects? Her mouth felt dry and it seemed her voice even cracked as she said, "My husband came to this colony from Montréal. He has thrown himself into his business. We haven't been involved in politics." Molly remembered Commander Andrews request for information. Now that she had it, she felt terrible about informing. Molly grew agitated by the battle raging with her conscience.

Mrs. Van Schuyler said, "The abuses flowing from London will change his mind about that. Who can abide these tyrannies? Oh, he will want to be involved."

Molly looked down. Her discomfort was making her stomach churn. Are these elitists retaining their resentment for losing New Amsterdam to the English she wondered. Are these valid grievances?

Mrs. Van Cortlandt asked, "What is your opinion of parliament's treatment of us?"

Molly swallowed hard. "I think taxes are a necessary evil. And I think that we should elect representatives to Parliament."

"But, darling, that would never work," said Mrs. Livingston.

Molly asked, "Why not?"

"Because Parliament contains the House of Commons and the House of Lords, and there are no 'lords' in New York.

Molly blushed and said, "Well, that is correct. I think that the king could appoint them in that case."

Mrs. Livingston said, "He will never do that."

Molly said, "Well, then, I shall place my hope in men, such as Isaac Barré."

Mrs. Van Cortlandt sighed and said, "If only there were more men like him. Unfortunately, there are not." Then Mrs. Van Cortlandt stood and said, "Ladies, please excuse us. I would like to speak with Molly privately outside."

Molly and Mrs. Van Cortlandt walked through the front door and stopped on the portico. For several moments, they watched the family's pet deer grazing by the side of the house and some ducks on the Croton River hunting insects in the reeds. Then Mrs. Van Cortlandt said, "Molly, a break with England is coming. The colonies in America must make their own path. I'm afraid parliament will not allow us to leave the empire without a fight."

Molly looked at Mrs. Van Cortlandt and said, "I hope it isn't in my lifetime. The thought of bearing arms against England is horrible. It is so horrible that I don't think I could." A tear welled and rolled down Molly's cheek.

Mrs. Van Cortlandt detected the turmoil roiling in her guest and embraced Molly. She said, "My friends and I have caught you unawares. I apologize for upsetting you. You and Jean-Luc must make your own decision."

Molly placed her forehead on Mrs. Van Cortlandt's shoulder. After a moment, she said, "Thank you for understanding. You see, I made many friends in the king's navy and the idea of taking up arms against those men makes me ill."

Mrs. Van Cortlandt Van Cortlandt patted Molly's back and said, "I understand, dear."

Molly turned and looked into the distance. Mrs. Van Cortlandt waited patiently for Molly to mull over her colony's future. Molly looked down and asked rhetorically, "Why did King George pick now to implement these changes?"

Mrs. Van Cortlandt looked at her sympathetically and said, "He needs money, Molly."

Down at the tavern, the men folk sat in the back room reserved for Pierre. Jean-Luc was relishing the attention from the lions and scions. However, at present, he concentrated on the unusual tankard before him. He looked around the table and saw the normal pewter tankards in front of the others, but his vessel was twice the size of the others and had one feature impossible to ignore—it had three mouths. "What is this?" asked Jean-Luc, smiling.

Philip Livingston chuckled and said, "Jean-Luc, we have an identical one at my home, Clermont. As you can see, Pierre's Fuddling Cup has three chambers, but from only one will the beer flow to your beer pipe. Selecting incorrectly results in a suds bath." All the patroons laughed heartily, since Jean-Luc faced a two in three chance of erring.

James DeLancey said, "Each of us has sat where you are and have confronted Pierre's Fuddling Cup. It's a Tarrytown tradition, and it is only beer, after all. Close your eyes and take a drink."

Understanding that if he escaped the beer bath the guys would be disappointed, Jean-Luc said, "Well, here goes." He placed his hands on the handles, closed his eyes, and brought the vessel to his lips. Beer splashed down his forehead and cheeks and onto his shoulders. He sheepishly looked around the table as the Hudson Valley clan chiefs roared in sidesplitting laughter. The golden liquid dripped from his eyelashes and nose as he said, "Delicious! And quite tasty! Why are you laughing? Did I not choose correctly?"

Philip Schuyler slapped Jean-Luc on his back and squeezed his shoulder. He exclaimed, "DeLancey's record stands as the only one to avoid the bath."

Van Cortlandt tossed Jean-Luc a towel. He had almost fallen off his chair he had been laughing so hard. "Are there any more trials, gentlemen?" asked Jean-Luc good-naturedly.

Pierre bellowed to the tavern keeper, "Hal, bring this gentleman a proper tankard. I think he is thirstier than ever. He has earned it." A moment later, the tavern keeper hustled in with a tankard, and after he placed the pewter mug before Jean-Luc, he regarded the wet stranger with bemusement. As he retrieved the fuddling cup, Hal chuckled at Jean-Luc's appearance.

Philip Livingston, who had laughed heartily at the prank, turned somber. "The next trial, Jean-Luc, is when you leave this tavern."

"What?" asked Jean-Luc, not sure whether Philip was joking. "I do not understand."

Livingston said, "We asked you here, because we think you are a man who can see through the clutter of daily life and recognize what is happening in this colony. After all, you have wisely selected shipping to earn your living, and you've moved to New York from Montreal —another shrewd move in my estimation, and you've chosen well a New York bride as your partner in life."

"You flatter me, sir." Jean-Luc sat upright and sat on the edge of his chair.

"Jean-Luc, we feel it is time you take your rightful place among us. You have become a man of considerable means, and, as I said, we also consider you a man of good judgment." Jean-Luc's hair tingled on his scalp. Philip continued, "We believe the day is coming when New York and her twelve sisters must strike out on their own." James DeLancey nodded vigorously as Pierre and Philip Schuyler leaned back in their chairs listening. All five patricians looked at Jean-Luc for his reaction.

"England will not allow New York independence, certainly not peacefully," said Jean-Luc.

Philip Livingston said, "We aren't talking about tomorrow, next month, or even next year. Our fellow colonists won't be ready for some time. But when they've become sufficiently unhappy with oppressive taxation and no political representation in London, they will yearn for liberty—and independence, and be willing to shed blood for it."

Pierre said sarcastically, "Oh, we do have representation, Philip. George Grenville calls it virtual representation."

Jean-Luc looked at Pierre with a quizzical look, but it was DeLancey, who asked, "Pierre, I don't understand."

Van Cortlandt said, "Grenville believes by assigning New York to one of his members of parliament, that person will look after our interests—even though he lives in England. So we are represented, you see, only in a virtual sense."

Jean-Luc asked, "Has our representative ever visited New York? Does he have any idea what is needed or how we feel about policies?"

Van Cortlandt took a swig from his tankard and said, "Of course not. Our representative relies on reports from our governor and on New York's colonial agent for information. And slanted reports the governor does forward, I fear. Cadwallader Colden is out to destroy our way of life far more than parliament. He is the worse threat. His acts are dangerous to the business interests of all sitting here, Jean-Luc—particularly up and comers such as yourself."

Philip Van Schuyler said, "In his youth he was quite interested in science and maintained correspondence with the leading learned men here and in England. Oh, Cadwallader began as most politicians, Jean-Luc; he was idealistic and wanting to do what is right. But he lost his way some time ago, and he is now trying to usurp local government's powers and centralize them in his office."

Stephen Van Rensselaer interjected, "He is envious of our wealth. We haven't tried to bribe him—yet. But I think he covets riches as much as the next public servant, but bribing him will only delay the inevitable. Cadwallader is a side issue compared to the future of New York and independence from England." Van Rensselaer's words hung in the air.

"I did not know any of this. I am disturbed by what I am hearing," said Jean-Luc. "I wish I could do something. I, I want to do something."

"That is how we all feel," said DeLancey.

Van Cortlandt said, "Though I'm twice your age, my boy, in my lifetime, New York will part ways from England."

Jean-Luc asked, "What of New Yorkers who wish to remain with England? Will there be a civil war? What happens to the families on the losing side?"

An awkward moment ensued as the patroons contemplated the dark side of rebellion and independence. Each man reached for his tankard and drank. The answers had ghastly implications. Wanting liberty was one thing; spilling blood to acquire it was another matter. Van Cortlandt said, "With so much at stake, families on the losing side—may lose everything—their businesses, their estates—even banishment from New York is a possibility—and we don't want to leave."

Jean-Luc looked down at the table and said, "That is a dreadful thought."

Van Cortlandt continued, "When it happens, as I believe it to be inevitable, there will be more demand than ever for maritime commerce."

DeLancey said, "We want our interests positioned for what comes in the aftermath. Obviously, you will, too. We think you'll be perfectly positioned, Jean-Luc."

Jean-Luc smiled and said, "Let's drink to independence."

"I just knew you would want to escape parliament's oppression," said DeLancey.

The men around the table slapped Jean-Luc on the back. Unlike the businessmen in the city, these Hudson Valley Dutch accepted him and his ethnicity wasn't an issue.

An hour later, he walked (perhaps stumbled would be more accurate) the gravel path to the pier. At the top of the plank he looked back at the tavern on the distant hill and thought of the discussion of liberty. Their prediction of a wonderful future for New York without the government of King George interfering made his heart soar, and yet this prophecy also made him uneasy. He wouldn't enjoy gaining at another's loss.

Inside the manor house, after dressing for bed, Pierre blew out the candle and slipped between the sheets. Mrs. Van Cortlandt rose to one elbow and asked, "How did you fare with the husband?"

"Very well, I think. He has a good head and will be an asset to the cause." As he nestled his head onto the cool feather pillow, he whispered, "What about the ladies' talk with the wife? Same?"

"I'm afraid not. We made her uncomfortable. It was obvious."

"Will she come around in time?" asked Pierre. When Mrs. Van Cortlandt frowned, Pierre asked playfully, "Some time this century?"

Mrs. Van Cortlandt said, "That I cannot predict." She blew out the candle on the nightstand, kissed Pierre on the forehead, and laid back. "Molly is young and her heroine standing is still fresh in her memory. What I like about this couple is the obvious love and respect they share. Did you notice how they look at one another? I wouldn't be surprised if they are talking now about the same subject we are."

Pierre lay on his back with his hands behind his head. He watched the fire's shadowy tails dance on the ceiling. "I need to go into New

York City and speak with our solicitor about that customs inspection I failed last month. I will be gone three days and will try to look in on the St. Alemberts while I'm there." Mrs. Van Cortlandt smiled and kissed her husband on the forehead.

On the schooner, Jean-Luc softly closed the door of the cabin and squinted in the dim moonlight shining on his cot. "Molly, are you asleep?" he asked in whispered French.

Molly, in their bed suspended from ropes attached to the ceiling, opened her eyes, but she did not respond.

"Henry said you had come aboard," he said standing by the bed and looking down on her. "How are you feeling?"

"Awful," said Molly.

Uh oh, thought Jean-Luc, something is wrong. "What is the matter, darling?"

"My stomach is bothering me. I can't sleep."

Jean-Luc didn't respond, but wisely waited for more information.

"It's because I am upset."

"What is it, darling?" Knowing Molly, the real cause would be mentioned second.

Molly said, "All evening, I heard one seditious comment followed by another. How can they talk like they're unhappy and dissatisfied? They're English subjects. They're rich English subjects, for God's sake. Being English is like winning a prize drawing. Would they prefer to live elsewhere? I find it unbelievable!"

"Did you not enjoy yourself?"

"They're going to get themselves into trouble. Sedition is serious, and I don't want them to drag us down with them. We cannot do any more commerce with these Van Frogs."

Jean-Luc's face flushed with anger at the ethnic slur. "Everybody off the ship," he yelled at the top of his lungs. The crew slowly rolled out of their hammocks and ascended the companionway. In Van Cortlandt Manor candles were lit in response to the commotion aboard the visiting schooner.

Mr. and Mrs. Van Cortlandt peered out their bedroom window and saw a dozen crewmembers shivering in the cold by the pier. Mrs. Van Cortlandt asked, "What is going on, Pierre?"

Van Cortlandt said, "I think the Lakes are discussing this evening." He and his wife started to put on their coats. They ran outside and stood behind the crew; all strained to hear, but to appear as though they were not trying to listen.

Back inside the skipper's room, Jean-Luc said in a loud hiss, "Molly, I... You know it upsets me when you use that term. In the future, please never use it again."

"Fine! I won't say Van Frog," said Molly in an angry whisper.

"Our colony cannot go on in this way. The government threatens our business and we have no say. This oppression must end."

"So, you are joining the ranks of the ungrateful," said Molly accusingly.

Jean-Luc remembered the crew waiting in the cold. "We must continue our discussion some other time." No matter what path the colony took politically, he cherished his marriage to Molly and did not want King George's taxation coming between him and his wife. He said, I am going to bring the crew back aboard."

As Jean-Luc motioned his employees to return, Henry Charles looked at Van Cortlandt and smiled knowingly. Pierre put his arm around Joanna and they walked back inside.

The spat earned its skipper some snickering amongst the veteran crewmembers as they filed aboard. Jean-Luc remembered something his mother told him before his wedding—'Any misunderstanding is always the man's fault. Apologize immediately.' He undressed quietly, slipped into their swinging bed and said, "I do not like to argue with you. I feel terrible, and I am sorry."

Molly whispered, "Kissing is still acceptable."

He said in whispered French, "We will get through this." He lay with his hands behind his head. After several minutes, he felt Molly's body gently twitch, signaling she had fallen asleep. He reviewed the evening's discussion. On cloud nine when he came aboard, he now felt his stomach churning from his wife's stand on the issue.

# CHAPTER THIRTEEN

OCTOBER 21, 8 A.M.

THE FOLLOWING MORNING, Jean-Luc rose early and busied him-self with his responsibilities for readying the schooner for de-parture. He avoided running afoul of his wife. The patroons and their wives came to the pier and waved as the vessel's bow gently turned in the soft breeze toward the Hudson River. When the schoon-er gathered speed, he steered her out of the Croton River's mouth into a wide area known as the Tappan Zee. Though the sail to Albany went smoothly, Molly remained surly. Her brusqueness lasted the entire sail, off-loading the cargo, and the trip overland to Schenectady.

It wasn't until her parents' cabin came into view that her frame of mind changed. As soon as Jean-Luc halted the rented wagon, Molly jumped down, ran to the cabin, and excitedly knocked on the door. Jean-Luc came up behind her. Molly's father, Peter Lake, opened the door a crack and peered out. Jean-Luc could see he held a musket at the ready.

Molly said excitedly, "It's me and Jean-Luc, Papa."

Peter flung open the door and hugged Molly warmly. Marie rushed over and hugged Molly and then Jean-Luc, and then Jean-Luc shook Peter's hand uneasily.

"Was your journey difficult?" asked Marie.

Jean-Luc removed his cockaded hat and said, "We had good wind, Mama."

Peter said, "We were hoping you'd make it up here on a business trip. We are moving and it will be a long while before we see you two again."

Molly looked at her mother but asked her father, "Where are you going?"

"We have been talking, Molly. We want to leave the area. There are rumors of the crown taxing everything in sight. They are saying we will have to put some kind of a stamp on official documents. I heard nothin' would be legal without this stamp. I'm only eking out a living from Van Rensselaer's dirt patch as it is."

Marie interjected and said, "Oh, we aren't as destitute as Papa makes out. Please, sit down. You have had a difficult journey. I'll get some cool water for you to drink." When she returned, she asked, "Did you bring any Stroudwater, Jean-Luc?"

Jean-Luc smiled and said, "Yes, we have your English wool in the wagon."

Peter paused for his wife to sit and then continued. "We know you have been struggling, too, but isn't everyone? We have had a real time of it. How are you managing with the tax increases?"

"We are in a bind, too," said Jean-Luc. "We either hand over the money and default on our loans or—"

"Or what, Jean-Luc?" When her son-in-law met her question with silence, Molly looked at him with irritation.

"Or I avoid customs as I have been doing," said Jean-Luc finally.

"They turn us into lawbreakers. Is that the thanks the colonists get for helping King George win the war?" asked Peter angrily. Then he remembered his son-in-law's French origin and said, "I'm sorry, Jean-Luc, I didn't mean to offend."

"What is your destination?" asked Jean-Luc, tactfully shifting the topic.

Peter said, "Well, I have talked it over with several neighbors.

We'll be heading over the Appalachians for sure — at a point along the Ohio River. We'll pick a fertile bottom area with pastureland nearby. Now that Pontiac's Rebellion is beat down, it is safer to travel on the rivers."

Molly glanced at her husband when her father mentioned Pontiac. She knew Jean-Luc would be concerned about his childhood friend, Opechwan, Pontiac's younger brother. Several years back, before hostilities broke out, Opechwan had visited Jean-Luc and Molly when they were still newlyweds. During that visit he acted distant and when he departed, he left Jean-Luc feeling that his friend didn't want to see him again. Since he hadn't heard from Opechwan, he worried about his getting caught up in Pontiac's scheme. He and Molly spoke of him often.

Molly asked, "But what about the Proclamation Act of '63? Won't the regulars on the border stop you from crossing the mountains?"

"Well, that's why they were put there, of course, but those boys aren't cut from the same cloth as the ones we fought with at Quebec, Molly. They pretty much stay in their fort and rely on paid Indian sneaks to tell them when settlers are entering illegally. Things could get ugly in the Ohio Valley with the English bribing the Indians and promising to keep us settlers east of the mountains. This Ohio country is too big for the army's scant numbers to control. They simply can't handle it. I sense the time is full. We need to go west now."

Molly turned to her father and said, "But the king hasn't lifted the ban on travel."

Peter said, "You're right, Molly, but we're going anyway."

"You mean you aim to defy the proclamation?" asked Molly incredulously.

Marie said, "Only thing we're afraid of is the king's Indian agent at Detroit may have made a deal with the Indians."

"If you're caught crossing the mountains, there will surely be a fine. Plus, you will be abandoning your farm here."

"We wouldn't be going if we thought we were going to get caught. Clearly, King George wants peace for financial reasons and doesn't give a hoot about the Lake's future or financial situation," said Peter. He then looked at Jean-Luc and noticed a distant look. "Is something wrong?"

"It is work." With a shrug, he added, "It is nothing really."

"Tell us, maybe talking about it will help."

"Well, making the business profitable is tough— tougher than I thought it would be. The established shippers ignore me—unless they want something. Then there are the customs agents who have started enforcing the Navigation, Sugar, and Molasses Acts. And like you just mentioned, they now want us to pay for stamps on everything."

"Everybody just ignored those laws in the past," said Peter.

Jean-Luc said, "Yes, they did, and I have been ignoring them, too. Molly's mouth fell open, but she didn't say anything. "The prime minister wants the colonies to help pay the war's costs. Those acts have been on the books for decades, but they mean to collect them now and have authorized their agents to confiscate our ships—well, I mean the shippers avoiding customs—they can then sell the ships and pocket the money."

Marie asked, "And are you two in danger of having your ship confiscated?" Jean-Luc guiltily looked at Molly. Marie quietly said, "I see."

Peter quickly added, "Good for you, my boy. Good for you."

"You think what he is doing is alright, Papa?" asked Molly, taken aback again.

"Of course, all of us should resist tyranny. He's actually doing it."

"Is it really—tyranny?" asked Molly, taken aback again.

Marie scolded her husband. "Peter, don't encourage the children to break the law. Please!"

Peter said, "If the young folk don't resist these unfair laws, then all the hard work of the last one hundred thirty years will be wasted. It looks like parliament intends to suck all the money across the ocean."

Molly said quietly, "That's what Mrs. Schuyler said, too."

"Lordy, are you two mixing in those circles? I never thought I'd see the sun shining when kin of mine would be mixing with the Hudson River's high and mighty."

Jean-Luc said defensively, "We have met them once. Before that, we thought they were standoffish, too. But I found them to be very nice people."

"Well, they're most of the reasons we are pulling stakes. Van Rensselaer owns the land around here, the mills, and the transport to the market, even the market itself. It's hopeless. I really want to leave New York." Jean-Luc looked down at the table and folded his hands.

Molly said, "What about grandchildren, Papa? You and Mama won't be here to spoil them."

Marie said, "Grandchildren? Are you expecting, Molly?"

Jean-Luc jerked around for the answer.

"Oh, no, Mama—not yet, anyway."

Marie asked, "Are you sure?"

Molly said, "Why, of course. I'd be the first to know wouldn't I?" Marie comically knitted her brows, and they both laughed.

Marie said, "Well, in a way, I'm glad. That is the only thing that could have changed our plans."

Peter walked to the window and looked out on the Adirondack Mountains. "I wouldn't want to hear of you two having young'uns and getting into trouble. Promise us you'll steer clear of trouble."

Jean-Luc said, "We don't carry stolen property. We charge what the market will bear with a profit, but—I under report tonnage and quantities on our official manifests."

Still skeptical, Marie asserted, "That is still risky."

"I would drown in red ink if I played by the king's rules. Our competition smuggles, too," said Jean-Luc defensively. After an awkward moment, he asked, "Do you think what I am doing is wrong?"

Peter said, "Resisting tyranny isn't wrong."

Molly said, "Well I think he is playing with fire."

Marie said, "But he just said he would never make it otherwise."

Peter said, "And Molly it's easy to evade the customs ship." Turning to Jean-Luc for support, he asked, "Customs ships are slow, aren't they?" Jean-Luc looked down and shook his head slowly. Peter cleared his throat, because (for domestic peace) he needed to back his wife. "You know this reminds me of the mouse we had last month." Molly rolled her eyes and looked at her father with a bemused expression. Jean-Luc smiled nervously as Peter rambled on with his fable. "I put out a trap with some bait, and the next day, I found that bait nibbled on, but no mouse."

Molly said, "He was too fast for you, eh, Papa?"

Peter smiled as he looked at Marie. "I checked the trap for five nights in a row and each time found the bait nibbled on — but no mouse."

"Well, there you go, Papa. There is much to be said for speed and guile."

Peter put his hand on Jean-Luc's shoulder. "Then one morning I checked that trap and found that mouse. He was dead as a door nail."

"What is your point?" asked Molly with a hint of annoyance.

"I understand his point," said Jean-Luc. "His point is — you can escape their custom ships today and maybe for many tomorrows, but one day, the king's customs ship will catch you."

"I would imagine the loss of a ship would hurt your pocketbook something awful," said Peter.

"It would devastate us." Jean-Luc looked crestfallen and added, "It would bankrupt us."

"You need to look down the road, son. If New Yorkers don't get our own representatives into Parliament, England's taxes will bleed us dry."

Marie said, "Peter, it upsets me when you talk like this."

"I know it does, but we cannot ignore what is happening in the colony." Peter turned back to Molly and Jean-Luc and said, "Have you thought of the consequences to your sailors if you are boarded and taken a prize?" Molly and Jean-Luc didn't answer. "Families will lose their fathers, because the navy will impress those seamen. And if they aren't impressed, they'll be jailed."

"I'm just trying to survive. I haven't thought through the nightmare of getting caught," said Jean-Luc.

Peter said, "The impact on New York will be higher prices from higher transport costs, a slowdown in delivery of critical supplies to the colony's interior. I also think confiscation of one of your ships would have a harmful impact on Hudson River commerce."

Jean-Luc said, "Just the other day, one of the big shippers in the city, Frederick Philipse, posted a flyer advertising a rate cut. If I do not follow suit, I will lose business."

"Philipse!" said Peter with disgust. "His tentacles reach into every corner of the Hudson and Mohawk valleys. Exercise care, son, but seek the company of men who also see the folly of being ruled by a king uninterested in the issues on this side of the Atlantic. We ought to be able to tax ourselves and use that money to improve our lot here in New York. We shouldn't have to send our hard earned money to an overseas king—especially one who doesn't allow us to be politically represented. I sure as heck don't want to pay to be oppressed."

Jean-Luc said excitedly, "I am glad you understand."

Molly asked, "Is that why you're moving? You aren't the type of man who leaves problem solving to others."

Marie smiled, because the subject was sure to agitate her husband. She said, "Well, that's one of our reasons."

"It's that, and I will not live beside the Van Rensselaers or the Van Cortlandts or any other damn Van Frog any longer than I have to."

"Papa, I must ask you not to use that expression. It hurts my husband's feelings," said Molly.

"I forgot myself—and didn't mean to be rude. It won't happen again." Peter tapped his pipe absentmindedly against the hearth. He then said, "There are a handful of families that control everything that moves or grows in these woods. They are standoffish and contentious. It is pure hell negotiating a lease or a produce contract." Molly had not seen her father emotional since the war, and it bothered her terribly to hear his voice crack when he said, "And I—I just can't get ahead farming as a tenant. We got a start here, but now we need to move on. Besides, with so few families nearby, we feel isolated. Pontiac's Rebellion recently drove that home. Plus, many of our friends have left already for the western parts. Some went to Kaintuck and others over the mountains into western Virginia."

"We just left Van Cortlandt Manor and we found them very hospitable," said Jean-Luc, trying to balance Peter's assessment of the local Dutch.

Molly added tersely, "I didn't enjoy their company quite that much. You are right, Papa; it is almost that bad in the city."

Peter said, "These Dutchmen control the farmland, the waterways, the mills, and the fur trade."

Marie said, "Speaking of fur traders, Molly, we saw Rhis Nance last month."

"How is he?"

"He's become quite prosperous as a *handlaer*. Though, he grumbled about being forced to travel farther and farther west for pelts," said Marie.

Peter said, "Rhis is a good man. His way of living with the proclamation is to move to Canada. Since that isn't an attractive option, Mother and I must leave New York if we are to prosper."

Jean-Luc said, "But New York will need men like you, if it is to overturn unjust laws coming out of London."

"I may be misjudging my fellow New Yorkers, but I don't think they are ready to resist in ways I think is necessary."

Remembering his meeting with the patroons, Peter's words struck Jean-Luc like lightning bolts. He asked, "Papa, it may surprise you to learn that some do think there will be violence. I just hope something is done before we find ourselves in the mousetrap." Jean-Luc forced a smile. He then said, "Do you think there will be violence?"

Peter looked at Marie and nodded. He added, "Not any time soon, though. I'll be an old man before New Yorkers are ready. It'll come to blows someday, but it won't happen for a spell. When New Yorkers decide to resist, it must come from young men like you, son, men willing to fight for a better future."

Molly looked at Jean-Luc and then at the floor. She saw the impact her father's words had on her husband. Molly didn't quite realize it, but Peter's words were having a powerful impact on her, too. She took her father's hand and they walked to the window. As they gazed upon the Adirondacks, Molly said, "Papa, do you remember we used to talk about finding the headwaters of the Hudson? When are we gonna make another trip?"

"Molly, we'll be postponing that trek for a while, sweetheart. You know where it is, anyway."

"You said as a boy you walked to Lake Tear of the Clouds. I remember your story of how you dammed up the streamlet with your foot and exclaimed to Grandpa that you had stopped the powerful Hudson."

"Stop it, Molly. You're making me melancholy. You and your husband can go; it's on the southwestern slope of Mount Marcy in the Adirondacks. Just ask some of the locals when you get near it."

A tear rolled down Molly's cheek as she said, "We won't see you for years. Kentucky and Ohio are a long stretch from the coast."

Marie said, "Molly, Peter and I have been talking about heading over the mountains ever since you left our nest to make your own family. We've decided that we just don't like the way George Grenville plays politics. He is using us folks on the frontier as his main bargaining chip with the Indians. We want to breathe free and live without King George forcing us to pay for his soldiers to keep us penned up—the very ones preventing us from improving our lot."

"Papa, I think you have always had a touch of wanderlust." Peter and Molly hugged fiercely. "Oh, I'll miss you terribly." Then Marie and Jean-Luc joined and the four New Yorkers put their arms around each other. As Molly hugged her father she wondered how much longer will her husband would be able to nibble the cheese and not become caught.

Downriver, Freddy and Elizabeth Philipse stepped down from their carriage in front of their Yonkers mansion. "It's good to be home. Isn't it, Freddy?"

"Quite so, dear."

"You seem distracted. Are you having misgivings?"

"No."

"Then pay a visit to that dour old Scotsman and have that chat we talked about on the ride down from the upper mills."

"I'll see him first thing in the morning."

# PART III

# Diamond Reef

# CHAPTER FOURTEEN

October 26, 9:00 a.m.

"Governor, Mr. Frederick Philipse is here," announced Dillon. Philipse strode into the office as the personification of self-assurance. Governor Colden walked around his desk to greet his distinguished visitor.

"What do I owe the pleasure of your company, Mr. Philipse?" He, too, was confident, and enjoyed playing cat and mouse with the patroons—especially this one. Governor Colden felt the political struggle had turned in his favor, and he intended to destroy the patroons' strangleholds on the courts of their vast landholdings. This was a plank in his governing platform, and yet, Governor Colden was attracted to the trappings of their wealth.

Freddy sensed the governor's diffidence toward him. He said, "It has been a long time since we last chatted, Cadwallader."

Governor Colden said, "That is perfectly understandable, Mr. Philipse. It is a long ride from Yonkers—and you are a busy man."

"And yet, I recently have become troubled by information that..."

"Are you here to discuss the king's stamps?

"No, not at all, Governor the new tax is a nuisance, nothing more."

"Please excuse my interruption—why have you come, Mr. Philipse?"

"I wish to negotiate your assistance on a matter of personal import."

"One moment, Mr. Philipse — Jeremy, would you please step outside?" Dillon nodded, put down his pen and paper, and hurried out. An obvious breach of the governor's policy, Governor Colden didn't want Dillon witnessing a political favor. "What can I do for you?" asked Governor Colden after Dillon had closed the door.

"I have recently learned of the presence of a smuggler operating on the New York wharf."

"How surprising," said Governor Colden with mild sarcasm. "I'll have one of my customs agents look into it. Who is he?"

"It is a criminal transporting Africans without proper paperwork."

"That is serious, who is this lawbreaker?" asked Governor Colden. He didn't really consider this matter serious, but he would play along.

"Not so fast, Cadwallader, this information would improve your customs collections record, would it not?"

Governor Colden's eyes narrowed as he waited for Freddy's quid pro quo. "Yes, of course, but I didn't think you would turn in another patroon for a trading advantage."

"I would never inform on a peer. This individual isn't — " Freddy stopped in mid sentence.

"Let's discuss what you want for this information, Mr. Philipse?"

"Very little, really, Cadwallader, I just want your criticisms to cease. As a legislator and as a representative of my lands, I should like a reprieve from your attacks on my, well, I mean, all our manors. The families that settled New York, cleared the land, and turned wilderness into civilization — you shouldn't attack us."

"I only criticize your autonomy in the courts. This colony has moved past that being appropriate. You cannot continue operating outside his majesty's government."

"Autonomy, as you say, is necessary to efficient control," countered Freddy. "The large landholders of this colony whose properties are adjacent to the east bank of the Hudson River had that autonomy long before you arrived."

Governor Colden steepled his fingertips and leaned back in his chair. The tension grew palpably, but in truth, Colden welcomed this confrontation. After watching Freddy squirm, he said, "We consider Philipse Manor a valuable asset. And you have been instrumental in stabilizing the region. But you must understand; any manor lord acting as judge and jury for tenants on his lands and the want of free and open elections are direct affronts to England's democratic model. The king alone has dominion over this land. I am duty bound to end these ill practices. I cannot barter away those reforms, Mr. Philipse. Indeed, they are overdue."

"I see," said Freddy icily. "I suppose you might be able to retain your post despite your dismal tax collection record. Personally, Cadwallader, I think you should step down and return to your botanical interests." Governor Colden refused to show emotion. "Then, Cadwallader, our meeting has no further purpose. Good day."

Governor Colden called out, "Jeremy, come back inside, please." Dillon immediately reentered, and Governor Colden said, "Escort our distinguished visitor to the door, won't you? And then come back."

When Dillon completed his errand, he said, "The meeting with Mr. Philipse didn't go well, I take it." "Not from his viewpoint, Jeremy. But from mine, it went splendidly." Governor Colden laughed quietly. To Dillon, it sounded ominous. "He offered a sacrificial lamb in exchange for self-government over his holdings. He tendered a smuggler's identity, but let it out which ship captain it was without ever saying his name. You see, Jeremy, the Hudson River families intermarry, and they are a cohesive community. They may cooperate with his majesty's government due to the English conquest a hundred years ago. No, Mr. Philipse was referring to someone other than a patroon. He came to sacrifice the new man, that Canadian hothead, St. Alembert."

Dillon asked, "Shall I send for John Robb?"

Governor Colden leaned back in his chair and smiled. "Would you please?"

Outside, Philipse stepped onto the sidewalk and reviewed his meeting with the governor. As he turned toward his office on the wharf, he heard a familiar voice hail him.

"Freddy! Freddy!" Philipse turned around and saw Pierre Van Cortlandt waving and walking in his direction.

"Pierre, it's wonderful to see you. It has been too long." Philipse shook Van Cortlandt's offered hand warmly. "What brings you into the city?"

"Business, Freddy, I am meeting with my solicitor."

"No squatter trouble, I hope. I could loan you some of my boys, if you need them."

"It is minor stuff, Freddy, and more an annoyance, to be truthful. The customs agent stopped my schooner, found a discrepancy with my cargo, and wants to haul me into court. Oh, there'll be a fine, I expect, but I am not terribly concerned. Before I forget, Joanna and I are grateful for you and Elizabeth loaning us Massy and Dina. They were helpful."

"We were only too glad to assist. As for Customs, I sympathize, Pierre. I hear of that happening more and more. I, too, came in for a meeting. I just left the governor."

"Did the meeting go well?" asked Pierre probing though displaying a disarming smile.

"Unfortunately, no, I have grown tired of the governor's carping about the justice I administer to my tenants—particularly those squatters from Connecticut. You know quite well, he doesn't like us holding court on our property. I offered to throw him a bone, if he would agree to back off."

"A bone, you say. Freddy, perhaps you should have met with the rest of us first? As a group, we might have offered—a bigger bone."

Freddy looked down the street pensively, "Well, I offered an inconsequential smuggler. If he could show the crown he could actually catch someone, they might ease up on him... and him on us."

Pierre stopped smiling and said, "But Freddy, though we compete hard against one another our shipping circle is small. I certainly hope you didn't accuse one of our friends or family. Did you?"

"Of course not, I offered the name of someone outside our circle.

But the governor wouldn't agree to it, so I never gave him the name. Pierre, you know me well. I would never betray another patroon."

Van Cortlandt said, "Well, Freddy, I need to get to that appointment. It is good to see you again." After watching Philipse walk around the corner, Van Cortlandt's mind raced as he eliminated the shipping firms one by one. When Van Cortlandt realized whom Philipse was talking about, he also realized that Colden would be able to deduce the smuggler's identity the same way. Freddy, what have you done, he thought.

When John Robb appeared in the governor's office, Governor Colden said, "I now know that St. Alembert smuggles. Do you know his whereabouts?"

"His trip plan on file lists the usual stops along the river. After his delivery in Albany he will return."

"I now have reason to suspect him. I want you to intercept and search him. I recommend you board him upriver if possible."

Robb said, "Yes, Governor." But his creepy smile unsettled Governor Colden, who watched Robb walk out of his office. That man, thought Colden, isn't working out.

# CHAPTER FIFTEEN

OCTOBER 30, 7:00 A.M.

THE *MARIE'S* SENTINEL in the crow's nest shouted, "Ship. Two points off the starboard bow." The call was more an alert to the fact than an alarm.

"Jean-Luc?" Jean-Luc stood at the helm staring into space. Molly walked up and asked, "What are you thinking about?" Her purpose was to redirect his attention to the helm (as the skipper could ill afford to allow his mind to wander). The Marie would be turning for the pier within the hour. Molly thought, Jean-Luc should be more focused.

Jean-Luc turned to his wife and said, "Oh, it is you." He laughed to cover his embarrassment and said, "I was just thinking about something your father said to us." He checked his sail trim and tell tails before continuing, "He said, 'When New Yorkers decide to resist, it must come from young men like you... men willing to fight for a better future.'"

"Dear, he also told us the story of the mouse. We have no need of fighting, and I'll have no talk of it."

"Molly, I am tired of running and smuggling. Every day I go to work I wonder whether I will be bankrupt at sundown. And I am tired of being scared—of losing our future."

"Jean-Luc, it won't be like this forever. This, too, shall pass. I walked over to you, because the lookout spotted a ship off the port beam. Look there, in the shadows by the Pocantico River." Molly pointed to ten o'clock.

"I see him. It appears to be the *Durham*, and he is blocking the entrance. I cannot return the servants because of this."

Fifteen minutes passed as the schooner Marie plowed through the water making wonderful speed due to a constant ten mile-per-hour wind blowing easterly. Jean-Luc's tension increased when the sentinel shouted, "The vessel is pulling his anchor and his bow is turning. It is now pointed due east, Skipper."

Molly looked at Jean-Luc and their eyes locked. The implication was clear—the distant ship had weighed anchor and intended to get underway. "Oh, no," gasped Molly. "Do you think he is coming for us?"

Jean-Luc said to Molly, "We are without cargo. We have nothing to hide." He then yelled to the men above, "Keep her full and by," meaning for them to sail as close as possible to the wind without the sails beating. Jean-Luc said, "If they are waiting for us, I think I will give them the chase they want." He altered the *Marie*'s course slightly away from the frigate.

"If they're after us," said Molly, "they observed that course change." Jean-Luc smiled. Molly knew he comported himself in this way during situations to keep the crew relaxed and focused. She turned to watch the distant vessel hoping it was destined elsewhere. Molly said, "It seems to be 'in irons.'" Unlike Jean-Luc, Molly didn't wish for a confrontation. "That gives us some breathing room. I see they're using the current to push the bow off the wind. As strong as the Hudson is, that maneuver will cost them time."

Jean-Luc said in a whispered aside, "I have the feeling they coming for—us. If we can just pass Diamond Reef with a decent lead I will circle the island and head for the pier."

Molly didn't look at her husband, but fixed her eyes on the frigate off the stern. Without looking at her husband, she said, "The crew's families are going to grumble."

"I cannot help that. If they are at the pier, they will be able to see the situation for themselves." Jean-Luc peered over his shoulder and saw the frigate's sails fluttering but then fill with wind. He frowned, but quickly caught himself and forced a grin. "See, we are lengthening our lead. We will be all right." As if reassuring himself, he repeated, "We will be all right."

The *Marie* sailed without the frigate noticeably gaining ground. Molly watched their pursuer's bow rise and fall in graceful, rhythmic tempo. Molly's greatest fear unfolded. She not only saw the distant customs ship gaining on them, but its superior number of sails gave it the speed to bear down faster than she or Jean-Luc had estimated.

The tension on deck coursed between crewmembers over possible impressments. Molly began thinking of the locations of their other vessels, their market values, and the principle owed on each. The math depressed her further. She bit her lip and then said to Jean-Luc, "They're gaining."

"We are at top speed, and he has not signaled for us to stop." He looked over his shoulder and observed the royal navy's ship had closed the gap. His shoulders slumped. "We aren't going to reach the pier—if that is the *Durham*, it is going to board us."

"Then the possibility exists they'll confiscate this schooner and—" Molly couldn't finish the sentence as the realization of five years of hard work might have been for naught when the customs frigate came alongside.

Jean-Luc said, "Wait a minute, we are not carrying cargo. We do not have anything on board they can use to charge us with for smuggling." Jean-Luc glanced at Dina and Massy huddling by the foc'sle, but didn't give them another thought.

"Still, let's not be overconfident," said Molly.

Jean-Luc said, "There! They have raised a signal flag. They want us to heave to. Any ideas, darling?"

"Anchor over Diamond Reef until we learn what they want. That warship can't follow us into shallow water."

"That will not prevent them from boarding the *Marie*." Jean-Luc decided Molly's suggestion had merit. "Prepare to tack," he shouted. He turned the wheel hand over hand several revolutions until the Marie turned slightly toward the New Jersey shoreline. He then ordered to one group, "Lower the main sails." And to another set of sailors, he ordered, "Raise the spanker." The spanker was the sail on the rearward mast and when raised would push his stern toward the Jersey shore just as he sent his rudder hard alee. The effect of this maneuver was to turn the ship into the wind and place it 'in irons' and radically slow the ship's headway. That would leave the bow with an easterly heading and he would let the current gently wash his schooner over the rocks of Diamond Reef.

"Well, done," shouted Molly. "I'm going forward to ensure the anchor sets." After Jean-Luc and the crew brought the schooner about ever so gently and its stem bumped the rocks running beneath the water's surface, Molly shouted to the crew on the capstan, "Drop the hook." Molly watched with fever-like concentration as the anchor plunged into the water and hit the reef several feet below the surface. Molly frowned when she saw the anchor lying atop the boulders. She called to Jean-Luc, "Bring her in again slowly." She then said to the men below deck on the capstan, "Bring the hook up halfway." The crew and captain did as Molly indicated, but when the anchor dropped anew and again failed to hold, she said, "I'm going down and set it myself."

"One of the crew can do that," said Jean-Luc.

But Molly shook her head and threw a line over the side and, hand-over-hand, lowered herself onto the reef. There she struggled to heft the anchor's fluke as a powerful wave washed over her. She tried to wedge it to get it to hold fast. As Molly pulled the shank with all her might, another wave rolled over her. Its power forced the anchor to roll several inches and Molly almost got her fingers caught between the anchor arm and the rock. With the tide rising, she would lose more than her fingers had she become stuck. "I need help. Send someone down," Molly shouted. She whistled softly at the thought of her near encounter with Davy Jones.

Jean-Luc told a sailor to go down to assist Molly. Though desperately wanting to go himself, Jean-Luc knew he could never allow the helm to be unattended. He considered that the first rule of being a skipper. With his wife in danger of drowning between the anchor's shank and the rocks, or worse, the hull and the rocks, Jean-Luc had a greater worry than the confiscation of his business asset. But he stood powerless. Molly had made her decision and was doing what she believed was required. She had to reset the anchor, and her life and the ship's existence now depended on her actions. As the moments passed without word from below, Jean-Luc glanced over his shoulder and saw that it was the *Durham* pursuing him.

Though Molly stood in cold water up to her chest and grasping the anchor rode, she and the sailor helping her stared transfixed on the *Durham* as the mighty frigate came about. She had a sick, helpless feeling in her stomach. As soon as the sailor let go of the rope and lent his strength to Molly's struggle with the anchor's shank, the sailor and skipper's wife wedged the Marie's fluke snugly. Now that the anchor was situated, Molly waded several yards further out on the reef to check the amount of water between the reef and keel. Since it was now low tide, she felt satisfied with the three-foot cushion she observed. She and the sailor climbed the rope ladder and joined the others on deck. A crewmember handed each one a towel and blanket.

The *Durham* slowed, turned into the wind, and with its prey cornered, ran up the signal flags that communicated her intent to board. Molly stood on the deck watching (and shivering) as the frigate dropped anchor three hundred yards astern. She felt her stomach knotting tighter. Now with a warm blanket about her shoulders, she walked to her husband's side and said in a whisper, "Since we don't have contraband, it will be interesting to hear their rationale. I can't wait to see their faces."

"But we do have the two Africans with us. Remember, we were going to drop them off at the Upper Mills, but when we saw the frigate I did not do it. That probably carries a fine, but I am more bothered by the timing of this. Call me suspicious, but I smell a rat."

Together the St. Alemberts watched the Durham's crew lower the captain's launch. Molly pulled out the spyglass and peered through. "I see those customs agents are on board." Molly slapped the telescope shut with her palm and stamped her foot in frustration. Turning to Jean-Luc she asked, "Will they confiscate the Marie?"

"We must wait and see," said Jean-Luc nervously. Five gut-wrenching minutes ticked by before Captain Mowbray's launch bumped the Marie's hull. Jean-Luc and Molly walked to the gunnel to meet with him. Robb and Lising were with the captain.

Captain Mowbray stepped aboard and confronted the couple. Robb and Lising stood behind him. "Are you the captain of this vessel?" Mowbray asked.

"I am."

"Do you know why I stopped you?"

"We haven't a clue," said Molly. "By what authority have you stopped this vessel?"

"Our authority comes directly from the royal governor. You are suspected of smuggling; I wish to see your ownership document, business license, manifest, and passenger list."

"One moment," said Jean-Luc.

As her husband turned to go below, Molly said, "I'll get them for you, dear." She disappeared down the companionway.

Jean-Luc said, "We off-loaded our freight, and are returning empty."

Captain Mowbray gave a disinterested nod; he then turned to John Robb and raised a brow. Jean-Luc noticed this silent communication and Robb's barely disguised glee. Tension-filled minutes passed without Captain Mowbray or Jean-Luc speaking. When Molly returned with the official documents, the naval captain glanced through them quickly, but to Jean-Luc it appeared he was not really interested and quickly handed the papers to Robb.

While Robb leafed through the documents, Lising went to the hold to search for contraband. When he returned to the quarterdeck, he whispered something to Robb. The customs agent looked over to Dina and Massey huddled by the foc'sle. He took Mowbray aside and said, "Except for the two chattels, there is only a barrel of flour below that isn't on the manifest."

Captain Mowbray asked, "What's a barrel of flour worth?"

Robb said, "Ten pounds, I think. The chattels are worth much, much more."

Captain Mowbray said, "Well, then, I believe a felony has been committed."

Robb whispered, "Yes, but—I am not sure this is enough for us to confiscate the ship. I rather doubt it."

Captain Mowbray said, "Let me handle this. The first step is to take possession of the vessel." Robb nodded and the pair returned to where Jean-Luc and Molly stood. Captain Mowbray said in an accusing tone, "You are smuggling chattels and flour. Smuggling is a serious offense."

"Carrying the two girls was a favor for a client," said Jean-Luc who began to suspect the reason behind his being boarded.

"A favor? Black marketing is a form of smuggling, too, ain't it, Captain?" asked Lising.

Captain Mowbray said, "Quite right, Lising. This captain could be classified as a slave trafficker, black marketer, or smuggler."

Molly said defensively, "My husband already told you we were doing a customer a favor. We can prove it."

"As I see it, you've no authority to transport those chattels, you have no passenger list, and there is a barrel of flour below not on your manifest either."

"We traded personal property for that. I can prove that, also."

"This vessel has all the indications of being involved in smuggling. However, you'll have the opportunity to explain these discrepancies."

Molly said, "And we will have a solicitor, you can rest assured."

Jean-Luc asked, "Are we free to go?"

Captain Mowbray said, "We will transport your wife and crew to the Manhattan shore. We will detain this vessel in its present anchorage until these legal issues are resolved. But you and that sailor standing next to you are under arrest and will go to the *Durham*'s brig."

"On what charge?" asked Jean-Luc defiantly.

"Smuggling, slave trafficking, and oh, yes, attempting to flee." Jean-Luc's expression changed and his defiant attitude deflated like a balloon. "Take them away."

Molly said, "My husband has done nothing wrong."

Jean-Luc turned to her and said, "I will be fine." The guard took Jean-Luc by the arm and led him to the gunnel. Molly knew her husband's demeanor was an act.

Robb watched the intimate exchange and became furious. He said, "Get him out of here."

While the royal navy transported the crew ashore, Molly remained attentive. She overheard Mowbray say to Robb, "You and Lising will remain with the prize. Take good care of her until I return to move her on the next favorable tide."

Robb said, "We'll be fine—there is plenty to eat and drink."

Lising piped in, "Yea, they must feed the crew well. There is a cask of spirits and food below. We'll have a celebration. Prospects are looking up."

Mowbray said, "Fine, but don't overdo it. Misfortune loves to visit men who don't keep clear minds." He motioned toward the open seas and said, "Overindulging and the briny don't mix."

Ever the skeptic, Robb asked, "We are not going to fall overboard, or anything. What can happen out here?" Within hours, he would feel differently.

# CHAPTER SIXTEEN

OLLY REMAINED AT the pier until the workers finished stowing gear, and then headed home. She worried that Jean-Luc was being mistreated. Molly knew well the duties he may have been assigned as a quasi-prisoner. On the road home, she passed a wooden, four-sided news board to which townsfolk had affixed newspapers, handbills, and civic announcements. A crowd stood about, talking in hushed, but excited tones. Curious, Molly approached a woman and asked, "Madam, what is causing this hullabaloo?"

"Col. Isaac Barré argued for us in Parliament. The newspaper carries his words. He and Townshend had quite an exchange. Sir Charles Townshend is wrongheaded. Barré said we should be allowed to set our own taxes and collect them, too. Wouldn't it be wonderful if the king permitted us to levy our own revenues and spend the taxes improving our lot?"

"It would." Molly then said under her breath, "I know Isaac Barré." She encountered him when Barré was a staff officer under Wolfe during the Quebec campaign, though only an acquaintance, For a moment Molly's mind was freed from worrying about Jean-Luc. She felt thrilled that someone she knew was generating such excitement. The man beside her turned to leave. "Sir, what is the date on the newspaper?" asked Molly.

"February 26 of this year, madam," said the man. Reflecting on what he just read, he added, "He is right, you know," and then walked away.

Molly pressed forward to read what Member of Parliament Barré said about the colonies. She first read Sir Charles Townshend's parliamentary challenge...

"And now will these Americans, children planted by our care, nourished up by our indulgence until they are grown to a degree of strength and opulence, and protected by our arms will they refuse to contribute their mite and relieve us from the heavy weight of that burden which we lie under?"

Running her finger down the page until it rested upon Barré's rejoinder that had impassioned her fellow citizens. The reporter described Barré leaping to his feet and responding like Thor hurling verbal thunderbolts one after another at his political rival.

*"They* planted by *your* care? No! Your oppressions planted them in America. They fled from your tyranny to a then uncultivated and inhospitable country—where they exposed themselves to almost all the hardships to which human nature is liable, and among others to the cruelties of a savage foe, the most subtle and I take upon me to say the most formidable of any people upon the face of God's Earth. And yet, actuated by principles of true English liberty, they met all these hardships with pleasure, compared with those they suffered in their own country, from the hands of those who have been their friends... *They* nourished by your indulgence? They grew by your neglect of them. As soon as you began to care about them, that care was exercised in sending persons to rule over them, in one department and another, who were perhaps the deputies of deputies to some member of this house—sent to spy out their liberty, to misrepresent their actions

and to prey upon them; men whose behavior on many occasions has caused the blood of those sons of Liberty to recoil within them; men promoted to the highest seats of justice."

Molly gasped and covered her mouth. Standing quietly as the significance of this exchange sank in, she heard the man behind her whispering the emotional words, *'sons of Liberty.'* Molly eagerly read Barré's concluding remarks.

*"They* protected by your Arms? They have nobly taken up arms in your defense. They have exerted a valor amidst their constant and laborious industry for the defense of a country, whose frontier, while drenched in blood, its interior parts have yielded all its little savings to your emolument. And believe me, remember I this day told you so, that same spirit of freedom which actuated that people at first, will accompany them still. — But prudence forbids me to explain myself further. God knows I do not at this time speak from motives of party heat, what I deliver are the genuine sentiments of my heart."

The crowd around the news board whispered to one another as they drifted away. Molly felt a chill in her scalp — gooseflesh from pride in being a New Yorker — proud of her colony's folk labeled 'sons of Liberty' — but she but also wanted her colony to have economic and political ties with England.

# CHAPTER SEVENTEEN

OLLY SAT AT her desk and feverishly scribbled out the scenarios of the family's financial position. Assuming the confiscation of the schooner, she reviewed the numbers in an attempt to find a way keep the family business operating. After evaluating assets, liabilities, mortgages, miscellaneous debts, and the like, Molly capitulated to the math spirit, tossed her pencil in disgust, and concluded the St. Alemberts would be insolvent by the end of the quarter. Alone with her thoughts, she blamed Jean-Luc for the financial fiasco they now faced. After working up a case of indignation at her husband's expense, Molly put her head in her hands and stared at the candle flame flickering on her desk. She knew the wine casks would have been tempting and impossible to resist, and visualized the celebration Robb and Lising were having at the St. Alembert'.

Molly normally loved watching the sun set behind the Jersey bluffs, but not this evening. Fighting the nausea that seemed to be haunting her, she pushed her chair away from the desk and stood. Her eye caught her husband's tool chest in the corner, and she regarded it for a moment. Then an idea came to her. Molly opened the neatly arranged chest and studied the tools. She gently moved her hand over the implements and stopped when her fingertips fell on the hand brace. She picked it up and examined it thoughtfully. Then she moved the hammer and a leather pouch holding his drill bits to one side until the bag holding his plug cutters lay before her. She took the hand brace and the bags holding his bits and plug-cutters, and set them on the desk. Then she put on a wool blouse and draped a leather cape over her shoulders, scooped up the tools, and left the house.

Robb and Lising sat in the schooner's cabin and enjoyed a feast gratis, which they appropriated from the cargo. Breaking off a piece of bread, Lising said, "This should get the old goat off our backs for a while." He stuffed the bread into his mouth, chewed with enthusiasm, and started to pour another cup of rum for his boss.

"I really shouldn't," said Robb putting his hand over the rim of his cup.

Lising stopped and set the bottle back on the table. "Lighten up, why don'cha? This is a night to celebrate. We are in the middle of the harbor with nothing else to do. Let's celebrate taking a prize. Can you imagine the satisfaction pirates must have felt?"

"Nobody is going to check on us, right?" Robb stood and walked to the window. As he looked on the harbor, he turned to Lising and said, "You think it will be difficult to sell this old boat?"

"Are you kidding me? Not at all." Giving in to the temptation to keep drinking, Lising poured himself a third cup of rum. After slurping down half the contents, he wiped his chin and asked Robb, "Sure you don't want some more? I hate to drink by myself."

"Nah, I'll pass." Robb continued gazing out the window. "You know, this—he opened his arms wide and gestured about the cabin, "is the start of our fortunes in America."

"Right you are, Johnnie," said Lising slurring his words in the first signs of tipsiness.

Robb looked at Lising and his obvious enjoyment of the liberated rum. "By Jove, maybe you've the idea after all. This *is* a night to celebrate." He walked back to the table and indicated to Lising he wanted his cup topped off.

"This is good stuff, too," said Lising.

Feeling pleased that today marked his rise in society and his exit from the governor's doghouse; he drank several swigs of the grog and closed his eyes. He wondered what that auburn-haired beauty was doing since her husband is away.

Molly walked to the wharf and lowered one of their firm's spare row boats into the water. The tavern lights down the street burned a golden, inviting hue. Molly paused a moment and questioned her plan's chances for success. She placed the tools into the dinghy, jumped in, and pushed away from the dock. Just as Alexander the Great had once burned his ships on an enemy's shore, Molly too had set a course with no retreat. Molly rowed past the army's artillery battery on the point with strong strokes and hoped against hope that the schooner had been left unattended. She had six hundred yards to cross between the southern boot of Manhattan to where the *Marie* lay at anchor. Molly glanced at the half-moon and wished there were clouds to cover her approach. She figured a person on deck could see her coming, so to cover that possibility she concocted a story of returning for something she had forgotten.

The harbor lights grew smaller with each oar stroke, and Molly turned her head from time to time to adjust her heading. She had three hundred yards to go when she heard voices coming from the schooner. Molly stopped rowing, silently raised her oars out of the water, and listened. Not hearing anything further, she carefully slipped the oars back into the ocean. She approached the schooner from astern and observed the yellowish flicker of a single candle in their quarters. That indicated the schooner had one or more guards aboard. Disheartened, she considered abandoning the idea. Having come this far, Molly believed Fortune would favor her audacious undertaking, and she pressed on.

Determined to foil the customs agents' plan, Molly decided to sneak aboard to check out the situation. She secured the dinghy, gathered her tools and lantern, and ascended the rope ladder. When she reached the deck rail, she peered over, and not seeing anyone, listened for several minutes. No more talking came from below, so she stepped aboard and tiptoed to the companionway and down the steps to the cabin door. She stopped to listen by the door, and heard loud snoring. She pulled back and remained motionless for a few moments to verify the drunken state of her persecutors. She peeked into the cabin and, seeing a burning candle, wondered whether those fools would torch the ship. Also on the table were two empty rum bottles, and the customs agents were slumped on the deck in drunken unconsciousness.

Molly's resolve turned to steel and her breast filled with righteous anger at the thought of these men confiscating their property and selling it. We worked hard to make the business profitable, and if these scoundrels think they'll get rich at our ruin, she thought, well I'm not going to allow that. Molly treaded softly to the companionway and descended to the orlop. Reaching the lowest deck she slowly raised a large hatch that covered the bilge. She carefully lit the candle inside her brass lantern and lowered herself into the wettest and foulest area of any vessel. There among the large oak ribs that formed the skeleton of the ship, Molly heard rat squeals and swallowed hard. Ignoring both her fear of rodents and her mild case of claustrophobia, she pulled the hatch down.

Molly's anger multiplied since the seizure, and she used it to steel her spirit. Looking for the seam where the hull's shiplap dovetails into the keel, Molly moved her hand about in cold, slimy bilge water until she found the joint between those key structural members. Molly wiped her hands on her dress and blew on her fingers to warm them. Then she attached the plug cutter to the hand brace in the mindset of an assassin loading a pistol, and placed the bit parallel to the side of the keel. Molly began slowly turning the handle. She felt the bit slipping on the wet, slimy Oakwood and leaned on the handle to put heft behind her effort. She needed to get the tool to bite. Molly tried turning the handle slower, but abandoned that, because it still made the splashing noises and wasn't achieving her purpose. Every thirty seconds, she stopped to listen for footsteps. The schooner's eerie silence reassured her Robb and Lising were still immobile. And yet, she was in mental turmoil at the prospect of being surprised.

Once the plug cutter bit into the slick wood her work went quickly. Not knowing the hull's exact thickness, Molly turned the handle slowly until she felt the wood giving way on the ocean side. She put her hand out to stop her fall as the ocean water began to geyser. The salt water splashed into the compartment and wet her front. Molly quickly extracted the tool, placed her palm over the two-inch plug, and after carefully extracting it from the tool placed it into her pocket. Wanting to escape the foul bilge, the chilly spray, and the prospect of becoming trapped by the slowly rising ocean, Molly grabbed her tools. She pushed open the hatch, and pulled herself up on the orlop deck. With the danger of drowning over, Molly lowered the hatch silently and felt a wave of self-satisfaction wash over her. She thought I'd give anything to see their faces when they awaken. Molly tiptoed up the companionway. At the top of the stairs she heard someone moving on the deck and gasped inaudibly when she spotted Robb standing on the gunnel holding a ratline and urinating over the side. To Molly, the water rushing through the borehole made enough noise that Robb could hear it. However the customs agent finished his nocturnal business, tied the drawstrings on his trousers, stepped down, and scratched his scalp with a yawn. He staggered in Molly's direction. She quickly, but silently backed down the stairs, and hid in the darkness of the lower deck until Robb made it into the cabin. After he closed the door, Molly waited a few minutes for the taxman to resume his stupor. When two distinct snores became audible, she crept up the stairs.

As Molly descended the rope ladder, she looked for an indication the Marie was listing. Seeing none Molly began to second-guess her decision. She bit her lip at the prospect that the *Marie* would somehow not settle on the reef, or worse, she would slide to the bottom of the harbor. She had passed a mental point of turning back and she knew she needed to get off the schooner. Molly stepped into her dinghy, and glanced around to verify her presence hadn't been detected. She then untied her boat and allowed it to drift away from the schooner. Molly continued to observe her vessel for signs of it taking on water; she didn't have long to wait. After rowing two hundred and fifty yards from the ship, she heard their schooner groan as it settled onto the reef. Well that ought to awaken the customs agents Molly thought. Now in a five-degree angle of repose, the *Marie* appeared as an overweight person fallen through a cane chair. And yet, the cabin darkness gave no indication that the customs agents had awakened.

Molly rowed to the pier without incident. Walking home, she patted the two-inch wood plug in her pocket and allowed herself a smile.

# CHAPTER EIGHTEEN

NOVEMBER 1, DAYBREAK

ROBB BLINKED AND tried to focus through his blood-shot eyes and squinted at a pesky sunbeam interrupting his intoxicated reverie. He scratched his nose and thought something isn't right. He rolled over and tried to kick Lising to waken him. But his assistant snoozed on the floor by the distant bulkhead. Robb groped for the table leg intending to use it to help him stand up. When he realized the deck was at an angle he sat up in a shot. Adrenaline surged through his body banishing his hangover, and he ran through the door. "Dammit, Lising, wake your sorry self up. We're sunk," Robb shouted as he staggered in circles with his hand on his forehead. He mumbled repeatedly, "Someone sank the ship."

From inside the cabin Lising called, "Hey, Johnnie, why is this deck tilted?" Then he rolled back and laughed hilariously.

Robb ran into the cabin and screamed, "We're sunk; didn't you hear me?"

Lising propped himself on his elbow and grinned sheepishly. He rubbed his scalp several times, and asked, "What did you say, Johnnie?"

"It had to be that vindictive wife! Or else—she sent her people to do this." There was a thump on the hull from a launch, and both agents ran to the gunnel to see who was coming aboard. Below was Captain Mowbray who from his ship had observed the schooner low in the water. "He's going to be furious."

A minute later, Captain Mowbray pulled himself over the slanted gunnel and stood with hands on hips scowling at Robb and Lising. "What happened?" asked Captain Mowbray angrily.

Robb looked down and stated the obvious, "Last night, while we slept, the boat sank."

"To prevent a problem is why I left you aboard. And neither of you heard anything? Pretty obvious you were celebrating prematurely."

"I slept through it, Captain, but I am certain responsibility lies with the shipper."

"The shipper?" asked Captain Mowbray incredulously. "He was on the Durham last night."

"We think it was his employees." Several moments passed in icy silence.

Looking about, Captain Mowbray said, "Check the bilge. I agree that someone probably came aboard and scuttled the ship. But if the St. Alemberts think there won't be hell to pay, they are sadly mistaken."

Robb nodded toward the companionway for Lising to check for damage. He and Mowbray followed Lising down the companionway. Captain Mowbray and Robb waited in silence as Lising thrashed about in frigid, hip-deep bilge water.

Robb slammed his fist against the bulkhead. He said, "Well, they did *something* to our schooner."

"We'll make them plenty sorry," said Lising.

Captain Mowbray glared at Lising as though he were loathsome spiders. With a shrug of his shoulders, he said, "You haven't searched St. Alembert's house nor audited the books yet. I'll give you Sergeant Johnston. He excels at house searches." He took his hat off and rubbed his scalp in frustration with the agents. Then he said with hope in his voice, "If there is contraband in that house, Johnston will find it."

Robb said, "Good enough, but we'll need permission—a Writ of

Assistance will make it legal." He turned to Lising and said, "Pick one up from the governor's office."

Lising nodded and said, "I'll see Dillon as soon as I get ashore."

"How many men will we need? Do you think five is enough?"

Captain Mowbray shook his head and said, "The wife could have employees around or misguided neighbors that might meddle. We'd better double that."

"Good—Johnston's men can search the house and I'll inspect any documents uncovered."

Captain Mowbray said, "Listen to me, if it's there, you boys better find it, because if you don't find contraband, we can expect St. Alembert's widow to tie us up in court over the derelict for a long time."

Unsettled, Robb asked nervously, "Did you say widow?"

"Don't get virtuous on me. Accidents happen at sea all the time; St. Alembert just hasn't had his yet." Mowbray looked about the deck like he was scrutinizing an article for purchase. "We can still make money through salvage, but we must reduce the time this schooner is on this reef."

Troubled by the captain's deadly intention, Robb looked across the bay toward Manhattan Island and thought of the shipper's wife. Then he thought of her loneliness and her net worth. He said, "I don't want to lead this search."

Captain Mowbray asked, "Why not?"

"I don't want to alienate the wife. I am going to let Lising conduct the search. I'll come in later and play a consoling role."

"So, you intend to move in on the widow. Well, she is easy on the eyes, although after we confiscate several more you could return to England with money in your pocket. There you would find a suitable mate. You would do better in England."

"I don't intend to return to England. Besides, I think marrying her would make my move into society far easier."

"Suit yourself," sniffed Captain Mowbray. "Just ensure the search doesn't turn into a debacle." He walked to the gunnel and descended the rope ladder into his launch.

Robb stared thoughtfully as Captain Mowbray exited. He forced his mind back to the task at hand and asked Lising, "If you were St. Alembert, where would you hide contraband?" The rhetorical question hung in the air.

Lising said, "I say start with his chest of drawers and closets."

His voice dripping with disdain, Robb said, "Chest of drawers and closets? Lising, if you want to catch a smuggler, you have to think like a smuggler. Would you hide contraband in those places?"

"Well, no, I..." said Lising reddening. He brushed his pants leg trying to clean up a bit and said, "I would have a secret area—like under the floor or between the walls."

"Now you're using your head."

Lising brightened at Robb's praise. He added, "We should check the ceiling, too."

"That would about cover the property, wouldn't it Douglas? Of course, we may need to schedule an entire week to finish the search. Will the house be standing when we depart?"

"What do you mean, Johnnie?"

"The key to a good search is to be thorough and efficient." Robb walked to the gunnel and tapped nervously with his fingertips. "Whether contraband is found or not, we'll send the other shippers a message. St. Alembert is without political connections. I think our goal is to force these shippers to pause the next time they think of smuggling or striking a customs official."

Lising said, "Let's get back to Manhattan. No reason to remain here." Robb nodded. As soon as they tied up to the pier, Lising hurried up the street to the governor's office. He rushed through the governor's door and approached Dillon. He said, "We need a writ of assistance."

Dillon looked up and tried to disguise his surprise. "I have never issued one, Lising, but I know where they are. I'll be right back." Dillon walked down the hall to a closet and retrieved the form. When he returned to his desk, Dillon asked, "May I ask what the date of the search is going to be and when you want to pick it up?"

"The search is for tomorrow night and I want to pick it up in the afternoon."

"Mr. Lising. I'll have the governor..."

"Look, I am in a hurry."

"I appreciate that, Mr. Lising, but this document requires the governor's signature. As I was saying, I'll have the governor sign it this evening, and it will be ready for you in the morning. I just have a few questions. Whose residence are you searching?"

"Jean-Luc St. Alembert's house," said Lising. Dillon's pen paused perceptibly. "Yeah, the same person that stormed in here demanding to see the governor."

Dillon asked, "And what is his address?" After Lising provided the details, Dillon said, "That about does it, Mr. Lising. It'll be waiting for you in the morning."

Lising said, "Now it is time to squeeze our prey."

Dillon put his pen down, nodded, and smiled politely. Lising exited the governor's mansion and walked down the street to the home of the Clifton widow where the governor had quartered the Royal Marines.

When Widow Clifton answered the door, Lising said, "I need to speak with Sergeant Johnston, ma'am."

Widow Clifton nodded sullenly and closed the door.

A minute later, Sergeant Johnston opened the wooden door and stood before Lising, bare-chested with his pants secured by suspenders. "What do you want, Lising?"

"The governor has ordered a search and the captain said for you to help us."

"Yeah? Keep talking."

"We're going tomorrow night after dinner, and here is the best part, we're going to the Frenchman's house, you know, the same guy you clobbered yesterday."

Sergeant Johnston pursed his lips and thought a moment. "Besides getting in my way, what's he done to deserve this?"

"He's a smuggler and we intend to catch him red handed. We'll be looking for contraband, and when we find it, we get to keep it. We have his ship, and after tomorrow, we'll have his real estate. But we want to make sure we have enough men to keep a lid on things while the search is underway."

"Fine, we've been ordered back to the ship anyways. Seems we'll be sailing day after tomorrow. We'll be ready."

The following evening, the wharf street vibrated from pounding boots striking the cobblestones. Frightened by recent events and in particular naval impressments of their neighbors, New York citizens rushed to their windows and peered through the curtains with trepidation. People holding candles and looking outside were indications to Sergeant Johnston that he and his marines were drawing unwelcome attention. On each side of the street one could see flickering candle flames marking the progress of the Royal Marines toward their prey. The detachment ran double time with their muskets carried across their chests. None knew their destination, but all knew it would be horrible for those unknowing souls who would play their hosts this night. Their footsteps seemed like thunder to the intimidated mothers who ran to comfort upset children awakened by the din. The echoes rebounded through the exteriors of the colonial homes, and the mothers collected their children. When the royal marines had passed a house, the relieved husband walked into the street to see which colonial family's home would soon be fatherless. Some even stepped onto their front porches to hoot and holler at the soldiers. "I bet they're going to the young Frenchmen's house," said one

"I think you're right. What a pity," said his neighbor.

But some began taunting the Royal Marines; as interest grew in who they had come for, the clamor increased. Hearing the crowd noise, Molly stopped undressing for bed and went downstairs to see what was causing the commotion. Opening her front door, she stepped onto her stoop. When she saw the regulars running in the street, she feared her home was their destination. "Oh no," said. Molly, "They are coming here!" She threw on her cloak and watched apprehensively as the Royal Marines double-timed up her street. She struggled to remain composed. As feared, the Royal Marines came to a halt in front of her door. She asked, Seconds later, the menacing royal marines came to a halt in front of her front door. Molly demanded, "What is the meaning of this?"

Sergeant Johnston glared at her. Robb and Lising rode up behind the royal marines on horseback, but held back across the street. Lising dismounted and walked through the Royal Marines and said, "We're here to search this dwelling for contraband."

"On whose authority?"

"But, of course, Madame." Reaching into his coat's breast pocket, Lising said, "Ah yes, I have it right here." He unfolded and displayed the Writ of Assistance.

Molly scanned the document and asked, "What is a writ of assistance?"

Lising said with disdain, "It is our authority to search your premises, woman. We are here to search for contraband."

Molly said, "You don't have any idea what you're searching for, but you intend to search anyway."

Snatching the writ from Molly and returning it to his pocket, Lising said, "We suspect your husband of smuggling, and we've come to find evidence of same."

Molly, who had many times defended King George's policies, stepped slowly back to her front door. "You won't find anything," she insisted.

Robb looked back at Sergeant Johnston and nodded. Johnston pointed at two of his royal marines and said, "You, two, keep that woman at bay."

Two men came forward and at bayonet point forced Molly inside her home and against the wall. Lising walked to the wall sconces and lit them. Molly fought to keep from crying. Distressed she watched the search party enter her home and fan out. One marine knelt and place his ear to the floorboards and began methodically tapping each one. Molly gasped and remembered Jean-Luc's hidden area under his desk. "He is searching for your hidden compartments," said Lising as he strutted through the foyer and stopped before a small circular table. He opened its small drawer, and finding nothing, slammed it shut. He then picked up a small vase. Molly's body tightened as the realization that the empire's customs agents would intentionally violate each part of their home. Lising glanced at Molly, and sensing the vase was dear allowed it to slip through his fingers. It shattered on contact. He said, "Oops, how clumsy of me."

Sergeant Johnston opened her husband's desk drawers, rifled the contents, and dumped their papers on the floor. Standing stoically against the wall, Molly watched the customs agent and his lobsterbacks go through their rooms. With the floor littered with paper, Johnston used the tip of a bayonet to methodically tap the walls listening for hollow areas. Molly figured his use of the bayonet was as much to intimidate as it was a tool for locating contraband. Molly's body shook with resentment and a sense of outrage welled within her breast. Her lower lip trembled. She looked beseechingly at her neighbors in the crowd. They slowly shook their heads as if silently saying, "We cannot do anything to help you."

So intent on damaging the St. Alemberts' possessions were the Royal Marines that they didn't notice the number of neighbors had been growing and had been inching closer to the house. Gathered in front, husbands and wives strained their necks to see what the royal marines were destroying. And each knew full well that one of them could be tomorrow night's search victims. These neighbors were aware of the St. Alembert's shipping enterprise, of his French heritage, and also of the lower priced goods they enjoyed as a result of his labors on the hazardous waters surrounding their island. With each sound of breaking glass and splintering furniture, the crowd's resentment ballooned until their sympathy for the St. Alemberts' predicament flared. Finally, their indignation exploded over this violation of a member of their street. First, Mrs. Sherman yelled, "Leave her be!" And then the rest began to chant, "Leave her be!" Their shouts echoed through the city streets. The pity they now felt for young Mrs. St. Alembert roused them to act.

Robb had been watching the crowd and decided the time had

arrived to dismount and play the role of knight in shining armor. He said to the crowd as he passed. "I'll put a halt to this."

But as he ascended the steps, a man shouted, "He's a customs agent, too."

Robb glanced back at the crowd and scurried inside, but the shouting increased in ever more threatening tones. He knew he would have to return through this angry crowd. He no longer felt comfortable about having sufficient numbers either to intimidate the rabble or provide protection.

Two blocks away, Captain Mowbray also could hear the commotion. Though he correctly assumed the fuss was coming from the searched house, he wasn't able to reinforce his marines because he was involved in the vital task of preparing the *Durham* for its mission to escort the ship delivering the king's newly arrived stamps to the New Jersey office.

Back at the house, Molly took courage from her neighbors' support. When Sergeant Johnston knocked a framed needlepoint off the wall and thoughtlessly toss it onto the floor. Molly's mother had cross-stitched a forest scene as a wedding present and it had immense sentimental value. Seeing her keepsake trashed, Molly could no longer continue to stand idle. Angry, she brushed past the surprised royal marine detaining her walked up to Sergeant Johnston and slapped him in the face. She then screamed, "Get out of my house."

As Sergeant Johnston raised his hand to strike Molly, Robb rushed between them and said in a chastising voice, "Be more careful." Surprised, Sergeant Johnston looked at him as if asking, 'What are you doing?'

Molly glared at Robb. She said, "You also. Get out of my house."

Watching Molly castigate Robb and Sergeant Johnson, Mrs. Sherman said to her husband, "Look! The Frenchers wife is standing up to them. She needs help. I'm going inside."

Mr. Sherman said, "Don't get involved."

When the neighbor's wife burst through the front door, Sergeant Johnston turned to face the new threat and raised the butt of his musket. Molly instinctively snatched a thick, wooden candlestick from a table and smashed it into the Royal Marine's shoulder blade a moment before he would have struck her neighbor. Molly whirled around; her eyes met Mrs. Sherman's, and both understood a threshold had been breached. Now they were in for serious legal difficulties.

Having watched two women confronting the empire's Royal Marines, The men in the crowd were embarrassed. One of them shouted, "The lobsterbacks are going to hurt our women." From across the street, the angry crowd surged toward the house.

Robb shouted, "Let's get out of here."

Sergeant Johnston just glared at Molly and Mrs. Sherman with his fists balled. But then he realized the crowd outside was entering the house, he joined his marines jostling one another in their haste to exit the St. Alemberts' back door.

Robb shouted again, "No, you have to leave through the front."

But panic had overtaken the search party and they abandoned Robb and Lising. Robb said to Molly, "I am truly sorry this happened." Molly didn't respond. He and Lising ran out the front door to reclaim their horses. The mob surged toward them, and Robb and Lising pulled their pistols. The crowd halted as they wildly swung their pistols with a bug-eyed look. Seeing their one chance to escape the mob, they quickly mounted their horses and galloped away. Several in the crowd pelted them with rocks during their getaway.

Neighborhood men surged into the parlor where Molly and Mrs. Sherman stood surveying the damage. They looked out the back door and saw the royal marines bolting down the back alley, and one declared, "This evening is not over by a long shot." The others angrily shouted their concurrence. Then the men ran out the back door after the search party.

A handful of men chased the Royal Marines down the alley. The others went back into the street. At the worst moment of her life, Molly walked to her back door and listened with Mrs. Sherman behind her as one man addressed the throng. He shook his fist and shouted, "We're not letting the king's thugs do this to one of *our* families. Follow me." He stepped down from the St. Alemberts' steps and began walking toward the wharf and the governor's mansion. The others fell in behind him. Their women, angry though they were, didn't follow and began drifting back to Molly's house speaking in low whispers and with worried brows. Several good-hearted souls approached Molly. One said, "Missus Alembert, we'd like to help ye tidy up." Molly forced a smile. She wiped away a tear and nodded. Molly sensed this was a breakthrough of sorts for her and her husband who had experienced difficulty being accepted by those living around them. Her fellow citizens viewed them as victims of the king's tyranny, and what Molly and Jean-Luc had failed to do in four years, Sergeant Johnston had accomplished in minutes. Molly hugged each neighbor, though before tonight they had been aloof strangers.

As they began to pick up the debris, the house was eerily quiet. Molly shook from the emotional toll and public humiliation of her home being violated. She stared at the crowd moving off and said between clenched teeth, "I must go." Molly dashed down the steps.

Mrs. Sherman said, "Don't!" The neighbor women watched Molly run down the street and disappear into the night's blackness.

Sergeant Johnston didn't realize the dangerous situation developing behind him. Several blocks away, he felt safe enough to order his men to halt. They stood in the same alley though a number of streets away from their ship. Johnston said, "I don't know about you blokes, but I'm tired. Take a few minutes and rest." Behind him was a fenced backyard containing one middling sized pig and four chickens in a coop. Inspired by his hunger and the availability of these easy pickings, he said, "Personally, I'm tired of eating oatmeal and old cheese. Let's steal us some meat and poultry. Are you blokes with me?" The marines mumbled their approval at their leader's suggestion. They tore down the wire fence and scooped up the animals. The squad ran down the alley, laughing at their mischief and toting the creatures under their arms. It never entered Sergeant Johnston's head that Schout Jack Freeman, the local constable, would construe their midnight requisition as a criminal act.

Having lost sight of the Royal Marines, the angry mob continued their advance on the governor's mansion. Their torches cast ominous glows divulging their movement.

From his office, Governor Colden had heard the mob shouting and had said to Dillon, "There is going to be trouble. Go home and await my instructions."

"What about you, sir? Where will you go?" asked Dillon.

"I'll take refuge on the *Durham*. I'll be safe there. There aren't enough troops to suppress a mob, but you can be sure that I'll be asking the prime minister for more troops when I return." Governor Colden watched Dillon limp hurriedly up the street toward his apartment. He locked the governor's mansion and was relieved to see Captain Mowbray and a small group of sailors.

Captain Mowbray's men were transporting chests containing the official stamps into his office. He looked up the street and saw the lights from the mob's torches dancing on the walls of the buildings. Hearing the angry shouts and observing the mob's shadows nearing, Captain Mowbray said, "Wrap this up, men." The sergeant in charge closed the door on the governor's storage cabinet, fastened the lock, and handed the key to Captain Mowbray. "Get to the ship," he said with obvious concern in his voice. He and his work detail hurried outside and hustled the two blocks to their frigate.

As the gangplank was rising, Sergeant Johnston shouted, "Wait for us." He and his men sprinted up the gangplank and onto the ship panting and laughing. With Governor Colden already on board as a precaution, the captain nodded to the officer of the deck who ordered the crew to release the lines, and the frigate swung away from the pier.

Captain Mowbray looked Sergeant Johnston over and asked, "Where did you get these animals?"

"They was loose in the streets, Captain."

"Did anyone see you take them?"

"No chance, Captain," answered Sergeant Johnston.

Captain Mowbray frowned and rubbed his eyes. After several tense moments, he looked up. Finally, he nodded. With permission granted, The Royal Marines whooped and accepted the congratulations of the ship's sailors.

# CHAPTER NINETEEN

November 1, 7:50 p.m.

A SHORE, THE MOB'S GROWING emotion exploded into fury. From years of enduring the empire's press gangs, tariffs from an overseas parliament, and now searches of their homes and businesses, they were intent on taking their frustrations out and making a political statement. Three individuals asserted leadership over the mob, these men, named Captain Isaac Sears, James DeLancey, and Captain Alexander McDougall, had moved to the forefront a block from the governor's mansion.

When the mob rounded the corner and approached Governor Colden's main entrance, McDougall gave the signal to halt. He could see the masts of the Durham leaving its berth and felt confident that the remaining soldiers in the barracks couldn't or wouldn't attempt to interfere. He turned to the men in the front ranks and said, "Burn down the door." Two men ran up the steps and held their torches to the wooden portals. Roaring their approval, men in the mob shook their fists and shouted insults and curses at the governor and the tax policies he represented. Though the door charred and became heavily discolored from the flames and smoke, the torches could not ignite the thick wood.

Losing patience, McDougall yelled, "Around to the back." There the mob discovered a building containing the governor's carriage. "Burn it," shouted DeLancey. The same two men ran forward and held their torches to the garage doors. Impatient and frustrated, one man hurled his torch through a side window; it landed on a hay bale. The flames quickly licked through the windows and flickered on the dark walls and support beams. When they broke open the carriage house doors, they pulled the blazing carriage into the street. Moments later flames could be seen leaping to the walls and then to the ceiling. The intense heat forced the crowd back several steps. The fire rapidly engulfed the carriage house.

Captain Sears raised his torch skyward and shouted, "Now, boys, we are going to the tax collector's house. Tonight New York will take its stand against tyranny. What say you? Do you feel like teaching the taxman a lesson?"

Someone in the crowd roared, "Damn right!" Sears walked at the head of the men as they surged up the street toward the house shared by Robb and Lising. Upon arrival they found the occupants absent from the premises. They immediately set about smashing furniture, dishes, and windows. When there was nothing left to break, they ate Robb's food and drank their beer. For good measure, they even ripped out the garden the customs agents had started.

Tired and ready to turn in after their failed search, Robb and Lising rounded the corner near their house. Smelling smoke, they stopped. Robb looked about trying to locate the fire. He heard shouting from the direction of his tenant house and it sounded ominous. "Let's check this out, first, Douglas." The customs agents ran around the corner and watched in horror as their apartment building burned. The city fire fighters had already arrived and were fighting to contain the blaze. In the street were fragments of the customs agents' furniture. The frightening implication was clear. Their home had been vandalized and torched. He looked up and down the street in alarm to see if the perpetrators were returning for him and Lising.

Out of breath, Molly rounded the corner of the Governor's Mansion and stopped. She watched as two carriage wheels burned off and crashed to the ground. The pathetic vehicle listed to one side and made a dismal sight. Standing quietly she watched the flames climb into the night sky. From behind her, Mrs. Sherman approached and said her name snapping her from her stupor. "Mrs. St. Alembert, you have had quite a night. I'll walk you home."

Molly slowly turned about and realized her kindly neighbor had followed her. "Yes, you're right."

# PART IV

# Peine Fort Et Dure

# CHAPTER TWENTY

NOVEMBER 1, 8:00 P.M.

SCHOUT JACK FREEMAN stood in the middle of the street with his hands on his hips staring at the razed coach house and smoldering carriage. He pushed his hat back on his head and muttered between clenched teeth, "Not in my town." He walked among the smoking debris kicking over ambers in his way looking for clues to identify the arsonists. He had suspicions, of course, but he was looking for something that might have been dropped or could link a culprit to the fire. He needed evidence that would stand up in court. He picked through some smoking pieces of wood hoping to find the nuggets of proof. As yet, he hadn't found anything but rubble when he heard running footsteps. He turned to face the approaching individual. He recognized the man and called, "What brings you out, Johnny Howerton?"

"Schout Jack, come quick!"

"What's this all about, Johnny."

Howerton pointed up the street and said between breathless pants, "All Hell is breaking loose couple of blocks over."

"Be specific, Johnny."

"Soldiers came and ransacked a woman's house. Then a mob

formed. So's the soldiers skedaddled, and in leaving they stole Rudolf Christmann's pig and his last four chickens."

"They took all of them, did they? Were these soldiers from the garrison or from one of his majesty's ships?"

Johnny said, "A ship—from the *Durham*, Schout Jack."

"I see." Schout Jack rubbed his chin deep in thought. "I should have known. That vessel's crew has caused me trouble since they arrived." He stared at the governor's mansion and thought a moment. Finally, he said, "I believe I'll speak with the victims." He mounted his horse, helped Howerton get on the horse behind him, and quickly galloped the two blocks to the scene of the ransacking.

Upon arriving at the St. Alemberts' house, Schout Jack surveyed a street filled with women standing about in twos and threes speaking in hushed voices. That's odd, thought Schout Jack, no men about, and where are their men folk? Howerton dismounted, and with his errand being complete, disappeared into the crowd. Schout Jack walked into the St. Alembert's house and found Molly, Johnny's wife, and Mrs. Sherman picking up broken items and scattered papers from the floor. "Which one of you ladies is Mrs. St. Alembert?"

"I am," said Molly.

"What happened tonight?"

Molly, whose face was streaked with tears, turned to the sheriff and said, "Customs agents, guarded by marines from the *Durham*, came and—"

Mrs. Sherman interjected, "Look around, Schout Jack. They deliberately broke up this woman's belongings."

Schout Jack nodded to Mrs. Sherman and said, "Yes, ma'am." He turned back to Molly and said, "Please continue."

"They showed me a writ of assistance and proceeded to turn my house inside out."

"Did they say what they were looking for, ma'am?"

"They accused me of hiding contraband, but when they didn't find any, they ransacked our home and left."

"Which direction did they go, ma'am?"

Molly pointed toward her rear door and said, "They went out that door and down the alley. They wouldn't dare go out the front—the menfolk of these women were waiting for them."

Mrs. Sherman said, "They took off plenty fast when they saw what was waiting for them in the street."

Freeman was aware of a writ of assistance, its purpose, and why the customs agents used it tonight. "Where is your husband, Mrs. St. Alembert?"

"They put him on the *Durham*. The customs people stopped us on our return voyage from Albany." Molly shook her head and said, "First, they impress our seaman, then they confiscate our ship, then they arrest my husband on groundless charges, and finally they've ruined our home. I'm sure they intend to impress him."

"So that is your schooner aground on Diamond Reef?" asked Schout Jack.

"Yes, it's ours," said Molly disgustedly.

Mrs. Sherman said, "This lady told me the custom agents and navy captain plan to take their ship and sell it. Can they do that?"

With her voice rising in anger, Molly said, "First, they have to find contraband."

"Pardon me for asking, but are they going to find contraband?" asked Schout Jack.

"No!"

"This is just the start, mark my words," said Mrs. Sherman butting in. "Those customs people are out of control. Whoever heard of confiscating an entire boat? Quite an incentive for mischief, I think. Don't you think so, too, Schout Jack?"

"Yes, ma'am."

"Well?" asked Mrs. Sherman.

"As soon as I read the Crown's implementation plans for the Sugar and Stamp Acts, you can be sure that clause caught my attention. Parliament wants tax money for sure." He figured there was nothing more he could do here. "I ought to move on to the Christmann residence." Turning to Molly, he said, "Ma'am, I can't get in the middle of your squabble with customs. However, I can investigate this invasion of your property. Thank you for your time, but I now need to talk to the Christmann family." He turned to Mrs. Sherman and whispered, "You'll stay with her a while?" Mrs. Sherman nodded grimly. Schout Jack exited the back door and walked the short distance down the alley to where Rudolf Christmann waited for him with hands on hips.

A recent immigrant from the Rhineland Palatinate, the slim, bushy-bearded farmer waved his arms as he proclaimed, *"Mein baueri ist aufgebrochen worden!"*

Schout Jack's Dutch is close enough to Deutsch to make out the man's meaning said in his pigeon German, *"Ja, Ja,* I understand that the soldiers broke into your pen and took your livestock. But please speak English, Rudy." After the farmer calmed a bit, Schout Jack asked the basic who, what, and when questions and jotted down Christmann's answers.

Christmann asked, "How am I to feed my woman? The sailors trampled my garden and took my livestock."

"I'll do what I can to get them back," said Schout Jack. He took his leave and retrieved his horse.

"What you gonna do now, Schout Jack?" asked Will Sherman from behind as Jack put his foot into the stirrup.

"I'm going to the *Durham* and have a word with her captain and the culprits."

Molly, standing on the porch, overheard Schout Jack, and said, "May I come with you. I must know my husband is safe."

"Ma'am, I understand your feelings, but it is better if I go alone. It ain't right to take civilians along on police matters."

"You don't understand. These men have dogged my husband for weeks now. I just want to know that he hasn't been beaten—or worse. I promise I won't be a problem to you."

"Well, I'll allow you to accompany me in the skiff, but I cannot allow you to board the *Durham*. Will you agree to that?" Molly nodded. Schout Jack offered his hand and pulled her up behind him in the saddle. After his horse began its trot, Molly's neighbors began to follow them on foot—at first just in ones and twos, but with each half block the crowd swelled. Many of the men who participated in burning the governor's carriage were still awake and word spread that Schout Jack was going to the frigate to speak with its commander, and had the lady whose house was turned upside down with him.

Captain Sears still was unofficially in charge. Wanting to observe the sheriff's actions, he kept the crowd in the distance—available, but not raucous enough to alarm the sheriff. The mood of the mob had turned unpredictably light and now carried the atmosphere of walking to the theatre for entertainment. They watched Schout Jack and Molly untie a government skiff from the pier and push off into the dark waters. As the small boat progressed toward the naval ship at anchor in the harbor, Sears exhorted the people to remain on the waters' edge. He used the time to continue sending men to find more citizens to boost the crowd's size. When the sheriff's boat disappeared into the night, Sears said, "Will Sherman, you and Howerton start a bonfire on the beach to keep the people warm." Sears didn't want them wandering off to the comfort of a tavern, or worse, heading home.

As Schout Jack's boat approached the Durham, the officer of the deck called down, "You, there, come no further."

Schout Jack answered loudly, "I am Sheriff Freeman. I wish to speak with your captain."

"He has retired for the evening," responded the officer of the deck arrogantly.

"Well now," said Schout Jack in his easy going drawl, "He will have to be awakened. I'm here on official business and I cannot postpone it." Schout Jack, not waiting for the deck officer's response, returned to his rowing. When the stem of the skiff bumped the frigate's hull, sailors on the night watch peered over the railing. Neither Schout Jack nor Molly spoke as the seconds ticked off without a response from the warship.

Several minutes passed in silence, and the standoff sorely tested the sheriff's patience. Finally, the officer of the deck came to the railing. With Captain Mowbray standing a few feet off the gunnel (out of view), the deck officer said defensively, "State your business."

Schout Jack answered loudly, "I wish to speak with your captain."

The deck officer disappeared, and after conferring with Captain Mowbray, returned to the gunnel. "As I told you before, he is indisposed. Tell me what this is about and I'll see if he can speak with you."

"It concerns the theft of livestock. I'm here to question certain members of your crew who participated in the raid on the shipper's house this evening. My purpose is to discover whether they were involved or no."

Jean-Luc and Henry Charles were on deck. It was the captain's habit to put new impressments to work doing the least desirable jobs. The purpose of that regimen was to illustrate that after they were assigned their permanent duties, such as sail furling or gunnery, they wouldn't consider it intolerable in comparison. Jean-Luc kept a close eye on the captain and the positions of the crew near the gunnel. In his mind there would never be a better time to escape.

After whispering with Captain Mowbray, the officer of the deck leaned over the railing and said, "There were no members of this crew involved."

Molly could hold her tongue no longer and shouted, "We know you have my husband and topman aboard. We want them returned."

Irritated, Schout Jack sternly said, "Please, Mrs. St. Alembert, I'll handle these talks."

"Yes, sir," said Molly chastened.

Jean-Luc whispered to Henry, "Follow my lead."

"Aye, Skipper."

Schout Jack said, "Farmer Christmann reported his pig and four chickens stolen. Witnesses I interviewed reported the thieves were from this vessel. Since his allegation has been corroborated, I must insist you allow me to come aboard and continue my investigation."

"With regrets, Sheriff, we cannot allow that."

Schout Jack sniffed the night air in an exaggerated manner and said, "What is that I smell?" Out of the corner of his eye he saw the deck officer's smirk disappear. "Could it be swine on the spit in the galley?"

When the officer of the deck didn't respond, Schout Jack became truly angry. "See here, Lad, my authority extends to this vessel while you anchor in our port."

The deck officer disappeared a moment and when he reappeared, asked, "To what authority are you referring, Sheriff?"

"In the name of the great Jehovah, sir, I refer to the agreement written in the royal charter concerning the legal status of the king's armed forces and their conduct in his colony of New York." Schout Jack emphasized his final point, "And particularly conduct criminal in nature —yes, son, the Royal Navy falls under my jurisdiction when anchored here."

Again the deck officer disappeared from the railing to confer with his captain. As the two officers talked quietly, Jean-Luc and Henry worked diligently at their cleaning chore, but inched ever closer to the gunnels. When the deck officer reappeared, he said, "We cannot allow you to board this vessel without a search warrant authorizing said search."

Schout Jack slapped the hull with his hat and said angrily, "Dammit, man, you seem determined as hell not to allow me to board, well now, when I return with that warrant I'll search every inch of this tub." Shaking his fist, Schout Jack hollered, "I'll be back!"

Molly watched Schout Jack sit and snatch the oars in a huff. She pushed an extra set of oars out of the way and stood in the boat to yell to her husband.

Afraid of swamping, Schout Jack pleaded, "Mrs. St. Alembert, please sit down!"

"Jean-Luc!" shouted Molly with her hands cupped.

Jean-Luc released his grip on his holy stone and whispered, "Now!" He and Henry jumped to their feet and dashed for the railing. A burly sailor grabbed for Jean-Luc, but the young husband easily sidestepped him and jumped upon the gunnel. He glanced back to check on his topman.

Two sailors with belay pins chased Henry. He bounded over a deck cannon and appeared cornered between the shrouds and the cannon on the railing. As his pursuers closed in, Henry slithered between the legs of the sailor with his back to Jean-Luc and dashed across the deck. Jean-Luc saw an officer try to grab Henry, but missed. The topman bounded onto the railing beside Jean-Luc grinning from ear to ear. Jean-Luc said, "Into the ocean," and jumped overboard.

Henry yelled, "Scrub your own stinking decks." The officer of the watch pulled his sword. Henry turned around and considered the distance from the gunnel to the ocean's surface. He looked at the armed naval officer coming at him and followed Jean-Luc in a headfirst plummet into the chilly, dark ocean.

The runaways splashed twenty feet from Schout Jack and Molly. The sheriff, hearing the tumult aboard the warship changed course and rowed to where Jean-Luc was holding Henry's head above the water. He and Molly hurriedly assisted the pair aboard. Though their teeth chattered from the wet clothes and cool night air, Jean-Luc and Henry eagerly took the oars, and Schout Jack moved to the transom. Molly sat in the bow and called out course corrections. Schout Jack kept a wary eye on the frantic activity aboard the frigate.

No sooner had the impressed sailors dove overboard than Captain Mowbray ordered the ship's launch lowered; he had the intention of recapturing the deserters. Two royal marines ran to the rail and aimed their muskets at the fleeing skiff. Captain Mowbray said crossly, "Don't fire. The sheriff is in that skiff. The last thing I want to answer for is a dead sheriff."

"Lower the captain's launch!" screamed the deck officer. Within seconds the sailors had the tarp off. The royal marines hustled to the poop deck and efficiently seated themselves with their muskets held straight. They were followed by the oarsmen who just as efficiently seated themselves and had been drilled to hold their oars upright in military fashion.

Captain Mowbray turned to the deck officer and asked, "Are the davits in working order?" The davits were the beams, lines, and pulley system for lowering the launch from its high perch.

"Yes, Captain, I checked them myself this afternoon."

"Good. When I return with our deserters, I want the ship moved behind Captain Rodney's *Dublin*." Captain Mowbray nodded toward the frigate anchored off Red Hook in the Buttermilk Channel. Captain Mowbray stepped into the launch. As the deck officer gave the signal to lower the launch and gently lower it onto the ocean's surface, he heard Captain Mowbray shout, "Double rum rations to all aboard when we catch the runaways. Put your backs into it, men."

"Huzzah!" shouted his oarsmen.

As soon as the launch had its buoyancy and cleared the frigate's hull, the sailors wetted their oars and the coxswain began his rhythmic chant. Their synchronized strokes quickly propelled the launch to top speed. "Listen, men, they have a 150 yard lead. Stay focused on the rum. We are catching them!"

During the chase's first moments Captain Mowbray's launch wasn't visible, but Molly could now see the empire's pursuers, and they were gaining. Jean-Luc, though concentrating on pulling the oars couldn't help but notice in the moonlight, that the *Marie* sat low in the water. "What happened to our ship?" he asked in a gasp.

Molly said, "Someone scuttled it."

Jean-Luc looked confused, and blurted, "What? Why?"

"We'll talk later, husband, but now, row!"

Twenty motivated men rowing in sync rapidly got the launch to top speed. Molly and those in her boat had heard the cheer from the king's warship and knew its implication. "Row, Jean-Luc, row!" shouted Molly, imploring her young husband to a greater effort. Henry maintained Jean-Luc's cadence and the skiff's stem sliced through the waves toward a beach on Manhattan's East River side.

Captain Mowbray shouted encouragingly, "We're gaining on them, men!" With the oars dipping in coordinated strokes the *Durham*'s contingent grunted in unison to their coxswain's tempo. "Remember, double rations of rum." The sailors put forth a super human effort on the oars, and the distance between boats began narrowing at an alarming rate.

The sheriff's skiff had a lead of twenty yards, but Molly mentally calculated the launch would close with them at its current speed and they would be overtaken short of the beach. Molly alternated checking the beach and their pursuers. Her mind raced to their future arrest and she felt despondent. She thought even if we get to the beach, Captain Mowbray's people will capture Jean-Luc and Henry there.

Just then, Molly heard shouting coming from the shore. She could make out several hundred townsfolk standing on the beach. In the night air, their taunts carried clearly and the mob screamed for Schout Jack's skiff to make it to shore. Though he had to squint in the moonlight, Isaac Sears followed the pursuit's progress keenly among the throng. As did Molly, Sears could see the launch's speed overtaking Schout Jack's skiff. Schout Jack had heard the crowd's noise and said, "Come on lads, put your backs into it. They're gaining on us."

Captain Sears shouted, "What's happening, Schout Jack?"

Schout Jack half stood in the skiff and hollered, "The *Durham*'s giving chase. I have our two townsfolk on board—the ones impressed today, but they ain't letting them leave easy."

Captain Sears addressed the mob and said in a bellowing challenge, "Are you going to let the king's navy keep stealing our fellow citizens?"

"No!" shouted the crowd.

"Are you going to let them steal your friends?"

"No!"

"Steal your husbands?"

"No!"

"Then grab yourself a cobble, because two New York sailors need an assist." Each person in the crowd picked up two rocks as instructed. Captain Sears also picked up two cobbles and began wading into the foaming surf with his gaze fiercely fixed on the pursuers' launch.

Now, Molly could see the sizeable crowd on the shore, but, looking back, also observed the launch a mere five yards astern. One sailor put down his oars and crawled to the stem and leaned over with his arm outstretched. "Faster Jean-Luc!" she implored.

"We are rowing as fast as we can," said Jean-Luc through clenched teeth.

"They are about to catch us!"

Jean-Luc slapped the oars into the ocean and pulled with all his might. The skiff surged with his new found power. Molly screamed, "They're coming really close." Schout Jack swatted away one marine's outstretched arm. The marine tried again and this time Schout Jack grabbed him by the wrist and twisted. His fall overboard caused his shipmates to veer around him and they lost some distance. Seeing the action going hand to hand, Sears waded even farther into the surf. The crowd followed him. Soon all were standing waist deep in the chilly ocean. "Now!" screamed Captain Sears as he chucked his cobble with all his might at the king's launch.

Molly's skiff raced under the hail of stones that showered down on the navy launch. The cobbles landed with fearsome force and accuracy. Within moments every pursuer had blood running from the blows. The launch faltered, since the empire's sailors found it impossible to row and to cover their heads.

Schout Jack yelled, "We're almost to shore. Don't slack up." The skiff plowed through the dark waters and came to a crunching stop when the stem met the seabed.

Captain Mowbray said angrily, "Keep after them!"

A sergeant behind him asked pleadingly, "Captain, can we use the muskets to defend ourselves?"

"No! We are only here to get our recruits back. Listen all of you —no one is to fire without my order."

When the second volley of cobbles rained down on the launch, followed by more hoots and screams from the Yankee crowd, a sailor behind Captain Mowbray said beseechingly "Cap'n, it ain't possible to catch them now."

Neither Captain Mowbray's wrath nor his rum rations could motivate the sailors to confront the fury of the rock-hurling New Yorkers. "Reverse course, coxswain," bellowed Captain Mowbray himself a recent victim of a cobble to the shoulder.

Molly and Jean-Luc leapt from the skiff, ran through the crowd, and didn't stop until they reached the first street fifty yards from shore.

They stopped though as soon as the crowd erupted into a triumphant roar as the *Durham*'s launch turned about in a display of flailing, panicky oars slapping the foamy water. Schout Jack and Henry pulled the sheriff's skiff onto the beach. Schout Jack placed his hand on Henry's shoulder and said, "You better get home." Then he turned to the withdrawing English sailors and shouted, "I'll be out to the ship with my warrant right soon." He turned around again and asked the crowd, "Where did my young couple make off?" The people obliged and parted so the sheriff could see the St. Alemberts by the street. "I'd like a word with you two."

As Molly and Jean-Luc stood quietly waiting for Schout Jack, Molly said in a whisper, "I scuttled the schooner, darling."

"You?" asked her surprised husband.

"I just couldn't let them take our ship. I have the plug. Whenever you're ready, we can refloat her."

Schout Jack sauntered towards them. "If I were you two, I'd disappear."

Molly said, "We will."

Jean-Luc said in his French accent, "Thank you, Schout Jack."

"Well, then, get going," said Schout Jack in mock sternness.

Molly and Jean-Luc held hands and ran towards their home. Captain Sears approached the sheriff from behind and asked, "Will you be need'n any more help, Schout Jack?"

The sheriff said, "Not from your friends, Captain Sears, but maybe from you."

Sears nodded and announced to the people on the beach, "That's all for one night. Thank ye kindly, good folk. And give yourself a round of applause for teaching the tyrant's lackeys an important lesson in Yankee liberty." The crowd laughed, and hurled another round of derisive shouts at the retreating launch.

As Molly and Jean-Luc neared their house, an older man stepped out from the shadows. "Jean-Luc, May I have a word with you."

The couple stopped. Jean-Luc asked, "Mr. Van Cortlandt? Is that you?"

Pierre Van Cortlandt stepped forward and said, "Good evening."

Molly inched closer to Jean-Luc. She asked, "Why are you here, Mr. Van Cortlandt?"

"I, too, am answering charges levied by the customs pair, and met with my attorney. While on the island, I couldn't help noticing your lives have grown quite interesting since Joanna and I saw you last."

Molly said, "When we returned from Albany, the customs frigate was waiting for us. It was like they knew we were coming, they even knew of our transporting the two slave girls to and from your manor." She looked at Jean-Luc a moment and continued, "Is there a connection, or is this all a horrible coincidence?"

Pierre said, "I think I know why you were stopped. I came tonight, because I am concerned for your welfare. Clearly the customs officials suspect you. Their campaign against you will escalate."

Jean-Luc said, "We share your concern."

Van Cortlandt said, "You can stay with Joanna and me for a while."

Jean-Luc said, "That is very kind, but my employees depend on me. My business cannot run itself."

"I was afraid you would turn me down. Then you'll be extra careful? Promise me you won't let your guard down."

Molly smiled and said, "We promise."

Van Cortlandt nodded and said, "The tax collectors are growing desperate."

# CHAPTER TWENTY-ONE

NOVEMBER 1, 9:00 P.M.

ROBB AND LISING sat in Montayne Tavern with two pewter tankards of porter ale on the table untouched. Having just left Governor Colden's presence they felt depressed and with their domicile destroyed, they viewed getting inebriated as a viable option. Robb ran his finger around the rim of the mug and stared at the foamy amber liquid. Lising stared at the table candle's flame; his thoughts elsewhere. A minute later Lising shifted in his chair and rested his rump on the front of the seat and his neck on the back support and stared at the ceiling. Neither man was parched, but tonight they intended to get smashed, because both knew that they had failed miserably and didn't want to be alone with their thoughts.

Robb broke the silence and said, "Bad timing, Douglas, what with us arriving at the governor's burning carriage the same time the old Scotsman shows his face." Lising grunted and crossed his legs at the ankles. Robb continued, "Life isn't working out as I had planned. You know—I had high hopes when I came to the Americas. Do you think it is too late to get back in the old Scot's favor?"

Lising didn't give the question much thought and said quietly, "I don't know. There was no reasoning with the son of a bitch. Face it,

Robb; we are in the wrong place at the wrong time and doing the wrong work."

Thirty minutes earlier Robb and Lising had arrived at their offices only to watch the governor's carriage smoldering in the street and the governor standing there in the early morning hours watching the glowing embers. Governor Colden turned around upon hearing footsteps and recognized his two customs collectors. He pointed at them and roared, "I want to see you both in my office—Now!" A dozen soldiers stopped relaying the fire fighting water buckets to watch the commotion.

"Yes, Governor," said Robb. He looked at the ground. Like school-children, they dragged through the governor's door as Dillon held it open. As soon as they passed, he quickly shut the door and hustled into the governor's office to take the governor's cloak and hang it properly. Having accomplished that task Dillon moved behind his desk where he arranged his paper, pen, and inkwell; he then sat quietly prepared to take notes.

"An interesting night we had, gentlemen, a very interesting night wouldn't you say?" asked Governor Colden in a tense voice. Robb and Lising nodded sullenly. "Yes, I'd say we nearly had as much mayhem as we can stand in one night. What say you?"

Robb said passively, "Yes, sir."

"Let's see, my carriage was burned, the apartment I provide for you was burned, too, not to mention the city suffered the danger of burn-ing to the ground." Governor Colden's eyes flashed the unmistakable fury he felt toward the agents. "Do you suppose these events are related to your raid on that young shipper's residence?" asked Governor Colden sarcastically.

Robb misinterpreted the governor's meaning and tried to actually answer the question. "Sir, I don't believe those people burned your carriage over our raid of the Frenchman's house. Those rioters don't care about him. He's a foreigner."

"Shut up, you miscalculating idiot. Are you under the impression this is a two-way conversation? Well, it isn't! I'll do the talking, and you will do the listening." Colden's bony finger stabbed the air in emphasis.

"Yes, Governor," the pair answered in unison.

"First Mowbray absconds with his employee and then you search his domicile with utter disregard for how the people of the colony would react. Could you have picked two more inflammatory acts to commit against this so-called foreigner?" This time, Robb and Lising kept their mouths shut. With the veins in his neck pulsing from anger and high blood pressure, Governor Colden's rant continued, "No that would be quite impossible. Perhaps, I could tolerate your bumbling if your collection record was decent, even below average, but it isn't, is it? No, I think you are too comfortable in your positions. That's what I think."

In the back of the room sat Dillon listening, enjoying every moment, and ready to scribble a note if the governor ever gave one. He thoroughly relished each verbal jab the governor delivered. The customs officers had earned this scolding and Governor Colden intended to carve his 'pound of flesh.'

Colden walked over to Robb and Lising, got right in their faces, and said, "I've matched you with a good naval officer and the fastest frigate in New York's waters. But have you increased customs collections? Have you rid this colony of smugglers? No and no! They're operating under your noses." Governor Colden walked back behind his desk. He slammed his palm down on its surface and bellowed, "Rid me of this problem, now, or so help me, I'll put you both on the next ship bound for London."

"Yes, Governor," said the agents. Each glanced at the other for an indication of whether they should leave or wait for more of the governor's dressing down.

"Now get out of my sight."

With chins on chests and drooping shoulders reflecting their emotions, they slowly shuffled out.

Dillon started to close the office door, but waited to ensure the two agents had exited the building. Satisfied they had left, he closed the door and said softly to his employer, "The governor was quite hard on them."

Governor Colden looked spent. "Yes, I was," he said softly. He closed his eyes and pinched the bridge of his nose attempting to calm his passions.

"Is the governor considering his statements might be taken out of context and misinterpreted by his servants?" asked Dillon carefully.

Surprised, Governor Colden asked, "I'm sorry? What do you mean, Jeremy?"

"Your wish for them 'to rid you of the problem' could be misinterpreted. The word 'rid' seems imprecise." Dillon glanced down, not wishing to make his question confrontational. "It concerned me. That's all."

"Perhaps, Jeremy, but really, now, even those idiots couldn't misconstrue my words."

"Yes, Governor, I'm sure you are correct." Dillon slowly closed his desk drawer, took his coat and hat from the rack and grasped the doorknob. "If the governor doesn't need me further, I'll take my leave for the evening."

Governor Colden watched his personal secretary quietly close the door. Sitting down at his desk, he turned in his chair toward the window and asked in a whisper, "Even those idiots couldn't screw my words around, or could they?"

By mid-evening Robb and Lising had finished their fifth tankard of ale. The governor's reprimand faded with each swig and their outlooks on the futures had improved dramatically. Robb wiped the foam from his lips and said in a raspy whisper, "Douglas, I think we should rid this colony of smugglers— tonight."

Lising had been giving Governor Colden a piece of his mind in his fantasy world and looked at Robb with a blank expression. "Wha'd you shay, Johnnie?" he asked.

Nodding toward the tavern door, Robb reiterated, "I said," and slammed his fist in mock anger on the table, "we should rid this colony of smugglers t'night." The two customs agents roared in laughter.

"I'm wit' ya' ole buddy," burbled Lising with drooping eyelids.

The customs agents staggered to their feet, grabbed their tankards and with bottoms up sucked the final drops of porter, and shook hands giddily as only the inebriated can. "Gimme those shillings in your pocket, Douglas, we're gonna buy ourselves a flagon of ale for the road. Ridding the America's of smugglers can parch a man somethin' awful. We're sure to need drink later."

When Lising struggled to find his pants' pocket opening, Robb started snickering. After purchasing their alcohol supply they stumbled out of the tavern. Too tipsy to understand the dire implication, he said, "Damn, Douglas, we are going to need a place to sleep tonight. Oh, well, our first stop is th' stable. We'll drive to the lumber yard and pick up some planks and tools we'll need to build a contraption for ridding towns of smugglers."

As they rolled up to the St. Alembert's home, they observed through the window a lantern's glow and the proprietor at his desk. John Robb smiled malevolently and thought good—he's in.

# CHAPTER TWENTY-TWO

November 1, 9:30 p.m.

Jean-Luc unlocked his front door and shut it behind him. He lit the candles in his hallway, put his coat and hat on the rack by the door, and sat down behind his desk. To Jean-Luc, events seemed to have spun out of control. He didn't like having to either continually scan the horizon for customs frigates or slipping into port on each business run. He intended to make some ledger entries before he retired for the evening, hoping to speak with Molly about selling the business; Jean-Luc thought she might like the idea of moving west with her parents. When he heard a wagon stop outside his door, he paused momentarily, but went back to checking his arithmetic. Even when he heard two pairs of boots dismount he didn't think the noise unusual.

Then the door burst open, and the customs agents rushed in with pistols drawn. "Put your hands up, St. Alembert!" said John Robb.

Jean-Luc's eyes widened and he dropped his quill pen. He quickly obeyed and raised his hands. The intruders reeked of the alehouse and the tacit implication was the customs agents weren't here on official business. "You have been drinking."

"That's quite perceptive of you, Laddie." Jean-Luc's eyes darted to his side drawer where he kept a loaded pistol. Though tipsy Robb sensed the young man's intent and he motioned with his pistol toward the drawer. "Don't even t'ink about it."

"What are the charges this time?" asked Jean-Luc struggling mightily to appear calm.

"Shut up!" said Lising. He slowly lowered the flintlock of his pistol and hung the weapon about his neck by its strap. Jean-Luc sensed an ominous intent and began to fear these men. "Now, stand up." Robb kept his pistol trained on Jean-Luc while Lising bound his wrists and ankles. The knots felt uncomfortably tight, and then Lising produced a third rope to bind Jean-Luc's arms tightly to his sides.

"Where are you taking me?" asked Jean-Luc. He was stalling for time hoping that Molly had awakened in the next room and had discovered the intruders. He also wished against reason that Count de Charnay would mysteriously arrive upon the scene.

Robb stepped forward and glared into his prisoner's eyes. He backhanded Jean-Luc snapping the young man's head back. The resulting split lip bled freely down the young man's chin and neck. "Another word from you and I'll pull this trigger and send you to hell. I swear to God I will." Turning to Lising, Robb said, "Shove a rag into his trap."

Jean-Luc's chest heaved in gasps. Observing this, Robb sneered at his nemesis's vulnerability. Lising crammed a rag into the ship owner's mouth to prevent a cry for help. Then Robb and Lising each took him by his arms and dragged him outside. While they pulled toward the wagon, Robb scanned around the neighborhood. He feared someone would see them and report the abduction. But since no candles or lanterns stood in the windows of Jean-Luc's neighbors all indications were that the residents were asleep. "The neighborhood seems peaceful enough," said Lising ironically.

Robb and Lising lifted Jean-Luc into the wagon and shoved him to the headboard. In the limited moonlight, the wagon's contents puzzled Jean-Luc. He saw two eight-foot long flat boards, two sledgehammers, a half dozen four by four posts, and a burlap bag. Fearing the worst, he felt relieved that there was no other rope visible.

"I still don't see why we aren't taking this chap to that boulder pit across the Hudson. You know the one. It's just inside New Jersey. There would be less chance of getting caught. The water crossing may be farther, but we could avoid the wagon trip."

"Shut up!" barked Robb trying to sound officious. "We're going to Blackwell's Island, and that's that."

Jean-Luc then heard one of his captors crack the whip over the horses and the wagon lurched forward. Only when the wagon hit a bump could Jean-Luc hear the bag's contents clinking ominously — nails! He drew some hope for an escape when Robb and Lising opened a large flagon of ale stashed under their seat.

Jean-Luc fought to compose himself. As the wagon rolled through the streets of the city, he occupied his mind by studying the buildings about him and concluded his abductors were traveling northeasterly. When the wagon stopped Robb glanced back at his prey and smiled spitefully. Lising had stopped the wagon on the bank of the East River. Jean-Luc smelled the salt air, realized he was beside a river, and the fear that they would drown him surged through his thoughts. The three and one half mile trip took forty-five minutes and the wind gusted on the water's edge. To his mariner's mind, Jean-Luc noted the whitecaps on the river's surface and calculated the wind was gusting at fifteen miles per hour. Lising put the wagon's hand brake on, and jumped down. Ignoring Jean-Luc, he began to unload the lumber, sledges, and nails. When Robb roughly pulled Jean-Luc from the wagon and pushed him to the cold ground, Jean-Luc spotted a rowboat nearby.

Lising carelessly threw the supplies into the rowboat. He turned and said, "I'm finished. Let's stow him amidships."

Robb jerked Jean-Luc upright and said, "We're a piece from town, monsieur. You cooperate and you won't get hurt."

Jean-Luc thought perhaps they do not intend to kill me, after all — since they are drunk; maybe this is all about frightening me. Feeling the small craft pitch from his weight on the shore, Jean-Luc nestled down between the bench seats. Still tightly bound, Jean-Luc couldn't do anything about his situation, and turned his attention to the crescent moon that, inexplicably, was comforting to him during this ordeal.

Robb wobbled a bit before he stepped aboard. He shoved a board that had the misfortune to be in his way and plopped down. Clutching the flagon, Robb guzzled a long quaff and handed it to his partner. He asked, "Say, Dougie, who you suppose was the last bloke given the pancake treatment?"

"Dunno, Johnnie, too far back for my mind to recall. God rest the poor fellow's soul, though." Lising pushed the craft farther into the water and jumped in managing to roll inside with a thud while keeping his feet dry. He grasped the oars and began an out-of-sync and poorly cadenced jerk propelling the rowboat off the intended heading. With much struggling, he finally brought the bow around and kept his stem pointed toward the river island a short distance from shore.

The brief passage went quietly save for when Lising carelessly slapped the oars into the water and the rushing wind sent the spray onto Robb. "Be careful, dammit." When the bow hit the sandy beach on the southern boot of the isle, the customs agents jumped out and muscled the laden dinghy onto the beach. Jean-Luc lay quietly while the agents threw the lumber pieces on the beach.

Robb was sure their abduction hadn't been witnessed, but he was mistaken. Back when the customs agents had loaded Jean-Luc into the wagon, Billy Sherman had witnessed it all from his bedroom. He awakened his mother and father and had told them what he had seen. With his father hurriedly dressing, Billy and his mother rushed across the street and pounded on Molly's.

# CHAPTER TWENTY-THREE

9:45 P.M.

IN THE GROGGINESS of sleep, Molly heard knocking and wondered who it could be. Well, she thought, Jean-Luc will answer it. She rolled onto her side and pulled the covers to her chin. Just as she snuggled into a comfy spot, the pounding on the door grew more desperate. As if stung by a wasp, Molly threw off the covers. She realized Jean-Luc hadn't answered, because he must not be home. She bolted from her bed and, after grabbing a robe, ran barefoot across her cold wooden floor and jerked open the door.

Molly recognized her neighbor. "Mrs. Sherman?" Concerned that her husband didn't seem to be home, Molly stole quick glances around her foyer trying to spot him.

"Mrs. St. Alembert, my son, Billy, saw two men take your husband from this house by force just minutes ago."

"That's right, ma'am," Billy said. "They had him bound up with ropes and was treating him awful mean."

"Oh, no!" Molly put her hand over her mouth and thought a moment. She mused out loud, "Think, Molly, where would they take him."

Billy said, "I know where they took him."

"Where, Billy?" Molly placed her hands on Billy's shoulders and asked with desperation in her voice, "Where?"

"They argued a bit about some where in Jersey, but then decided to go to that old quarry pit on Blackwell's."

"Blackwell's Island?"

"Yes'm. You know, that abandoned quarry down on the boot."

"How many men were there, Billy?"

"Just two, but Blackwell's is where they said they was going."

Mrs. Sherman said, "My husband will be here in a minute, and he'll know some fellows that can go with you. We all saw what the government did to your home. A lot of folks were scared by it, and plenty more are fighting mad. It won't take my man long to have some men rounded up."

Molly said, "There isn't time. I'll ride ahead, but, please, send your husband and his friends to the quarry as soon as possible. Now, I must finish dressing."

As Molly turned to throw on some clothes, Billy shouted after her, "Good luck."

Molly dashed into the bedroom and threw on some cotton leggings, linen trousers, a blouse, and jacket. She grabbed a pistol from the closet and looped its lanyard around her neck. I'll need a second pistol if there are two of them she thought. She snapped her fingers and said, "Jean-Luc keeps one in his desk drawer." Rushing into the parlor, she opened the drawer and grabbed that pistol. A quick glance into each frizzen indicated the weapons were loaded, but she noted Jan-Luc's pistol had no lanyard. She shoved it inside her leather coat. As if she was talking to another, she said, "Let's go."

Fifteen minutes later, Molly had her horse saddled. Leaping on she spurred the stallion toward the street. Sensing her urgency during the saddling her horse jumped the fence without protest. Molly pulled the reins and headed up the alley to the major thoroughfare. The shadows on the empty moonlit street seemingly pointed the route to the river. She galloped on a northeasterly heading. Repeatedly she slapped the reins on her mount's hindquarters to maintain his gallop. Her husband's life was at stake and she was willing to sacrifice this horse if it meant saving him. She cut the corner of each street gambling that the next thoroughfare would be deserted this time of night. With the wind blowing her hair back she thought ahead to the time when she would catch up with the men who had her husband. Molly knew from experience that when guns and knives are involved, someone was going to get hurt. Am I prepared to kill, she asked herself. Spurring her horse onward was her silent answer. Coming to a fork in the road she had a decision to make. Deciding to take the right fork, she whipped the lathering animal. Spotting the East River at the end of the road, she gritted her teeth and twice whipped the horse's flanks. The stallion sprinted the final two hundred yards. Upon reaching the river's edge she pulled the reins with all her strength to halt the beast. In a cloud of billowing dust, she sat up in her saddle and strained to look through the darkness toward the island she knew lay a short distance from the riverbank. Desperate to locate the abductors beyond the dark ribbon flowing before her, she listened for the sounds of men talking, but only heard a repetitive pounding or hammering. That must be them she thought. She looked up and down the riverbank trying to find a boat she could use. "How can I get across the channel," she asked her horse.

Not finding a boat, she decided her only recourse was to swim the horse. She spurred the stallion northward heading upriver to account for the current. She stopped again and quickly looked about for something, anything, to use to cross to the island. But still not finding a dinghy, Molly looked about her surroundings and spotted a solitary farmhouse about a quarter mile from her spot. Maybe they have a boat I could use she thought. At that moment she heard a muffled scream come from the river island. I am wasting time she thought. She mentally calculated the river's current and how far it would carry her and the horse before she could reach Blackwell's Island. Disregarding the dangers, she spurred her stallion into the river until he began to swim. She fought to keep her pistols out of the river and retain her tenuous grip on the saddle. She knew that she must keep her powder dry. She held the pistols above her head, the reins in her teeth, and squeezed the animal's flanks with her thighs as tightly as she could. Ignoring the water's chilly temperature, she steeled her mind to guiding her horse to the island that was before her in the moonlight.

As she neared the island, she could hear the voices of her husband's captors. Molly kept a close eye on the current and grew concerned that it might sweep her horse past the boot before her mount found the shallow ground. As they neared the southern tip of the island still ten yards away, her horse found solid ground beneath his hooves. Relieved, Molly's reprieve lasted but a moment. Yes, she had crossed the dangerous East River in the darkness, but having arrived near her husband's location, Molly steeled her mind for the anticipated confrontation with the abductors. She focused on the task at hand. With the reins still in her teeth, she cocked her pistols' flints back until she heard the ominous second click. With the water cascading off her horse's flanks, Molly grew apprehensive about the abductors hearing her approach. Being forewarned, they would arm themselves. Even worse, during the channel swim she considered the possibility of being too late and discovering herself a widow. Molly spurred the horse into a gallop.

Back in the city, Billy Sherman and his mother rushed back to their house. They found Billy's father pulling on his shoes. "You've got to help Mrs. St. Alembert," said Mrs. Sherman. "Time's short, Will. Those men have a head start."

"I know. I've been thinking about who could help me. I believe I'll try Isaac—keep your fingers crossed he is home." Will Sherman bolted out the front door. Racing onto Isaac Sears' front porch, Will knocked in desperate raps. As he waited for Sears to answer, he gulped oxygen with one hand on the wall of the house and one hand on his knee. Almost too drained to turn around, he heard Sears ask from behind, "What can I do for you, Will Sherman?"

"Isaac! Can you round up some of the boys?" asked Will.

"Will, I just sent them home. What's happened?"

"You gotta get them back? We have a situation. It's serious."

"Yeah, I suppose so."

"Those customs agents snatched my neighbor, St. Alembert.

They're going to Blackwell's Island to do God knows what. He needs help, Isaac."

Captain Sears's face contorted in anger. "We'll make those rats rue tonight, Will. Why don't you come with me? That way the recall will go faster."

Having heard commotion outside his window, Dillon, tiptoed to his window to listen. He began eavesdropping; after overhearing Sears's instructions, he let the curtain fall from his fingertips. He rubbed his jaw thoughtfully, and then walked into his ally's bedroom. He rapped on the doorframe and said, "Geoff, wake up. There's trouble brewing."

De Charnay sprang from the bed with his pistol drawn. He had been resting for thirty minutes and had entered the deep cycle of sleep, but his paladin training served him well, and he was ready for battle. "What is it?" he asked in French. He blinked several times trying to shake off the sleep.

Minutes later, both men were galloping in the night toward Blackwell's Island. Dillon and de Charnay whipped their lathered mounts to the breaking point. The steeds snorted, and yet each time the reins were laid to their flanks they responded as though they knew a good man's life depended on them.

When they arrived at the riverbank they encountered the identical problem Molly faced earlier. After hastily looking up and down the riverbank for a skiff and not finding one, de Charnay said, "Let us ask that farmer." He pointed toward the isolated farmhouse on the far side of the field. Dillon nodded and both riders reined their mounts in the direction of the farmhouse. Just then they heard a gunshot echoing in the night air from Blackwell's Island. With only a nod as communication, both riders reversed direction and jumped their horses into the East River.

As he rode his horse through the cold waters, de Charnay heard a rumble and looked back. He saw a dust plume rising in the distance from the same road he and Dillon had taken. As he was certain it an alarm had been sounded, he figured it was Sears's men driving hard to lend their help.

Ten minutes later Sears's group arrived at the river having been delayed in rounding up supplies, besides their aims were both saving St. Alembert and the punishment of the customs agents. And when they approached the riverbank, Sears' local knowledge of an available boat became critical. He veered the wagon off the main road toward the solitary farmhouse sitting back from the river. When they stopped the wagon, every man jumped down and knew just what to do. While Sears spoke with the farmer (the man's wife listened from behind) his men loaded the small boat sideways across the wagon. It only took moments and they were speeding back toward the river. However, they had lost precious minutes, and Sears feared events on the island would play out before they arrived.

# CHAPTER TWENTY-FOUR

10:20 P.M.

ROBB AND LISING tied their boat to a tree on Blackwell's Island. While Robb kept an eye on Jean-Luc, Lising carried the lumber supplies to the abandoned quarry. In the cool night air, Lising constructed a small bonfire inside the island's rock formations.

While Robb guarded his prisoner, Lising located what they needed: level ground. There he positioned one of the large boards. He next sited and dug the postholes around the plank. After placing the post, he filled in the holes and tamped down the earth around each. Though didn't realize it, he was safe as long as Lising labored on his project. Never had silence sounded as frightening as when the building noises ceased.

Robb rubbed his pistol's barrel along Jean-Luc's cheek and delighted in the young man's fearful reaction. The gesture reinforced in the captive that his life rested in Robb's hands. Robb laughed when Jean-Luc's eyes widened at the sounds of Lising working in the quarry. Jean-Luc could not imagine what Lising was building a short distance away. Jean-Luc didn't think they were going to hang him, since he hadn't seen sufficient rope.

"All set, Johnnie," called Lising.

"None too soon," answered Robb. "I want to get warm by that fire."

Lising joined Robb and together they picked up their captive and transported him to the quarry. As they approached the board and posts, the fire illuminated the area and gave Jean-Luc his first hint of their intention in bringing him to the river island.

Robb placed his pistol against Jean-Luc's temple and said, "The more you cooperate, the more kindness I'll show. Now I'm going to remove your gag, but listen closely. If you cry out, your life will become excruciatingly painful. Understand?"

As sweat beads rolled down his temples, Jean-Luc nodded slowly. When Robb removed the rag from the prisoner's mouth, Jean-Luc gasped for air and then spit, attempting to expunge the nasty taste. "What do you want from me?" asked Jean-Luc with desperate resignation in his voice.

"Let's start with a confession that you're a smuggler. That would please me to no end, Frenchman." Robb found it difficult to contain his hatred for and resentment of the young shipper.

"Fine," said Jean-Luc. "I am a smuggler. Now, please let me go."

"Well, smuggler, we have made arrangements to avoid a costly trial to the taxpayers of New York. Tonight we're reviving the infrequently used punishment men of the bar like to call *Peine fort et dure*." In the background, Lising sniggered.

Jean-Luc easily fell backward when Robb shoved him in the chest. Lising caught him at the halfway point and Robb whisked him into the air by grabbing his ankles. They lowered him onto the plank that lay amidst the six posts on the ground.

As Jean-Luc was laid on his back, his alarm heightened when Lising walked over to the second plank and picked it up. "What are you going to do?"

"*Peine fort et dure*, Monsieur St. Alembert," said Robb sarcastically. "In the language of the courts it translates into "hard and severe punishment. And for the crimes of smuggling and striking a public official, this court sentences to death by crushing!"

Lising placed the second plank on top of Jean-Luc. They forced his wrists into straps on the bottom plank to prevent his escape. Then they fastened two leather straps (resembling trouser belts) to gird the two pieces of wood, sandwiching the prisoner.

When Lising and Robb finished securing the captive between the boards, they sat down using the top plank as a bench. Jean-Luc squirmed and struggled mightily, but the customs agents mocked his efforts. Robb opened a flagon, and began passing the bottle between them, joking, and hooting at Jean-Luc's discomfort. Though he squirmed and struggled, the plank and the weight of the customs agents held him fast. Now Jean-Luc had to fight for a breath. He worked his wrists desperately trying to loosen the straps.

Lising, feeling Jean-Luc's thrashing about under the board, bent over and looked between his legs and said, "If your wriggling causes me to spill my drink, I'll—" The threat hung in the air. Jean-Luc's anxiety gave way to the realization he was about to die. As he lay there, his mind raced; he held to the belief someone was coming to help him.

When their bottle's contents had been consumed, Lising stood and wiped his sleeve across his lips. "Let's get started, Johnnie."

Robb said, "While sitting here, I noticed some splendid stones lying on the other side of the fire. Bring one here, Dougie."

Lising stood, wavered a moment as he fought the effects of the alcohol, and then staggered past the fire to where Robb was pointing. When he reached the large stone which weighed about seventy-five pounds, he stopped and pointed at it. Robb laughed and nodded his approval. Lising giggled, but struggled to pick up the rock more from the effects of the ale than the heft. Robb said, "Come on, Dougie, let's get this execution started." When Lising lugged the stone to where Robb sat atop Jean-Luc, the senior customs agent patted a spot on the plank beside where he sat and said, "Just place it nice and gentle right here."

When Lising allowed the rock to fall the last 12 inches, Jean-Luc groaned loudly. That sent Robb and Lising into a new spate of snickering. Lising wobbled back to the rock pile and returned with another comparable stone. After several large rocks had been set onto the plank over Jean-Luc, Robb knelt beside Jean-Luc.

Jean-Luc's raspy whisper, "I cannot breath. Please stop. You are killing me."

Robb moved his ear closer and asked, "I'm sorry, I couldn't quite make that out. What did you say, smuggler?"

Jean-Luc used his waning strength to lift the weighted plank to take his next breath. He screamed a raspy muffled whisper, "Please, stop—." Each breath he took required a supreme effort to lift the stones. Each exertion for a breath made the ensuing more difficult. Jean-Luc mounted all his strength and grunted out the words, "I—I'm dying."

Robb said, "Why, monsieur, isn't that what *Peine fort et dure* is about? Oh, I realize, crushing criminals is a wee outdated and hasn't been done in decades, but Dougie and I think your crimes and their effects on our lives merit this—sanction." Turning to Lising, he said without emotion, "Only a few more. He won't last much longer."

"Let's do him in, Johnnie. I don't want to listen to him whinin' no more. I'm still thirsty and want to open another flagon. Whaddya say, Johnnie? We got another flagon, haven't we?"

"Get that large rock over there," said Robb pointing across the quarry.

Lising nodded, walked over and picked it up. He hefted the boulder over his head and wobbled a step under its weight. He fought to remain upright. He struggled to carry it. Finally, he stood over Jean-Luc with the boulder held high. As Jean-Luc's life faded, Lising's stone certainly represented the death blow. Jean-Luc's strength was virtually spent—he was down to his final minute alive.

When Molly's horse found the solid ground of Blackwell's Island, horse and rider exited the cold river dripping water. The fire's glow a few hundred feet away was a beacon to her husband's location. Molly pondered two courses of action as her horse swam the river channel. One was to sneak up on the men holding her husband. The second tactic was to ride into their camp with her guns drawn. The head start the captors had on her directed her thinking that she should choose the latter course. She still held the reins in her teeth, but once on solid ground, Molly shifted the reins into her hands and held both pistol and leather strap in each of her hands. The customs agents, two sheets to the wind, never heard her mount's hoof beats. Thundering into the camp, Molly completely surprised Robb and Lising.

Robb's mouth fell open at the unexpected sight of a nightrider in their midst. Adrenalin shot through his system and his mind's haze began clearing. "What do you want?" asked Robb, not recognizing Molly.

"Release him," said Molly angrily as she slid off the saddle and landed on her feet.

He now could see Mrs. St. Alembert clearly. "Oh, you mean this smuggler?" asked Robb as his arm made a wide arc toward his captive. He recognized the shipper's young wife on the horse and believed he could handle her. "Hand me that rock, Douglas, I'll drop it." Robb couldn't imagine Molly being capable of pulling the trigger.

Molly watched horrified as Robb prepared to deliver the *coup de grace* to her husband. Molly said, "Drop that boulder or I'll—" Robb hesitated and looked at Lising.

His voice dripping with disdain, Lising said, "She's bluffing."

Molly squeezed the trigger and her muzzle flash lit up the quarry walls. The musket ball struck Robb's left ring finger, and he screamed in agony. The boulder fell harmlessly to the side. Holding his hand, Robb said through clenched teeth, "She shot off my finger."

Molly took a step toward the customs agents, nodded at Jean-Luc under the plank, and screamed, "He had better be alive, John Robb, or so help me, God, I'll put the next ball through your black heart."

"Help me with these rocks," screamed Robb to his partner. Molly's demonstrated wrath convinced him to do as he was told. The boulders rolling off Jean-Luc were stained with Robb's blood. As the customs agents discarded one particularly large stone, Molly heard Jean-Luc softly groan. She gasped and lowered her pistol barrel. Lising saw his chance and leapt for the pistol. He snatched it from Molly's grasp.

Just as Lising disarmed Molly, de Charnay and Dillon emerged from the river on horseback. They saw the fire and three figures standing inside the quarry. After dismounting, cautiously approached the quarry to assess the situation. From behind a boulder formation, de Charnay and Dillon observed the customs agents holding Mrs. St. Alembert at gunpoint and the crushing mechanism holding Jean-Luc.

Lising asked, "How did you find us?"

"A neighbor saw you taking my husband and came to me after you had left."

"Who was it?" asked Robb between clenched teeth.

"I won't tell you," said Molly defiantly.

Lising waved the pistol inches from Molly's face in threatening little circles and said, "Oh, you'll tell us all right." He turned to Robb and said, "Can you hold this pistol?" Robb nodded. "I'll get a rope and bind her. We'll give her a taste of *Peine fort et dure*."

"I'm bleeding bad. I cannot use my left hand, Douglas. Let me think." With his voice cracking with pain and emotional agony, Robb softly said to Molly, "I never meant to hurt *you*." Lowering his voice to a whisper, he added, "In fact, I wanted to call on you once —"

"Once what?" asked Molly. Pouncing on the vulnerable revelation, she said accusingly, "Once you killed my husband?" Molly glanced at Jean-Luc, and their eyes met. Molly shouted, "I love *him*. Don't you understand?"

"Now I have to kill you, too. You've seen too much," said Robb.

"I want to die if my Jean-Luc dies."

Lising pointed the pistol at Molly's heart.

Dillon said in a whisper to de Charnay, "I've seen enough." He took aim and fired. Shot in his back, Lising staggered a step, and pitched forward. Robb dropped the pistol and held his arms up. He began to sob. Molly looked in the direction of the shot.

To preserve his identity, Dillon remained behind the boulders, but de Charnay sprinted forward. Molly faced the approaching paladin. In French, de Charnay said, "I am a friend of your husband's." He quickly untied Molly's hands and said, "I'll guard this man while you untie your husband.

Molly quickly knelt and shoved away the stones. She felt confused and a little scared of the tall stranger. She said, "I recognize you. You are the beggar that sits outside the tavern. But just now you said, Jean-Luc is your friend. How do you know my husband?" De Charnay didn't answer. Molly hastily flung aside the remaining boulders. She again asked, "How do you know my husband?" Molly threw off the top plank. Jean-Luc's lips moved, but the night wind whisked away his inaudible message.

Molly gently lifted Jean-Luc by his shoulders. "Oh, Jean-Luc," she said. De Charnay rapidly untied the ropes binding Jean-Luc's ankles. The young shipper coughed weakly, and Molly said, "Thank God, he is alive." Jean-Luc was still too weak to speak or move. He had struggled for every breath, and he was exhausted.

De Charnay said, "His will to live accounts for his survival.

From behind cover, Dillon yelled, "The other one is escaping."

Molly looked up and saw Robb running for the boat. He had too great a head start and she could never catch the fleeing customs agent. Molly lifted the pistol and took aim, but then smiled and slowly lowered the barrel.

De Charnay asked in French, "Why did you not shoot him?"

"I didn't have to," said Molly.

A group of men had snatched Robb just as he reached the boat. De Charnay felt certain it was Sears's people. Upon arriving, Sears and the others beached their boat, and started toward the quarry. The unfortunate customs agent fleeing in the darkness had blundered into them.

De Charnay said, "I will take my leave now."

"Please, tell me how you and my husband are friends."

De Charnay again ignored the question. Instead he said as he pointed at the far shore, "I will take your horse and tie him to a tree on the far side. These men will assist you with Jean-Luc and the boat."

Molly knelt and placed Jean-Luc's head in her lap. She brushed a lock of his hair out of his eyes several times. Molly looked up at de Charnay and said, "You saved my husband's life, and mine, too. Whoever you are, thank you."

"Will he live?" asked de Charnay.

"He's exhausted, but with rest, he should recover." Molly watched de Charnay take her horse's reins and walk to the river and noticed another man join him from behind the rocks; she realized the man's companion accounted for the other shot.

Two of Sears' men came over. One asked, "Who are they?"

Molly answered quietly, "Friends—I don't know their names."

The man nodded grimly and said, "Let's use this plank to carry him." They lifted Jean-Luc and laid him along it. The other man said to Molly, "Ma'am, we'll put him into the boat."

Molly nodded and smiled gratefully. After Jean-Luc was placed in the boat, she gathered her pistols from the ground as Sears' other collaborators returned to the fire where the group held Robb. The men stripped him to his drawers and bound him using the same ropes he used on Jean-Luc. When Molly reached the riverbank, she paused to see what was happening. She observed a man place a small, black cauldron over the embers. A man holding Robb's feet yelled over his shoulder, "Lucas, that bag of chicken feathers is by the large rock to your right. The pitch will heat up quickly enough."

It didn't take long for the pitch to reach the proper temperature for brushing. Molly had no curiosity in the proceedings and stepped into the rowboat. After pushing off and rowing several strokes, she looked back and saw Sears's men brushing Robb with the dark, steaming goop. His blood curdling shrieks pierced the night as the heated pitch blistered his chest, back, legs, neck, and face with each brushstroke. She heard one of Robb's captors ask loudly, "Excise man, are you going to show your face in New York again?" The group's hooting drowned out Robb's answer. Molly heard the tormenter repeat his question louder indicating that he didn't like the first answer. Then the sound of Sears' men derisively clucking like chickens filled the night air—a tarred and feathered tax collector simply wouldn't return to work.

Molly settled into a rowing rhythm. Jean-Luc laid his head in her lap. She felt his soft breathing on the back of her hand as she brushed his cheek. Molly heard Robb's cries piercing the night, and she glanced again at the quarry and saw the frightening silhouettes of his tormentors. She could see Robb writhing in agony like a worm on a hot rock. Molly turned her head when she saw him clenching his fists and shaking his head as his captors continued applying the hot tar to his upper body. Molly felt torn between her relief that her husband had been spared a gruesome murder and the pity she felt for Robb's agony.

Unaware her life was again in peril, Molly pulled the oars and propelled the boat toward a tree on the shore.

# CHAPTER TWENTY-FIVE

11:45 P.M.

COMMANDER ANDREWS, SCHOUT JACK, and two deputies, galloped up the coastal road toward Blackwell's Island. "About a half-mile more to those lights," said Schout Jack to his posse. Schout Jack slapped the reins on the animal's hindquarters. He thought back to thirty minutes earlier when this naval officer entered his office and described the two foreign agents. He would enjoy ridding his town of a couple of subversive troublemakers. How will I recognize them, he wondered.

In the river, Molly rowed and Jean-Luc huddled beside her. She shivered in the cool night air. Though in wet clothes, Molly's exertions kept her warm during the short row across the East River. She knew the near-death crushing her husband survived had sapped his strength, and she wanted to get him home and in bed as soon as possible.

Emerging from the cold, dark river ahead of the St. Alemberts, Dillon and de Charnay rode their dripping mounts onto the riverbank. De Charnay tied Molly's horse to the tree as promised. Then he walked back to the riverbank and watched her in the approaching rowboat. He calmly drew his pistol and checked his frizzen. Puzzled, Dillon watched him with interest. "Geoff?" De Charnay did not respond, but continued his preparation in silence. "Geoff, are you going to kill her?" asked Dillon.

The paladin walked to the riverbank and stood motionless watching the approaching boat. Count de Charnay turned to Dillon and said, "I take no pleasure in this, you understand."

"Geoff, please don't."

"You were there—you heard him," said de Charnay in a whispered hiss. "My sovereign wants his paladin avenged."

"We need to leave. You are not going to kill St. Alembert's wife, are you?"

Irritated by this ill-timed debate, de Charnay said, "I have orders, Colonel Dillon."

"Murdering her will not help France. Her death will steel her husband's heart against us. The king means well, but on this matter he is misguided. Think this through—besides, the river will carry the rowboat out to sea, and then we'll lose your contact. Look, the authorities will be coming here, and we need to leave—while we can." Dillon looked uneasily around the area. Then he added, "St. Alembert survived and is now positioned to do what we want. That wife of his will be a huge asset for him and for us. Leave well enough alone."

"I have my orders." Oblivious to the imminent threat, Molly pulled the oars and drew close to the bank. She knew that in a minute she could begin coasting. Count de Charnay raised the pistol.

Dillon approached from behind and placed his hand on the barrel. "You saw what I saw. She fought like a lioness for her man—a man you worked hard to recruit." He slowly pushed it downward. De Charnay said, "You are right, my friend."

Dillon said, "We need to get out of here." They ran to their horses, mounted, and spurred them into a gallop. After riding down the coastal road for a several minutes, they saw horses' dust plumes in the distance. "Who do you think they are?" asked Dillon.

Count de Charnay reined in his horse. After pausing to read the situation, he said, "It could be anyone." As they squinted into the darkness for a clue to the identity of the horsemen, he then said, "It could also be the authorities."

Schout Jack's group spotted two riders between them and Black-well's Island. They, too, stopped to assess the men in the road. "I see two. What about you?" asked Schout Jack.

Commander Andrews agreed. "I see two. It could be the men who abducted St. Alembert?"

Schout Jack said, "Maybe." Tension grew as both groups hesitated in this uncomfortable nocturnal circumstance.

Dillon whispered to Count de Charnay, "If it is the sheriff, I am compromised. Let's ride to the right and take the Palisades Road. Act like nothing is wrong, but be ready to make a dash for the trees." De Charnay flicked the reins and his horse turned right and started a trot. Dillon immediately followed the paladin's nonchalant manner.

Commander Andrews said, "They're turning."

Schout Jack said, "Maybe we should let them be. They don't seem hurried."

"Still, we should find out who they are. They could be the men we want," counseled Commander Andrews.

Schout Jack said, "Let's go talk to them, boys." The posse spurred their horses.

When Dillon and de Charnay saw the riders start their pursuit, they quickly turned their horses for the woods.

The lawmen had ridden hard for a short distance when another horse appeared on the road to their front. The dismounted rider waved at them.

Commander Andrews said excitedly, "It's a woman. It might be Mrs. St. Alembert."

Schout Jack said, "You check on it, Commander. Me and the boys will keep after these two."

Commander Andrews pulled the reins and peeled off. He stopped in front of Molly, but Schout Jack and his deputies continued their chase. Commander Andrews asked, "Are you alright? You look in shock."

Molly said angrily, "My husband—they nearly killed him. I must get him in bed." Molly led the horse several steps and stopped. "Rocks! Can you believe they tried to crush him with rocks?" Shocked by this statement, Commander Andrews walked over to Jean-Luc whose exhausted body slumped in the saddle.

The staccato blasts of five gunshots shattered the night's stillness. Commander Andrews whirled toward the sounds and stared worriedly into the darkness.

Two minutes earlier, Dillon and de Charnay put their horses into a sprint. Riding side by side, Count de Charnay said, "We cannot outrun them."

Dillon said, "They will not take me alive. I'll be dammed, but I'll not swing from an English gallows."

Count de Charnay said, "Shoot the mounts then—we'll kill the riders, if necessary."

Schout Jack and his deputies couldn't see Dillon and de Charnay rein their horses in the meager moonlight. The fugitives had pistols in both hands. The first two shots dropped the deputies' horses and the riders slammed into the ground with such force that they lay in the road unable to rise. Dillon's second shot nicked Jack's left ear lobe; Count de Charnay's second shot zipped through his vest.

Schout Jack's ear burned and he felt warm blood trickling down his neck. He stopped his horse in a dust cloud. Furious, he fired his pistol at one of his attackers, but didn't see or hear anything. "I missed!" He not only needed to reload but didn't like his chances of pursuing two armed horsemen; he decided against continuing the fight outgunned. He galloped back to aid his fallen deputies.

A half mile away Molly and Commander Andrews listened to the sounds of the gunfight. Molly said, "Those two men were among those that helped my husband tonight."

Commander Andrews asked, "Do you know them?"

"No, I only saw one and that was a fleeting glimpse. Between the firelight and the commotion, I couldn't identify him." Molly turned back to the sound of the shooting and said, "I hope the lawmen aren't hurt."

"Andrews! Are you still there?" yelled Schout Jack.

"Yes! I'm with Molly."

"I need help. My men are injured."

They rode the short distance to where Schout Jack had been ambushed and Commander Andrews assisted him with placing the injured deputies on Freeman's and Andrews's horses.

Schout Jack walked over to Molly, sitting on her horse holding Jean-Luc, and asked, "I know it is late ma'am, but I need to know what happened tonight."

Molly related the customs agents' attempt to murder her husband, her shooting Robb, and the mystery men shooting Lising. Schout Jack pushed his hat back and said, "So you didn't kill Lising; one of our ambushers did. Is that it?" Molly nodded. "And you don't know what happened to Robb?" Molly sadly shook her head. "Well, I gotta go back to that island tonight. I cannot wait 'til morning."

After shooting it out with the lawmen, de Charnay and Dillon rode into a forest glen. It surprised de Charnay when Dillon slid from the saddle. Count de Charnay dismounted in an instant and ran to his friend. He asked, "Are you hit, Jeremy?"

Dillon didn't answer; he sat on the ground and stared into the night. Count de Charnay could see from Dillon's empty expression that something was terribly wrong. He put his arm around his shoulders, and could feel Dillon softly coughing. As he knelt on the forest floor, Count de Charnay brushed away the perspiration glistening on his friend's forehead.

The old Irishman said, "I'm shot through, Geoff. I never thought it would end this way."

"Do not say that," said Count de Charnay. Feeling the angel of death little by little taking his friend, Geoff knew his rescuer from Fontenoy had but moments remaining. He kissed Dillon's forehead tenderly. Dillon smiled weakly. A battler all his life, the old man fought to keep his eyes open. He grabbed Geoff by the lapels and buried his face in the paladin's chest. Geoff said, "Do not close your eyes, my friend. Stay with me, please."

Dillon said, "Geoff, I am cold." Count de Charnay wrapped his arms about the Irish nobleman. Then Dillon stopped breathing and his body went limp.

Count de Charnay said, "Brave friend—rest in peace. It is a sad day for the world. We have lost the leader of the Wild Geese." Count de Charnay sat in the dark field holding his friend in his arms. Tears rolled down his cheek.

# CHAPTER TWENTY-SIX

November 2, 8:30 a.m.

**M**OLLY STUDIED JEAN-LUC resting in the bed. She considered it a good sign that he had eaten his oatmeal and fruit. Once Mrs. Sherman came to give her a rest, and since Jean-Luc was napping, it seemed a good time to sneak down to the shore and check on their schooner. When she arrived at the beach, she walked to the water's edge and stared at the scene before her. There rested their scuttled ship, and several hundred yards to the east floated several of empire's warships. Though the *Durham* was among the anchored ships, the harbor appeared serene—all the more so in contrast to the nightmare of the evening before. And yet the frigate radiated malevolence as it stood guard over their wounded ship and colonial city. Molly placed her hand in the dress pocket and felt the wooden plug. She turned away with a heavy heart and walked home.

When Molly entered the house, she found Jean-Luc sitting up and smiling. "You look better, darling," said Molly.

"Yes, I feel better. I feel like going to the office and doing some work."

"That's out of the question. If anything, we should be making an appointment with the solicitor. There is a good chance we can prevent them from confiscating the schooner. But you need to take it easy for the remainder of the day."

"We will go when my strength returns," said Jean-Luc.

Meanwhile, at breakfast in Widow Clifton's dining room, Sergeant Johnston pulled the end off the bread loaf, slathered it with butter, and stuffed it into his mouth. As he chewed, he noticed Schout Jack Freeman pass the window with a body draped over his horse. "Oh my god!" exclaimed Sergeant Johnston, and he dropped his knife onto the pewter plate. "That looks like..."

When he jumped up, one of his squad members asked, "Where are you going, Sarge?"

Sergeant Johnston ignored the question and dashed into the street where he hailed down Schout Jack, "Constable! Wait a minute, if you please." Sergeant Johnston ran up to Schout Jack and took the cadaver by the hair and raised the head for a better look. "Who killed Lising?"

Schout Jack said matter-of-factly, "I'm working on that. Whoever it was prevented the customs agent from killing St. Alembert and his wife."

Sergeant Johnston dropped the head and took a step backward. "Where is Mr. Robb?"

The sheriff said, "Oh, he was there, but I haven't found him. After I drop off this stiff, I'll be looking to find the taxman. *Ja*, for sure, I have questions to ask Robb." Schout Jack looked down the street in a non-confrontational posture and said, "You know, Johnston, if you're involved in this, I'll find out. You could save us both a lot of trouble and tell me right now."

Sergeant Johnston said, "No, Constable. No way am I involved. Yes, everyone knows I helped Mr. Robb on occasion, but always on orders from me Cap'n. You can ask Widow Clifton me whereabouts last evening."

Schout Jack turned in his saddle and said, "So's your alibi is set, is it Johnston? Well, you were part of the raid on the St. Alembert's house. And then Lising here tries to murder them. It doesn't look good, you know. Were you aware of the murder plot?"

Sergeant Johnston said animatedly, "No, no. Robb talked about seizures; always talking about seizures. So we finally gets one, and now this happens." Sergeant Johnston's expression turned to disgust. "I suppose I ain't getting' no prize money now."

"Your expression of sympathy for the deceased is touching. As for the grounded schooner, the court will dispose of that, and there isn't any paperwork submitted. I wouldn't be spending that prize money ahead of schedule," said Schout Jack. "I'll see you around, Johnston." The sheriff spurred his horse, but reined him in after a few steps. "Oh, and one other thing, Johnston, did you ever square things with Farmer Christmann?"

"Not yet. Those livestock are expensive. I was kinda waitin' for the prize money to come in, Schout Jack."

"Then tell me how Christmann is going to feed his family. Can he do it on your good intentions?"

"Alright, Constable, on payday I'll take a collection and square things with the farmer. Sergeant Johnston frowned as he watched the sheriff ride away. Intending to tell the captain about this, he retrieved his coat from Widow Clifton's and walked to the wharf. There, he caught a ride with a government replenishment boat whose coxswain said he'd drop him off at the *Durham*.

Once aboard, Sergeant Johnston asked the officer of the deck for permission to see the skipper. After the junior officer left, Mowbray asked, "You wanted to see me?"

"Aye, Cap'n." Sergeant Johnston said. "I came straightaway when I got the news."

"To what news are you referring?"

"Mr. Lising is killed and Mr. Robb is missing. It happened last night. The sheriff said Robb and Lising tried to murder the couple whose house we raided the other night."

Captain Mowbray pursed his lips. With a pensive expression, he leaned forward and placed his hand over his mouth and tapped his upper lip with his forefinger. After several moments, he asked, "Robb is missing, you say?"

"Missin,' Cap'n, aye. Sheriff said 'e was in on it, too. But now—'e's disappeared into thin air."

Captain Mowbray looked out the window deep in thought. When he turned back, he said, "Thank you, Johnston. You may go."

Sergeant Johnston said, "Oh, 'ere is one other thing, Cap'n." Mowbray turned back. "The sheriff told me I 'ad to repay that *Deutscher* for the pig and chickens."

"Johnston, I'll direct the ship's purser to take care of it. After all," he smiled wistfully, "The entire crew enjoyed the meal."

"Thank you, sir. Thee constable also told me not to leave the area, you know, because Robb tried to kill that shipper."

"Why? You weren't involved."

"Snug under me own covers last night, I was, sir."

"Well, don't you worry about the sheriff, Johnston. His jurisdiction ends at the water's edge. As far as I'm concerned, this frigate's deck is English soil."

"Couldn't agree more, sir. But still, maybe the boys and me should move back aboard."

Captain Mowbray nodded. "That would be advisable. I don't want any more unauthorized requisitioning of supplies from the local farmers." Sergeant Johnston smiled and saluted, did an about face, and hurried out. Captain Mowbray walked to the window and stared at the schooner aground on Diamond Reef. I was to use that money to fund my son's medical practice, he mused. Turning away from the window, he looked over at his swinging wooden cot, which would double as his coffin if killed in battle. He thought I think I'll lie down—I haven't been feeling like myself lately.

At midmorning, Commander Andrews stopped by the sheriff's office. He entered and approached the sheriff's desk. There, sitting with his face in his hand, sat Schout Jack. Commander Andrews said, "You look tired."

"I got in an hour ago. I took Lising's corpse to the morgue, but I never did find Robb—or his cadaver."

"Any leads? I should like to know the identities of the men who shot at you last night."

At the mention of his close call the night before, Schout Jack felt the scab on his tender earlobe. Then he said, "No, nothing. I returned to the quarry at daybreak to take another look around—this time in sunlight." Schout Jack stared out his office window. "What I find strange is that there was dozens of footprints on Blackwell's Island. Who were all those people? There isn't normally much activity out there. There shouldn't have been but four or five sets out there." Schout Jack spat into the spittoon nearby and with concern in his voice said, "If there are groups in this city willing to kill customs agents and law enforcement, this town may be in for a rough spell."

"One reason I was sent here was to gauge the reaction to the new taxes."

"Looks like your worst scenarios are occurring."

"My worst scenario is for loyal subjects to conclude their king doesn't have their interests at heart. That is a recipe for rebellion."

Schout Jack said, "Rebellion can be an ugly thing. I hope it doesn't come to that."

Commander Andrews took his hat and walked toward the door. He turned and said, "I should like the use of your skiff for an important errand."

"What? I was about to head home for some rest," said the exhausted sheriff.

"Still, I must confer with Captain Rodney."

"Where is he to be found?"

"His ship is anchored off Red Hook in Buttermilk Channel. He must have brought the tax stamps over."

"Oh, the *Dublin*, well now, that's not far. It is about one and one half miles. The currents are tricky down there. I don't recommend you going by yourself. Would you like me to come with you?"

"Why, yes, I'd like the company. You could catnap on the way."

The passage in the channel took fifty minutes. Schout Jack found himself waiting on the *Dublin*'s quarterdeck for Commander Andrews who was conferring in private in Captain Rodney's cabin. When they emerged from the office, a grim-faced Rodney asked the officer of the deck to lower the launch. Commander Andrews, holding his hat in his hand, looked unusually somber as well. As Captain Rodney and Commander Andrews boarded the captain's launch, Schout Jack stepped in and tied his skiff to its transom. With twelve sailors propelling their vessel, the launch quickly retraced the mile and a quarter to the mouth of the East River where Mowbray had the *Durham* anchored.

As the launch passed the Lakes' schooner and approached Mowbray's frigate, Schout Jack realized the significance of this errand. It was reflected by the expressions of his fellow passengers. The officer of the deck on the *Durham*, once he realized Captain Rodney was in the launch, quickly dropped the boarding ladder and sent the duty runner to alert the captain. Again Schout Jack remained in the launch and did not participate in the proceedings. Captain Rodney and Commander Andrews knocked on the captain's cabin door and entered.

Inside the compact cabin, Mowbray took a chair across from Rodney and Andrews. Captain Mowbray said, "It's always good to see you, George. But what is the purpose of this visit? I didn't expect you."

Captain Rodney said, "I'm afraid I have bad news, Melton."

"I don't need any more of that, George. I haven't been sleeping well anyway." Mowbray tried to force a smile, but he pursed his lips and braced himself.

"This officer," Rodney gestured toward Commander Andrews, "has outlined a convincing argument that you've been overzealous in pursuing Yankee smugglers."

Captain Mowbray pounced on that statement. "Overzealous? George, on the contrary, I have only attempted to support the customs office. I've followed my orders exactly."

Commander Andrews said, "Captain Mowbray, attempting to destroy a businessman and his home is serious, the damage inflicted on the delicate relations between England and her colonies is something quite difficult to measure."

"See here, my orders were clear enough. Parliament wants money wrung from these lying Yankees. I only attempted to obey their orders as I understood them."

Commander Andrews said, "I am quite certain the Navy Board will view your complicity in murder with a jaundiced eye."

Captain Mowbray's voice rose slightly as he said, "George, for God's sake. What is this man talking about? Murder? I haven't murdered anyone!"

Commander Andrews said, "Perhaps, but you plotted a man's death."

"You are referring to the French shipper. The man you speak of is an enemy of the crown."

"Melton, this St. Alembert is a citizen now and English Law says he is innocent until proven guilty, and certainly, as an Englishman deserves no less than a fair trial," said Captain Rodney.

"The bloke is no Englishman, George. He is a French *émigré*."

"Still, you will have the chance to defend yourself against the charges. It sounds as though that is more than you gave this émigré. And if the allegation is proven, you will have disgraced his majesty's government. Any proof of his smuggling, Melton, will aid your defense. Do you have such proof?"

"It's right here." Captain Mowbray swiveled in his chair and held up St. Alembert's confiscated manifest. "We caught him smuggling chattel. Oh, I realize the quantity is miniscule, but remember, we wanted to make an example of someone."

Commander Andrews said, "He transported two African girls as a favor to a customer. There was no defrauding of the government involved."

"How would you know that?" asked Captain Mowbray.

Now it was Commander Andrews' turn to feel uncomfortable, because he didn't want to compromise his informant.

Captain Rodney glanced at Commander Andrews for a response, but then impatiently said, "You'll have the opportunity to plead your case directly to Admiral Boscawen. The admiral wishes the Durham to remain in American waters. You will return with me to London."

"You're relieving me of my command, George?" asked Captain Mowbray incredulously. "I don't believe this."

"Melton, you have given me no choice. Gather your things. The Dublin is sailing on the morning tide. You'll be my guest during the passage."

Captain Mowbray irately crumpled the manifest and flipped it onto his desk. Rodney and Andrews waited as Mowbray told the officer of the deck to have the launch take his trunk to the Dublin.

Captain Mowbray looked like a beaten man. "George, I could do with a few moments to gather my things?"

"Of course, Melton, I'll wait for you by the foc'sle."

Commander Andrews and Captain Rodney chatted for several minutes as they waited for Captain Mowbray to join them. With growing impatience, Captain Rodney suggested, "You better look in on him, Commander."

"Aye, Captain." Commander Andrews opened the door and saw Captain Mowbray seated staring at two pistols before him on his desk. "Don't do it, sir."

Captain Mowbray looked up. His face contorted into rage and he screamed, "Get off my ship." He pointed one pistol at Commander Andrews. Startled, Commander Andrews jumped back, slammed the door shut, and ducked to one side.

The pistol blast echoed off the cabin walls and the musket ball blasted through the oak door sending splinters over the deck. Commander Andrews and Captain Rodney looked at each other in shock. In a crouch, Captain Rodney drew his own pistol and turned to Lieutenant Evans, the ship's master, and said, "Bring the marine detachment." Lieutenant Evans nodded and ran down the companionway. Rodney shouted through the door, "This is fruitless, Melton. What are you trying to achieve?"

A second blast shattered the morning. Commander Andrews opened the door and looked warily inside. The first thing he saw was blood splatters on the wall and desk. Captain Mowbray sat slumped in his chair with a pistol dangling in his limp hand. Captain Rodney rushed in, and said in an anguished lament, "Oh, Melton."

The following day, a fatigued Commander Andrews sat in Governor Colden's office. Concluding his description of the previous night's activities, he said, "So those are the reasons Captain Mowbray was relieved of his command. Though the *Durham* will remain in New York waters, I felt it necessary to make the move before he did irreparable damage to the relations between his majesty's colonists and Parliament. Admiral Boscawen is concerned about this—even if other members of the government do not appear to be."

Governor Colden glared at Andrews and drummed his fingers. About to pounce on the innuendo, he instead allowed it to pass. He grimaced as he asked, "You did say that the Durham will remain in these waters to assist with revenue enforcement, didn't you?"

Commander Andrews nodded and said, "Yes, Captain Rodney appointed Lieutenant Evans to command the frigate in the interim."

"What else can go wrong today?" Governor Colden asked. He placed his head in his hands and stared at his desk. "My secretary did not come to work, the customs agents are missing, and now I have an inexperienced officer in charge of the frigate."

"Actually, you should have fewer headaches with Evans in charge. He is an up-and-comer and a good officer."

Governor Colden asked, "By the way, did Captain Mowbray give you any papers for me?"

"No, I am afraid not. If you are referring to St. Alembert's manifest, he accidentally destroyed it. Is that what you meant?"

"Yes! Without the manifest, we have no case against St. Alembert."

Commander Andrews asked, "Do you believe St. Alembert is a smuggler?"

"I've spoken to prominent businessmen who thinks so. That is good enough for me."

"That's not proof though."

"I know, and without proof..." Governor Colden's voice tailed away. He picked up a letter. "This," he said, "makes it all moot. This correspondence strongly implies Parliament will rescind the Stamp Act."

Commander Andrews said, "I'm glad they have come to their

senses. Perhaps, we can avoid a tax rebellion, after all." Andrews stood, took his hat, and walked to the door. "I certainly hope so." When he opened the door he was surprised to find Molly standing there. "Molly, I, uh, mean Mrs. St. Alembert, how nice to see you."

"Good morning, Commander." Turning to Governor Colden, she said, "Sorry to disturb you, sir, but your secretary wasn't around and I need to speak with you."

"What do you want?"

"I came to ask for your permission to recover our schooner."

Governor Colden coughed nervously and said, "Actually, since no charges are pending, I see no reason for you not to." Looking puzzled, he asked, "How do you intend to recover your ship?"

Molly said in a white lie, "We won't know until we get out there and assess what caused her to take on water."

Governor Colden knitted his brow and asked, "Was the ship scuttled?"

Molly said, "I really have no idea." Governor Colden nodded pensively. He evidently didn't wish to pursue that line of questioning.

Commander Andrews smiled and said, "I would love to stay and observe, but I am leaving for England."

# CHAPTER TWENTY-SEVEN

OUNT DE CHARNAY splashed cold water on his face in his boarding room. After toweling his face dry, he looked about the room and spotted Dillon's personal effects. The possessions belonging to his old friend made him melancholy. I have rested enough he thought, it is time to settle a score. To blend better into the city scene, he put on clothing of an English sailor. He shoved two pistols into his blouse. And with blood in his eye, he walked through the door. First stop, he thought, is the sheriff's office.

To maintain appearances, he hobbled down the street. Demonstrating the patience required of an assassin, he halted a block away from Schout Jack's office. He leaned against a building to observe the pedestrians and street activity. With the exception of several shopkeepers sweeping the sidewalk and some well-heeled bankers bustling to and from loan appointments, there was no sign of the lawman or his deputies. Deciding to move closer to the jail, he approached the sheriff's window. He peered in, saw the building was empty, and decided to hunt for him around the wharf.

De Charnay found no sign of the sheriff or his deputies there either. As he passed a group of sailors parbuckling barrels up the side of the hull, a group of idle royal marines on break eyed him suspiciously, though none accosted him. He walked along the dirt street toward the mansion, approached the front door, and decided to walk the perimeter. With hands on hips, he stood in the alley and thought I wonder where the sheriff could be found.

While walking the street along the Fields, the paladin finally spotted his prey. He recognized Schout Jack's familiar gait in the distance and quickly formulated an escape route. Positioning himself near an alley leading to a jumbled grouping of storage buildings, he ducked into the back street to reconnoiter alternative routes. He became confident his getaway path afforded ease of movement, concealment, a place to change his clothing, and anonymity; he reached inside his blouse and gripped a pistol. He watched Schout Jack stop and chew the fat with a shopkeeper. Soon the lawman resumed his sauntering toward the paladin's location oblivious to the danger. De Charnay ran his thumb over the flintlock and his forefinger touched the cold barrel; he wanted vengeance and his thumb tightened around the flintlock.

Schout Jack glanced at the sailor on the street, scratched his chin, and then walked toward Count de Charnay. Closing his fingers around the stock, Count de Charnay began to draw the pistol. At that moment he spotted a deputy round the corner of the bank building. Imperceptibly, the paladin frowned and released the pistol's handle. Schout Jack stopped in front of de Charnay and asked, "What's your name? I don't recollect seeing you around."

Count de Charnay employed his well-rehearsed Essex accent, "My ship sailed on the tide, Constable. I missed the departure."

Schout Jack looked the man over. He said, "I asked your name, sailor?"

"My name is Horatio Hutchinson."

"What is your ship's name, son?"

For an instant, de Charnay drew a blank. Recovering his wits, he said, "It be the *Dublin*; sir. A fine ship if I am allowed to say."

As the sailor praised his ship, Schout Jack observed a button on the sailor's blouse beneath the cloak. It caught his eye because the image of a rooster had been pressed into the metal. Schout Jack said, "You make your own buttons, don't you?"

De Charnay's mind raced. "Aye, Sheriff, us common ratings make our own—That we do."

"That's an interesting button on your cloak. Did you make that one?" Count de Charnay realized the peril this harmless subject posed. He mentally chided himself for his carelessness and allowing the button to be seen by the sheriff. But this paladin was no ordinary agent. Thinking quickly, he said, "In our last action, I took it from a dead 'Frog,' seein' as how he didn't need it no more. Do ye fancy it, Sheriff?" Schout Jack didn't answer. "I'll be happy to cut the threads and hand it over. Ye fancy it, sheriff, don't ye?"

Schout Jack smiled and said, "Your situation gives you difficulties enough without losing a button to boot." Schout Jack turned to his nearby deputy and said, "We should be moving on, Joshua." The deputy nodded. Schout Jack turned back to de Charnay and said, "When you sober up, come down to my office and I'll arrange passage for you to get home."

"A kind offer to be sure, Sheriff. Take you up on that I will."

Schout Jack nodded to his deputy, because he wanted to speak in private. As they walked away, Schout Jack whispered, "That fellow is no sailor, and he isn't even hung over."

"How can you tell?" asked the deputy.

"That button—it's an emblem of the Bourbon kings."

"A rooster? Schout Jack, I know the Frogs wear that lily flower a lot, but ..." The deputy stroked his jaw trying to piece together Schout Jack's rationale. What did the tar say about it?"

"He said he lifted it from a dead Frenchman, but French sailors' buttons don't carry the Bourbons' emblem. Only royalty are allowed that. He might be one of the foreigners we've been looking for." Schout Jack touched his tender ear and recalled his close call the other night. "We're taking him in for questioning." Schout Jack and Joshua turned around and approached de Charnay. They pulled their pistols and said gruffly, "You, there, raise your hands." The deputy frisked him and discovered two pistols and handed them to Schout Jack. The sheriff examined the nice weapons and their obvious quality. To Schout Jack that was another indication this was no common rating.

Arriving at the sheriff's office, Schout Jack shoved his prisoner into a back room and into a wooden chair. He and his deputy, a large man named Joshua Clay, stood glaring at him. De Charnay, experienced in interrogation techniques himself, sat helplessly. Dreading what he knew was coming, he looked up and weakly said in protest, "You have the wrong man."

Joshua glanced at Schout Jack. The sheriff nodded. "Liar!" screamed Clay and slapped de Charnay with his open palm. The paladin's head jerked to the right.

Schout Jack asked, "How old are you?"

De Charnay's eyes moved up and to the right. "I am thirty-eight."

"What is your name?"

Count de Charnay's eyes moved up and to the left. "My name is Horatio Hutch ..." Clay slapped de Charnay before he could finish his answer.

"You are a French agent!" bellowed Schout Jack.

"No, no, Sheriff. I be a sailor. I swear. My name is Horatio Hutchinson."

"Liar!" Clay pulled back his hand to deliver another blow to the suspect.

Reflexively de Charnay closed his eyes.

Schout Jack caught his deputy's wrist and said, "Now, let's not be hasty, Joshua." Turning to the suspect, Schout Jack smiled and said, "Look here, I will restrain my impatient deputy, but only if you answer my questions truthfully. You are not a good liar. Your name is not Hutchinson. And by telling me your real name, well, that implies you are the person I am looking for." Schout Jack went face to face with de Charnay's and said, "If you don't start answering my questions truthfully, I will walk out of the room, and Joshua here, will employ some unusual techniques to convince you of the health benefits of truth telling."

De Charnay's eyes widened at the prospect of being left alone with the deputy. "But, Sheriff, I'm not lying."

Clay slapped the paladin hard.

Schout Jack put his hand on the paladin's shoulder and said soothingly, "Yes—you are."

Every denial met with a stinging blow to his face or head, de Charnay's eyes became puffy, his vision blurred, and his cheeks became splotchy with black and beet red areas. He stopped answering Schout Jack's questions, because he received a beating whether he did or not. After three hours, his resolve waned. His shoulders hunched and his chin rested on his chest.

Schout Jack said, "There is nothing wrong with being a French agent, mind you. You are just trying to help your own country. You love you country, don't you?" Schout Jack's voice dripped with reassurance. "France is a good country, isn't it?"

De Charnay said in a hoarse whisper, "I do love my country."

"Of course you do. That wasn't such a hard thing to say, now, was it?"

De Charnay looked up and saw Schout Jack smiling appreciatively. "I know that slapping stings. Look, you've held out a respectable amount of time. Joshua and I admire you for that. You obviously love your country, and no man will hold it against you for owning up to it."

De Charnay said, "I love my country... I love... France."

Schout Jack looked at Joshua and the two smiled. Schout Jack said, "Joshua, get this man a piece of paper, a quill, and some ink. I want a written confession."

Molly sat on the side of their bed and nursed Jean-Luc. Exhausted from his nightmarish attempt on his life, she fed him oatmeal and pulverized beef to reduce the energy needed to chew and swallow. After he took one spoonful, she poured a glass of buttermilk and handed it to him. "Dear, you were lucky last night. They came close to killing you." Jean-Luc tried to smile, but his eyes told Molly he appreciated the lengths she had gone to save his life. "But you know, I've not pieced together who those two men were behind the rocks at the quarry. They helped me save your life; they even swam my horse across the river for me. They disappeared after that, but I think they were the men Schout Jack went chasing after in the middle of the night."

Slurring his words Jean-Luc asked, "How long have I been in this bed?"

"Jean-Luc, you must rest. You cheated death last night, but if you don't take it easy, I may yet lose you."

"You just said something about two men helping you. I think they need my help. Schout Jack will be looking for them, too."

Do you know those men, darling?" asked Molly.

Jean-Luc hesitated as he remembered his promise to Count de Charnay. Then thinking it better to divulge his association with the agent, he said, "If it was who I think, he was Captain d'Alquier's replacement."

Molly asked derisively, "Another paladin? Who has he come to kill?"

"No, no, he came to help New York resist Parliament's tyranny. He came to help New York. But now I think he is the one needing help. If the sheriff is after him, I need to get him out of the colony."

"Why do you say that?"

"He risked his life to save mine."

"Yes, but ..."

Jean-Luc narrowed his eyes and Molly knew he was serious. She tried a second argument. "Jean-Luc, there was shooting last night; this paladin could be dead for all we know. Besides, I don't like getting involved with a paladin. They are ruthless and dangerous men."

Jean-Luc struggled to one elbow and angrily threw off the blanket. He said, "I can see that I must take care of this matter myself." He tried to sit up, but teetered unsteadily, and fell back onto his back.

"You are not able to help anyone in your condition. Husband, I will make a deal with you; if you will remain in bed, I'll find one way or another to get him out of the colony," said Molly exasperated. Impatiently, she said, "Describe him." After Jean-Luc provided a detailed description Molly said, "He *was* the man who helped me at the quarry." She pondered a moment and then said, "I will need Henry's assistance."

She took her quilted hood out of her dresser and wrapped a heavy woolen cape about her shoulders, and walked to Henry's house. When Henry answered his door, Molly said, "I need your help." Henry cocked his head. "Bring the *Fiona* to C Dock."

Surprised, Henry asked, "That little derelict?"

Molly laughed and said, "Yes, her condition will add to her credibility. Be sure to reserve that space beside the French trader."

Henry nodded and said, "I know the one. No one is using that space; I'm sure the harbor master will give it to us. Then what"?

Molly clued Henry in on the rest of her plan. Now Molly felt prepared for the dangerous task ahead. Henry jogged down the street to get some of the crew to help him. Molly hurried down the street to the wharf. There, she searched for the ensign of the French trader. Spotting him in the distance, she hurried down the pier to speak with the captain.

# CHAPTER TWENTY-EIGHT

NOVEMBER 3, 10:00 A.M.

"I T IS TO *your* benefit if you transport this individual," said Molly in French. She stood with her chin jutted out and her hands on her hips.

Captain Guy de Fleury looked askance at the insistent young woman. "Can you not see that I am occupied at the moment? I have precious little time before the tide begins to fall and if we miss it, our voyage to Cherbourg is delayed another twelve hours, which will make me unhappy." He returned to supervising the loading of the last dozen barrels into the hold of his ship, *St. Jean Baptiste.*

"Monsieur, you are in the business of carrying cargo for money. All that I'm asking you to do is to carry one additional passenger to France. Since you are sailing to Cherbourg, why not enjoy the company of this Frenchman? I promise you that you will not regret saying yes."

Captain de Fleury turned to Molly, shrugged, and said, "I would like to help, but ..."

"Did I mention you will be rewarded handsomely?"

De Fleury stopped jotting entries on his manifest and turned to Molly. He asked in a low voice, "Who is this," he hesitated and looked about the wharf for eavesdroppers, "Frenchman?"

"Only he is at liberty to divulge his identity. I can tell you that your reward will significantly exceed your small effort." Molly studied the captain's face for signs that she had aroused his interest.

His expression showed some interest in anticipated gain, but mostly resignation. Captain de Fleury sighed heavily and said, "Fine. Have this passenger here in one hour."

Molly's body language revealed her frustration with de Fleury. With her hands on her hips, Molly's aggravation with the skipper bubbled to the surface. "Monsieur, if only handsome rewards were earned that easily."

"What else do you want?" asked de Fleury warily.

Molly said, "Send two of your men to the corner of Wall Street and Fir Street."

Captain de Fleury looked at Molly and snorted. He asked, "The crew is readying the ship for departure. What are you planning?"

Molly smiled sweetly and said, "You will be able to deny everything if you don't know."

Captain de Fleury said, "Go on."

"In one hour, I will signal them by touching my cheek. They are to begin a loud argument and then start fighting. You will be a short distance away, and when the sheriff arrives, you rush over and help him break up the fight." Captain de Fleury looked unconvinced. Molly said, "Fights happen all the time between deckhands. You tell the sheriff they are your sailors, take them by the collars and act like you are taking the roustabouts off his hands. The sheriff will be glad he doesn't have to do paperwork on two roustabouts." Shortly afterward, I will bring the passenger to the ship."

Captain de Fleury said, "You did say handsome reward?"

"I did say that, yes," said Molly. "We have reached an accord then?"

Captain de Fleury said, "Yes."

"You will never regret this. Molly turned to leave and stopped. "Oh, one other thing, the better you treat this man on the voyage, the greater the reward."

"I understand."

An hour later, Molly approached Schout Jack's office. She stopped at the window and glanced inside. Sitting at his desk, Schout Jack sat writing a report; Clay, sat nearby cleaning a pistol. Giving her signal to the crewmen, Molly touched her cheek and then walked inside.

"Good morning, ma'am, what can I do for you?" Schout Jack asked.

Molly smiled sweetly and said, "I stopped by to thank you for saving my husband's life."

"Why, I appreciate that, Mrs. St. Alembert," said Schout Jack standing for the lady. Clay remained seated and continued cleaning the pistol; the sheriff kicked his chair leg causing Clay to jump up and smile sheepishly. "We don't hear folks say that much. We were glad to help your man out of a jam."

Molly spotted the cell keys hanging on the back wall and said, "Well, I won't keep you from your duties." She glanced inside the cell block trying to see the paladin, but could only distinguish a man lying on a cot in the cell.

Schout Jack blushed as he said, "It was kind of you to drop by. Good-bye, Mrs. St. Alembert.

At that moment, a youngster burst into the sheriff's office and said excitedly, "There is a fight on the corner, Sheriff!"

Schout Jack muttered, "Oh, great. Ain't it always something? If you'll excuse me, ma'am, I have work to do." He bowed his head slightly, grabbed a nightstick, and bolted out.

Molly waited to see whether Clay would follow the sheriff, and was relieved to see him dash through the door on Schout Jack's heels. She, too, rushed outside, glanced down the street to ensure the actors in the diversion were still brawling. Seeing two sailors rolling in the dirt and throwing punches, Molly sneaked back inside the jail and grabbed the keys. Count de Charnay was standing in his cell wondering what the excitement was about. Molly hurriedly unlocked the iron door, and said in French, "Meet me in the alley behind Montayne Tavern in ten minutes."

The paladin squinted through his bruised, puffy eyes and asked, "Who are you?"

"I am Jean-Luc's wife. I believe you know my husband."

Count de Charnay nodded cautiously. Then realizing the magnitude of this opportunity, he hobbled into the office and took his pistols from the gun cabinet. Then he limped out the back door.

Molly knew the next sixty seconds were crucial to the plan's success. She hurried outside and saw Schout Jack and Clay jogging toward the melee. Molly lifted her dress to mid-calf and sprinted after them.

Running at full speed, her youth and athleticism served her well. Molly arrived at the fight scene only seconds after the lawmen. Standing behind Schout Jack, she gave the impression she had been running behind them the whole way. Relieved, Molly observed Captain de Fleury approaching as planned. Her risky scheme might work after all.

Schout Jack and Clay separated the fighting sailors.

To ensure she was noticed, Molly, "That was quick work, Schout Jack."

Captain de Fleury rushed forward. As Schout Jack held the two sailors apart, de Fleury addressed him. "*Merci*, Sheriff I apologize for the disturbance. You see, these men belong to my ship. We are due to sail with the tide."

Schout Jack asked, "Isn't that is within the hour?"

"If it is acceptable to you, I will escort them straightaway to the wharf and they will be out of your city by midday. I personally assure you they will not disturb the peace of your city again."

An old hand at breaking up fights between sailors, Schout Jack said, "That will work, but don't let them out of your sight until you have them on board."

Captain de Fleury took the two sailors by their elbows. The three walked quickly in the direction of the pier.

Molly said, "I must be going, also. I am late to the office, already."

Schout Jack tipped his hat and said, "Good day, ma'am. Stop in and see us anytime."

Noticing Clay for the first time, Schout Jack asked, "Who is guarding the prisoner? I'll skin you alive if anything happens to him. Clay ran back to the office and his jaw dropped when he saw the cell door open.

Schout Jack walked up, took one look at Joshua's expression and said, "Don't tell me he isn't in his cell." Joshua stood there quaking. The sheriff shook his head, and then began to look up and down the street.

Clay said, "Must have been that woman that stopped in, Sheriff."

Schout Jack said, "Couldn't be the St. Alembert woman; she was with us the whole time."

"Who in thunder let him out?"

"He has an accomplice. Let's hit the streets and find them."

# CHAPTER TWENTY-NINE

M OLLY ROUNDED THE corner and approached Montayne
Tavern. Count de Charnay, in pain from his beating and
looking pathetic, had been debating whether to shoot his
contact's wife as his last act before escaping. When Molly walked into
the alley, the paladin spoke French and asked with a suspicious tone,
"Where are you taking me?"

Molly answered in French. "I have a ship, the *St. Jean Baptiste*,
waiting to transport you to Cherbourg. Follow me."

"Why are you helping *me*?"

"My husband asked me to. He feels I need practice smuggling,"
said Molly revealing her mischievous side.

De Charnay said, "I have grown fond of your husband." Feelings
of betrayal of his sovereign troubled him; he concluded he could still
kill St. Alembert's wife in one of the alleys.

Molly looked up and down the passage; and seeing no one smiled
and said, "I'm fond of him, too." She looked at the paladin's lacerations
and said, "They worked you over something awful. The sheriff tried to
get you to talk, is that it? By your appearance, I would say you held out."

Count de Charnay looked at the ground and involuntarily smiled, but his swollen cheeks made the expression painful. He felt thankful the young lady's assumption left his dignity intact. He put his hands over his eyes. I do not wish to do this, he thought, but this is my last chance to fulfill the king's wishes.

Molly said, "If we use the alleys, we will lessen the risk of running into Schout Jack."

De Charnay nodded. "How much time do I have?" he asked.

"Twenty minutes at most. Your ship will sail on the tide."

"Then there is not much time."

Looking around the corner again, Molly didn't see Schout Jack or any of his deputies, and said, "The street is clear."

De Charnay took Molly's arm. Startled, she looked at him with alarm. Kill her now, he chided himself as he looked deep into Molly's eyes.

Molly said, "You're hurting my arm."

He said softly, "You could get into trouble helping me.'

"I've considered that possibility," said Molly testily.

Allowing his last chance to slip away, he loosened his grip and released her arm. Rubbing the spot where he had held her, Molly said, "You hurt my arm." De Charnay looked down. He felt ashamed at allowing his last opportunity to assassinate Captain d'Alquier's nemesis lapse. With his decision behind him, he said, "I am sorry. I just had to know that I can trust you."

Molly said, "Follow me." They walked quickly to the corner. She paused at the first cross street. Knowing that traversing in the open increased the chances of recapture, she whispered, "I'll go first. And if I see it's clear, you follow immediately."

As soon as she indicated the street was clear with a head nod, de Charnay crossed briskly and they resumed their rapid pace toward the wharf. Molly and de Charnay rapidly navigated three intersections in this fashion. One street remained and the masts of the ships were visible. Then Lady Luck turned on them. One block from the wharf, Molly spotted Commander Andrews walking toward the intersection.

Molly turned to Count de Charnay and said, "An English naval officer I know is heading this way." She watched horrified when the paladin gripped his concealed pistol and cocked the flint.

"Now you're in a spot," Molly said under her breath. Turning to de Charnay, she said, "Don't shoot. He is a friend. I'll cut him off. When his back is turned, cross the street. Remain in the alley. The ship you want is on C Dock—you can't miss it. The skipper's name is de Fleury. You have only one more block. Soon you'll be homebound." Molly looked at the pistol in de Charnay's hand and said, "Don't make me regret helping you."

Count de Charnay's eyes fell. He said, "I will not hurt your friend, unless ..."

Molly nodded. She stepped into the open and walked nonchalantly in Andrews's direction. She stopped for a horse and cart to pass, and then proceeded.

"Molly," hailed Commander Andrews.

She stopped and looked up. Acting surprised, she smiled and waved. He jogged toward her. De Charnay pressed his back against the building.

Commander Andrews said, "Molly, one moment please."

"Hello, Commander. It's nice to see you?" It took all of Molly's self-control not to glance at the alley. She knew that giving in to that notion might draw Andrews' attention to the spot.

"Molly, I have just left the sheriff. He said a French agent escaped. his custody. I have been looking for you. I wanted to alert you."

Molly forced herself to smile even though she felt worried. "Whew, that sun is sure bright, isn't it? Would you mind if I turned my back from it?" she asked. Her move caused Andrews to turn his back to the alley. She asked, "Why would I be in danger?"

Commander Andrew laughed and said, "Oh, probably not. It is just that—well, you are a block from the wharf, and the sheriff thinks the agent will try to catch a departing ship. You will be careful and on your guard, won't you?"

Molly said, "Yes, of course. Thank you for going out of your way on my behalf."

Commander Andrews motioned toward the alley and asked, "Did I just see you coming out of that side street?"

"Yes, why?"

"As I said, you could be in danger. I don't think it is safe for you to use the alley. Please remain on the main roads."

"I—I just wanted to make better time."

"Keep to the main thoroughfares, will you? Just until this person is apprehended?"

"Yes, of course.

De Charnay shook his head in appreciation. He had observed her manipulate the Englishman's attention and smiled when she turned him. *You are an ingenious woman, Madame St. Alembert,* he thought. *I understand why Jean-Luc left Montréal.*

Commander Andrews said, "I wanted to tell you I am being assigned to a ship when I return to Portsmouth."

"Congratulations. What is the name of this lucky boat?"

"The *Indefatigable*."

Molly brightened and said, "I want to hear all about your ship. Let's walk while we talk, shall we?"

Commander Andrews said, "I also stopped by the governor's mansion and learned the government is dropping all charges against you for that innocent slip up concerning your manifest and the chattels."

Molly's expression brightened. "Does that mean we can recover our schooner?"

"That is exactly what it means. I'm sure the news has made your morning."

"Yes, it has. Why don't we have a cup of tea? You know—to celebrate." said Molly excitedly. She took Commander Andrews by the elbow and pulled him into the café.

Back in the alley, de Charnay knew time was running out. If he missed this ship, it was not a case of simply catching the next vessel. He quickly disappeared into the shadows and came to the end of the back street. He peered around the corner. Not far from his hiding place, a sign covered in seagull droppings read, "C Dock." He turned his attention to the ships and spotted the nameplate *St. Jean Baptiste*. Just as she said, he thought, I am in the right location. And just as Molly also said, there stood a countryman supervising the loading of supplies onto the ship.

Then he saw his brutal interrogator, Deputy Clay, standing fifteen feet from the gangplank. He mulled over a plan to eliminate the lawman. He knew he couldn't use deadly force, since the Royal Navy could easily stop the French trader before it left New York's waters.

In the grog shop, Molly appeared anxious as they waited for their tea. Commander Andrews asked, "Is anything wrong?"

"Oh, no," Molly said. "I wanted to stay and chat, but there is something I need to do and should be going."

Commander Andrews said, "That's too bad, but if you must go, I understand."

Molly stood and said, "Congratulations on your assignment."

Commander Andrews stood and said, "I will mention you prominently in my report to the Naval Board. Until we meet again."

Molly hugged him and said smiling, "Have a pleasant voyage." She departed and hustled around the corner.

As she entered the street that ran along the wharf, Molly halted to observe the street scene. There stood Captain de Fleury supervising his crew, and Deputy Clay stood nearby (though off to the side). Molly had anticipated a lawman would be watching the French trader. Molly then glanced left. The paladin stood at the alley's corner watching her with an anxious expression. And just beyond the deputy, she could see her firm's small ship, *Fiona*, docked alongside de Fleury's trader.

Squinting into the sun, Molly strained to see if Henry had the barrel of flour loaded into the sling of *Fiona*'s davit, the crane used to hoist stores. She could see the davit straining, but holding the barrel aloft. Playing her final ruse, Molly took a small looking glass from her pocket and palmed it. She then used the looking glass to signal Henry to be ready

Molly tried to appear nonchalant as she walked down the wharf. She approached the *St. Jean Baptiste*. Henry began the slow swing of the davit's load on its pivot.

When Captain de Fleury noticed Molly, he stopped writing and watched her. Count de Charnay had no idea what Mrs. St. Alembert had planned.

Henry continued rotating the davit until the load was poised. As the barrel swayed in the wind over Clay's head, Henry waited for Molly to walk closer to the Deputy. When Molly was twenty-five feet from the deputy, Henry released lines holding the barrel.

As the barrel dropped, Clay could hear the rope screaming through the pulleys and looked around. Molly screamed, "Look out!"

Not seeing the danger, Clay ducked into a crouch. The barrel landed on its side ten feet behind him and exploded into a giant, billowing cloud of white powder. The flour cloud engulfed Clay and some of the powder even landed on de Fleury and Molly.

Molly backed up a few feet and gave Henry the thumbs up gesture; Jean-Luc's favorite employee broke into a wide grin.

De Charnay didn't need a signal from the shipper's wife. Seeing the deputy was incapacitated, he dashed across the street. As de Charnay approached the ship, Captain de Fleury was coughing and slapping at his clothes. He, too, was covered in flour and looked comical with the white powder in his mustache, eyebrows, and clothing. He put out his hand and said gruffly, "Where do you think you are going, Englishman?"

De Charnay lowered his voice and said in French, "You are expecting a passenger?"

Captain de Fleury looked at the man and was shocked to see the bruises and lacerations. "*Mon Dieu*, what happened?" Taken aback, Captain de Fleury asked, "Are you the passenger?" De Charnay nodded and glanced nervously in the direction of the deputy. Captain de Fleury said suspiciously, "I was told by the young woman that I would be handsomely rewarded for transporting you to Cherbourg."

Count de Charnay motioned with his head toward the gangplank and said, "Let us speak from the safety of your cabin? I will show you just how handsome your reward will be.

The self-assured manner of the mysterious passenger convinced Captain de Fleury to take him aboard. He hustled his passenger into his cabin and shut the door. He said, "Fine, now show me my handsome reward."

Count de Charnay said matter-of-factly, "I am an Emissary of the Master."

Captain de Fleury's eyes widened. He dropped to one knee, kissed de Charnay's hand, and said, "I am at your service, excellency. Command and I shall obey." He remained on one knee and avoided eye contact with his aristocratic passenger.

Count de Charnay said, "I am anxious to see France. High tide has arrived."

"Of course, excellency. How shall I address my paladin?"

"I am Count de Charnay."

Captain de Fleury left the cabin to supervise his crew. De Charnay walked to the window and tensely looked about for Schout Jack. He could see Mrs. St. Alembert brushing flour off Deputy Clay, and he smiled at the memories of his encounters with her. The St. Jean Baptiste's crew turned their ship from the pier and, when clear of the other ships, unfurled their sails.

As the vessel gained speed and approached Governor's Island, Count de Charnay placed his forehead against a beam, breathed deeply, and allowed himself to relax. Schout Jack had been a formidable enemy, and he felt fortunate to be escaping from Manhattan Island. As the ship passed the St. Alembert's schooner resting atop Diamond Reef, a small boat caught his attention. He observed a small dory with a solitary occupant rowing toward the schooner. Count de Charnay studied the rower, but he didn't recognize the person, and yet he seemed familiar.

While de Charnay watched the dory heading for Jean-Luc's boat, a knock sounded on the door. Captain de Fleury stuck his head inside the room and asked, "Does his excellency require anything?"

Count de Charnay said, "Actually, yes, captain. Please allow me the use of your desk, stationary, and a pen." Captain de Fleury hustled into the cabin, opened his drawer, produced the desired objects, and then hustled out. De Charnay sat at the desk and composed a letter for

King Louis that the contact's wife was not the individual that had wounded his predecessor. He also described the progress he had made getting a person inside the New York resistance movement. When finished, Count de Charnay folded his report. Upon arriving in Cherbourg, he would send it by courier to the king.

# CHAPTER THIRTY

NOVEMBER 4, 12:00 A.M.

"I AM, TOO, COMING!" Jean-Luc threw off his blanket and struggled to stand. Situated between him and the door with hands on hips, Molly scowled, stooped, and slowly picked the blanket off the floor. She began folding it in measured movements. Still wobbly, Jean-Luc tried mightily not to give away his unsteadiness and felt deeply the disapproval emanating from his spouse across the room. Her knit brow made him nervous. He said in protest, "I know I am being hard headed, darling, but, really, I feel much better."

"Perhaps you do, but I don't think it would be good for you to get out on the water in this chill. You could catch pneumonia. You should stay in bed."

"If we lose the schooner, I may as well be dead. Though I admit to being fatigued, I will not remain behind. Wild horses could not keep me from our schooner's recovery. We will be dead financially if something goes wrong," said Jean-Luc. "Besides, I was not the St. Alembert who sank her."

"I guess you'll be throwing that in my face for the rest of our lives."

"Look, all of our other boats added together don't equal the schooner in value, said Jean-Luc with a bit of exaggeration. "We have to raise her at least enough to sail her into dry dock."

"Indeed, we do, but I am the one who sank her, and since you are in no condition, I'll be the one who raises her," said Molly firing back. She started to walk away in a huff, but Jean-Luc caught her by the elbow.

He said softly, "If it will make you feel better, I will only watch. I will restrict myself—and only observe."

"Oh, no you won't, darling; I know how much our enterprise means to you, and it means just as much to me."

"If you know how much it means, then you also know I cannot stay here."

Molly slapped her apron with both hands and said in exasperation, "Oh, I give up."

Jean-Luc said, "While you round up the crew, I'll get dressed. Then, while they gather materials you row ahead and fire up the galley. That way everyone will have something to eat after the *Marie* lifts off the rocks." He took her into his arms and kissed her. As she stepped away, he asked, "Are there white-caps?"

Molly studied the garrison's flagpole down the street; it hung listlessly. "No wind, no white-caps—easy trip," she said.

Molly went straight to Henry Charles's house and knocked on his door. When Henry opened the door, she said, "Thank you for helping me this morning, you handled the davit perfectly." Henry laughed. "But we have more work. Gather the deck crew and meet me on the pier in an hour."

Henry smiled. He asked, "What supplies will we need?"

"Jean-Luc will meet you at the warehouse. We'll use lumber we have stored there. Join us as soon as you can."

"The boys would enjoy a Whitney once she's in dry dock."

With an indulgent smile, Molly said. "Yes, we'll celebrate like pirates once we've gotten her into dry dock. But not until I see her high and dry. Bringing her in will be dicey."

Henry said over his shoulder running down the street, "Good, the boys love a challenge. And I love a party."

Molly walked to the pier and set a rowboat into the water. She stepped in, took the oars, and began to stroke towards Governor's Island. Approaching the *Marie*, she became aware of a rowboat beached on the sands of Governor's Island. "Must be boys fishing on the far shore," she said to herself. When her rowboat bumped the schooner's hull, she secured the lines and quickly climbed aboard. Upon entering the galley, she had to strike a match to light her lantern. It took a few moments to locate the items she needed and lost track of the time. As she worked, she heard a boat bump the hull, but she thought it was Henry arriving early. She tied an apron around her waist and ascended the companionway to the quarterdeck. She stepped out onto the sun-lit deck and called out, "Henry, is that you?" No one answered. Thinking it odd, Molly walked to the gunnel. Next to her rowboat was the boat that was beached on Governor's Island earlier; *but it was empty*. Molly's stomach knotted and, instinctively, she spun around.

There stood John Robb. "Who were you expecting?" he asked.

Molly gasped. Standing before her was a parody of a human being; his face, hands, and neck were covered in monstrous scabs. His eyes appeared empty of life and had dark rings encircling his sockets. From his appearance, Molly could only wonder how long he had to live. Tar-matted strands of hair hung from his splotchy scalp; his face, hands, and neck were beet-red and numerous blisters oozed puss. Unsure, Molly asked, "Are you the Mr. Robb?"

"Was—no longer," said Robb.

"You look dreadful. Won't you let me tend to your sores?" Molly instinctively took a step forward intending to help and to comfort the pitiful creature, but Robb shook a large pistol at her to indicate he would not allow her approach. Molly stopped and placed her hands at her side. She asked sympathetically, "What do you mean was?"

"Those friends of yours—they did this to me. They damn near burned me alive with their hot tar. After they finished, they left me there to die. I waded into the river and found relief for my burns. Then I caught this god-awful cold. Achoo!" Robb sneezed.

"I have no idea who did this to you, and I am sorry for your nightmare. You must be in intense pain."

Robb blinked and his eyes welled with tears. "Aye, I am."

"However, it isn't as though you are an innocent victim. You tried to murder my husband."

Robb ignored her and said with a distracted look in his eyes, "I lay in the water for hours. It was cold, and yet nothing relieved the burning. Do you know what I thought about as I lay there?" Molly shook her head. Robb said, "I hated myself for it, but I thought of you."

"Me?" Molly placed the back of her hand up to her mouth in shock.

"I took a fancy to you the first time I ever laid eyes on you."

Molly said, "Sir, I am married!"

"So? People have been cheating for a thousand years. What makes you different? Besides, you're a smuggler, so I didn't figure you for a virtuous woman."

"I see you feel well enough to be insulting."

"Oh, never mind, it isn't important. The more I'm around you Yankees, the more heartless you seem."

"Well, if it isn't the pot speaking," said Molly. "How did you get off Blackwell's Island?"

"A boat passed the next morning, and it stopped to help. Once they saw the feathers stuck to me and figured I was a customs man, they took me to the riverbank and left me there." Robb sneezed again.

Molly blurted out, "Bless you." To her it was something you just said when someone sneezed.

"Shut up! None of this would have happened if it weren't for you, dammit." Robb tried to wipe his nose with his forearm, but the dried scabs felt like sandpaper to his inflamed skin.

Molly thought this man's out of his mind; I must keep him talking —must stall. "How have I caused your misfortune?"

"How?" asked Robb. "He snorted and lowered the barrel slightly,

"I fancied you once. And just when I thought I had this schooner as a prize and could use the proceeds to woo a proper lady—someone scuttled her. I figured your husband was behind it." Robb looked about suspiciously and asked, "Say, where is he?"

"Your logic is twisted, Mr. Robb. You can't kill a woman's husband and then come courting. You can see that, can't you?" Out of the corner of her eye, Molly spotted two familiar skiffs approaching Diamond Reef. Seeing hope, Molly thought please hurry, darling.

In the lead boat, an unsuspecting Henry sat near the transom manning the tiller. As the boats approached the schooner, Jean-Luc waved at his wife on the deck and shouted, "Molly."

Robb's eyes widened in alarm and he said in an angry whisper, "Come here." Molly took a few steps toward Robb. He grabbed her by the wrist and pulled her to him; he put his hand over her mouth and put the pistol to her temple. Molly glanced down and saw his finger on the trigger. Afraid his pistol might accidentally discharge, beads of perspiration formed on her forehead. He forced her to the gunnel and looked over at the two skiffs bobbing on the waves below him.

"*Mon Dieu*," whispered Jean-Luc when he saw his wife with a pistol to her head.

Robb shouted down, "If you don't want a dead wife, take those boats and get out of here. This ship is government property."

Molly said in a hoarse whisper, "That isn't true. It has been returned to us. It's all legal."

"Shut up!" said Robb gutturally.

From the water's surface, Jean-Luc said, "I beg to differ. My schooner has not been legally confiscated. It is you who are trespassing."

Robb angrily waved the pistol to emphasize his warning. "I guess you don't hear so good. This is my ship. If you don't leave, I'll kill her."

Jean-Luc said, "No, no, we are leaving."

When Robb pulled Molly back from the gunnel, he said, "When I see they've gone, we'll sail out of here."

"The belly is half-filled with ocean water. We can't sail anywhere."

Robb didn't answer; he just glared at her. She understood now this man was delusional.

Jean-Luc threw off the blanket and unbuttoned his coat. He rolled over the side of the skiff into the frigid chest-deep water of Diamond Reef. Holding onto the side of the skiff, he whispered through chattering teeth, "Act like you are returning to Manhattan, but do not row over halfway. Await my signal. I will wave when I want you to return."

Henry glanced up to see if Robb was watching from the gunnel. Seeing it clear to speak, he said, "Skipper, let me go. I can board the vessel faster. I think you are still weak."

"Henry, it is my wife's life at stake. You keep that coat and blanket dry, because I will need them later."

Henry turned to the crew and said, "You heard the skipper." Then he handed a pistol to Jean-Luc. "Take this."

The crew in the second boat wasn't happy. They understood the perilous situation of the skipper's wife and wanted vengeance. But Henry's leadership prevailed, and they reluctantly complied. The two skiffs slowly separated from the half-sunken schooner, although the current made headway difficult. Finally, Henry had both skiffs making their way toward the beach.

Jean-Luc grasped the rope ladder, but before he placed his foot in the first rung, he let the air escape from his trousers to prevent the gurgling sound from alerting Robb to his presence. As Jean-Luc slowly ascended the ladder with the pistol in his teeth, he half expected the gunman to detect him in this vulnerable position and he would be defenseless. When Jean-Luc reached the gunnel, he gripped the pistol from his mouth and peered over the railing. Robb and Molly were standing near the port gunnel in the same posture watching the skiffs return. With Robb's arm still around Molly's waist and the pistol to her head, any false move would end in with Molly's brains splattered on the deck. Jean-Luc also noted the companionway lay between him and the customs agent lengthening the distance he must travel to reach Molly's captor. He thought, if I slowly roll over the gunnel, I could sneak up on Robb, and disarm him. At that moment, Robb began a hacking cough, but still held Molly tightly. Jean-Luc slithered over the gunnel and began tiptoeing toward the customs agent and his wife. He had gotten within fifteen feet when Robb heard Jean-Luc's wet clothes brushing the deck. He whirled about to face the armed husband.

Jean-Luc raised his pistol.

Robb said, "Place your pistol on the deck and step back." Jean-Luc hesitated. "Do as I say or her brains will be wetting the deck."

"And then I will kill you," said Jean-Luc. He continued to point his pistol at Robb.

"I'm a dead man anyway."

Shaken, Jean-Luc asked, "What do you mean?"

Robb's voice was a ghoulish screech. "Look at me! I am disfigured and alone in the world." He began sobbing, and then said, "I'll always be alone."

Molly said, "You must see a doctor. Put the gun down and we'll take you to the hospital."

"Both of you shut up." Robb pointed with his pistol barrel and nodded for Jean-Luc to place his weapon on the deck and back away. Bending down, Jean-Luc laid the weapon on the deck, raised his hands, and stepped back.

Molly realized that if Robb gets that pistol he'll kill us both. Robb forced Molly forward and they moved within five feet of the pistol. The instant Robb took the pistol away from her temple and bent down, Molly stomped hard on his foot with her heel.

Robb screamed loudly enough to be heard by the men in the skiffs.

Molly shoved his shoulder, causing him to lose his balance and fall against the gunnel. She grabbed the pistol and pulled back its flintlock. She had the drop on him and said with a firm voice, "Put down the gun!" Robb hesitated, but reasoned that being shot by the shipper's wife was more than his heart could bear. His grip loosened and he dropped the pistol on the deck. Jean-Luc ran to his wife. Molly handed him the pistol and walked over to the shivering John Robb. She kicked his pistol across the wooden boards and backed away slowly. Molly said, "What you have done to my family is twisted, and you caused much anguish. I doubt Governor Colden approves of your tax-collection methods. You really ponder your actions in a prison cell for a while."

Robb coughed but didn't respond. Jean-Luc picked up Robb's pistol and walked to the gunnel to signal his sailors.

Molly turned to her husband and said, "I thought we agreed you would only watch."

Jean-Luc smiled weakly and said through chattering teeth, "Are you not glad that I am here?"

Molly smiled and said, "I forgive you—this once. I'm going below. I'm going to fire the galley up, and get some food started. When I get the fire going, you and I can switch places so you can get warm." Jean-Luc nodded, and she stepped down the companionway.

Robb started to stand. Jean-Luc said, "You, there, stay where you are!" Robb ignored him and stood. Jean-Luc said sternly, "Sit back down. I am warning you."

"I want you to put me out of my misery. Shoot me. Go ahead, I want you to." Jean-Luc was confused. Robb began another fit of hacking coughs and lost his balance. He fell backward against the gunnel and plunged over the side of the ship.

"No!" cried Jean-Luc and ran to the gunnel. Robb's body lay motionless on the rocks of Diamond Reef.

"The poor devil," said Jean-Luc. He lowered the pistol, dropped a coiled line, and descended. He dropped into the shoulder deep water and pulled Robb to the surface. From his misshapen neck, it was evident Robb died from his fall onto the reef.

The two skiffs approached, and Henry Charles yelled, "We saw the whole thing, skipper." The skiffs pulled alongside Jean-Luc, who was holding Robb's body in his arms. Henry looked at the customs agent and shook his head sadly. "What a way to die."

Jean-Luc handed Henry the corpse, and several of the crew pulled Robb into the boat. Jean-Luc said, "He told me that he wanted to die. Whoever did this to him showed no mercy to a fellow human. It is sad."

Henry said, "What are your orders, Skipper?"

"After you off-load the supplies and crew, send two men back to the city with the body to tell Schout Jack what happened."

Henry raised his voice and said, "You heard the skipper. Get moving."

# CHAPTER THIRTY-ONE

"WE'VE BROUGHT UP the supplies as you wanted. What are we going to do with this lumber?" asked Henry who was standing on the deck in front of the deck crew.

Molly looked over the material and mentally ticked off the items —lumber planks, ring chain, double-block pulleys, ten oaken buckets, iron hooks, tar, and sisal. She put her hand on Henry's shoulder and said, "Let's get started. Take this to the orlop and I'll join you shortly." Molly pulled out the three-inch wooden plug and descended the companionway to the orlop.

With the crew reassembling into a tight semi-circle, Molly said, "The first thing we need to build is a twenty foot pump dale."

Henry asked, "What's that?"

"Think trough. Make it one plank wide and place oakum and pitch in the seams. Then position the pump dale between those two portals," Molly pointed to two openings on the port and starboard sides. The men nodded and got to work. Handing the plug to Henry, Molly said, "Take this string, cover it with tar, and wrap it around the edge. I want to waterproof this plug."

When completed, Henry said, "I've got her ready." Molly walked over to examine his work. He said, "It's going to leak a little."

"I know. I just want us to get to the pier now. We'll need a dry dock repair after that." Molly pointed to a rib near the stem and said, "Its six inches to starboard from that spot. She waded into the cold waist deep water and felt about for the hole. "Right about here?" When she found the hole, Molly said excitedly, "Got it!" Henry handed her the oakum-wrapped plug and Molly worked it into the hole. "Hand me the mallet." Molly, on her knees, tried to hammer the plug in the water, but couldn't drive it snugly enough. She stepped on the plug and felt it sink into the opening half-way. She jumped up and down on it and attempting to use her weight to push the plug a little deeper into the opening.

Jean-Luc stuck his head through the opening again and holding a lantern asked, "How is it going, little girl?"

Molly grinned. She and Jean-Luc laughed. She enjoyed their marital give and take. "I almost have it."

"Do you want me to come down and help?"

"No, I want you to stay wrapped up."

Jean-Luc observed with a concerned expression until Molly finally announced, "It's in." She pointed to a companionway and said to Henry, "I want a pulley system set up. Attach the buckets at six-foot intervals. Use the ring chain in the pulleys, the sisal, and the hooks to attach the buckets."

Henry said, "I see what you're wanting."

Molly supervised the crew attaching the buckets to the ring chain they would use in the pulleys. While the sailors toiled on the pulley system, hammering could be heard from the quarterdeck. When a loud thud sounded, Molly said, "They must have finished the pump dale. Let's see how it looks." After inspecting the trough's seams and finding them well caulked, Molly said, "Fit for service. Place two men at each end of the pulley; one will fill the buckets and the other will empty them. Rotate the hands regularly to keep them fresh, but keep that chain moving."

"You heard Mrs. St. Alembert, men. The *Marie*'s been on these rocks too long! We want to start making money again, don't we?"

The crew cheered and threw their backs into the laborious work of removing the ocean water inside the bilge. For six hours, they filled the buckets and emptied them into the trough, which discharged into the ocean. Molly checked the falling water level with a measured stick, but after six hours of bailing the *Marie* remained on the reef. Wrapped in a wool blanket, Molly's brow furrowed.

"Do you think we're taking on water somewhere else, Mrs. St. Alembert?" asked Henry.

"Henry, give her a little more time. We removed a lot of water, but if it still is on the reef in another half hour, we'll consider the possibility of additional damage."

Jean-Luc stuck his head down the companionway and asked, "We're about to regain our buoyancy, right?"

"Jean-Luc, be patient."

As Jean-Luc started to turn away, the *Marie* shuddered and groaned. As if in slow motion, the schooner lifted off Diamond Reef. Molly broke into a wide grin, and the crew started cheering so loudly that they could be heard on Manhattan. But though the schooner was buoyant again, the danger hadn't completely passed.

Henry bellowed, "Keep working them pulleys, ye swabs. We haven't emptied the sea from her belly jes' yet. We could lose her yet, with this much water sloshing in the bilge."

Moving over to her senior employee, Molly said in a low voice, "Before we weigh anchor, I want to double check the plug and ensure it is seated."

Henry nodded. He directed part of the crew to move some of the ballast about to give his interim skipper room to inspect the wooden cylinder. Molly knelt in the puddle of bilge water still rolling about and found what she was looking for. The plug felt flush to the keel and seated nice and tight. She clasped both hands together as a signal to Henry who asked, "Ready to weigh anchor, Skipper?"

Molly shook her head, stood, wiped her wet hands on her blouse, and said, "Let's get a good night's sleep and take her to the pier in the morning."

The following morning, Cadwallader Colden walked to the window and peered out to sea. His jaw fell when his eye caught movement near Governor's Island; the scuttled schooner was under sail and coming in. Colden slowly allowed the drape to fall, shook his head, and returned to his desk.

Also watching the *Marie* under sail, Isaac Sears, Alexander McDougall, and James DeLancey stood in the tavern's door and beamed at the spectacle. Sears slapped his accomplices on the back and said, "Did you see today's news board?" DeLancey and McDougall shook their heads. "The king and Parliament are considering repealing the Stamp Act."

DeLancey said, "I think it is time we brought St. Alembert into our society. He's proven himself, wouldn't you say?"

"Yes, he has. Let's make a call on him this week. The Sons of Liberty need men like him," said Captain Sears in a whisper.

That evening, as Jean-Luc prepared for bed. Molly sat brushing her hair in front of the mirror. Suddenly, she stopped, put down the brush, and put her palm to her forehead. Jean-Luc asked, "Dear, are you feeling ill again?"

Molly said, "Uh-huh. I feel a little sick to my stomach."

"You ought not to have been wading in cold bilge water. Now you are ill because of it. I knew all these troubles would be too much. And to think, you were worried about me. Shall I get the doctor?" asked Jean-Luc.

"No, I will go in the morning." Molly tried to make light of it to keep Jean-Luc from worrying. "Besides, you are in worse shape than I."

# CHAPTER THIRTY-TWO

NOVEMBER 6, 10:00 A.M.

LATE THE NEXT morning, Molly entered Jean-Luc's office and sat in the chair next to him. She folded her hands in her lap and smiled. To Jean-Luc, her grin looked like a cat with canary feathers in her mouth. He placed his quill pen into the inkwell, and closed the ledger. "What did Doctor Ellet say?" he asked apprehensively. Molly placed her hand on his and her grin widened. "Why the coy look?"

Molly's face radiated happiness. "We're going to have a baby. Doctor Ellet thinks it will be a girl."

"A girl! *Magnifique*—I mean, a boy would be nice, too." Jean-Luc quickly added.

"I had no idea I was with child. But I figured I would be in his office a while and I knew you had to take care of important business."

"But why does he think it will be a girl?"

"He did *tests*. They all indicated girl."

Jean-Luc said, "Intriguing," and leaned forward.

"And my feet have been warmer than usual, and that means girl." Jean-Luc's eyes widened. "Plus, I had morning sickness early on, and, yep, that means girl. But do you want to know what clinched it?"

Jean-Luc laughed and said, "Of course."

"It was when I laid on my back and Doctor Ellet dangled a needle over my tummy."

Jean-Luc knew this test and said excitedly, "It went back and forth?"

"Not a hint of a circle," said Molly beaming.

Jean-Luc snapped his fingers. "Doctor Ellet is correct. It must be a girl. My mother told me about such a needle test." Jean-Luc's expression changed from elation to concern. "Perhaps it is not a good time to bring a baby into the world." Jean-Luc stood and stared out the window. "There will be more trouble between England and New York. You will see."

"Jean-Luc, a newspaper tacked to the news board said Parliament would likely repeal the Stamp Act. That should make everyone happy."

"Temporarily, yes, but Parliament will not leave New York alone. They will press the issue to show they have political and taxation authority over us."

Molly walked over to her husband and hugged him. "There has never been a better time to bring a baby into the world. You'll see."

*Finis*

# THE MOLLY LAKE SERIES
*continues in*
# The Treasure of
# Le Nain Rouge, 1773

# Acknowledgements

I gratefully acknowledge the historical information generously shared by the staff and interpreters along Hudson Valley Historic District, especially the Van Cortlandt Manor, Philipsburg Manor Upper Mills, and Philipsburg Manor in Yonkers. With appreciation, I recognize the rich trove of family history my friend in Chicago shared concerning a relative who commanded the regiment of Wild Geese during the War of Austrian Succession. I am also deeply grateful to Kieron Punch and Gerry Regan of the Wild Geese Association who also assisted me with details that improved the story.

I am appreciative of the historical information generously shared by the staff and interpreters along the Hudson Valley Historic District, especially the Van Cortlandt and Philipseburg Manors. With heartfelt appreciation I recognize the rich trove of family history my friend in Chicago shared concerning his relative who commanded the regiment of Wild Geese during the War of Austrian Succession. I am deeply grateful to Messrs. Kieron Punch and Gerry Regan of the Wild Geese Association who also assisted me with details that improved the story.

# About the Author

**SAMUEL ENDICOTT** served in the United States Army as a combat engineer from 1975–1995. A Ranger and paratrooper, he is a graduate of the University of Mississippi, University of Southern California, Command and General Staff Officer Course, and the Naval War College. Samuel is the author of the *Molly Lake* Series, www.mollylakebooks.com. Born in Louisville, Kentucky in 1949, he now resides in Mt. Pleasant, SC with his wife, Elaine, and English Setter, Probie.